A NIAGARA NOIR MYSTERY

IN THE WEEDS

LIZA DROZDOV

ISBN: 978-1-7776142-4-9
eBook ISBN: 978-1-7776142-5-6

Cover design by Damonza

BOOKS BY LIZA DROZDOV

Blood Relative

Dark Water

The One That Got Away

In The Weeds

IN THE WEEDS

I DON'T NEED the headlights to drive, thanks to waxing moon and the straight gravel road. The driveway and yard are illuminated with a ghostly light as I ride slowly past the house and then coast down the gentle slope to the pen. I turn off the engine and pull on the handbrake, then get out to open the gate. The thick humid air hits me in the face and it feels like I'm trying to breathe underwater. I'm sweating and I can feel beads of moisture trickling down my spine and into the waistband of my shorts. The backs of my thighs are slick with perspiration and I stick to the truck upholstery as I slide across the driver's seat.

I open the gate in the electric fence, satisfied that it doesn't make a sound. I oiled it a few days ago to make sure. Then I coast through and close it behind me. Once I'm away from the house and well into the pasture I'm able to turn the engine on again. I turn the truck around and back it up as far as I can before my rear tires start to sink in the soft ground near the wallow. I keep my headlights off, but the light of the moon is enough to let me see where I am going.

This summer has been the hottest on record, and the rainfall the lowest in memory; the scorching sun has hardened the earth in the pasture and I'm able to turn the truck without leaving tire marks. It doesn't matter anyway; I'm sure that whatever tracks I leave will be obliterated by sunrise.

I slip out of the truck and let down the tailgate as quietly as I can, then pull the heavy tarp out of the truck bed until it teeters on the edge. It's caught somehow on the tailgate hinge and I can't pull it any further. I'm about to climb up into the truck bed and give it a shove when the tarp tears free and falls, hitting the dirt with a sickening thump. I drag it as far as I can toward the boggy stream, my ears straining for any sound. I peer into the darkness but all I can see is the tiny lights of fireflies flickering in the brush.

I untie the tarp and roll the contents onto the earth.

He is naked. He lies facing up, staring at the moon. I don't want to see his face, so I roll him over with the toe of my boot.

As I load the tarp back into the truck, I hear a faint grunt, followed by a snuffling sound. I don't have much time and I start to move faster.

I drag the first ten-gallon bucket out of the truck and open it. The smell of corn mash and strawberry Kool-Aid makes me retch. I pour it over him then go to get the second bucket, this one full of corn mash and beer.

By the time I've poured that out I can hear them. Low growls and resonant rumbles that make it feel as if the earth is vibrating. They are getting closer, coming through the brush and the long grass by the stream, snuffling, rustling, breaking twigs and snapping branches. The hair on the back of my neck stands up.

I run back to the truck, drop the buckets into the back and start the engine. The noise won't matter now; they have caught the scent and nothing will scare them off.

As I drive slowly back toward the gate I can see them in the moonlight. Their eyes and tusks gleam as they run out of the dense brush at the back of the wallow. The large one in front is a sow. She scents the air, her massive head bobbing up and down. She snorts loudly—a warning to the rest in case of any threat. She can't see very well, but the scent draws her closer to the corn and she pauses, listening for danger. Then she squeals and trots toward the mash. The rest of them hear her signal and follow. I can see the humpbacked silhouette of dozens of the hairy beasts, trotting across the pasture in a thunder of hooves.

When I'm safely on the other side of the gate I pause to listen to the excited squeals as they smell the corn mash and the deeper growls and roars of the boars as they tear him apart. And under the contented grunts I hear the steady crunch of corn kernels, the tearing of sinew and muscle and the snap of bone.

I look up and can see every star in the clear night sky. I listen to the crickets in the field and inhale the aroma of new mown hay. Then I drive back to the road. I don't turn on my headlights until I'm a mile away.

ONE

Wright

I'M SITTING IN my car checking out the gardens planted along the front entrance of the restaurant. I don't know anything about flowers, but it's obvious someone here cares a lot. They are blooming all over the place, with roses climbing on trellises, trained along fence posts and pillars and archways, and all over the sign—Thorny Rose.

I'm glad I came early, before the place is open. Less chance of anyone being around to get in my way. I recognize her the minute she pulls up in her old pick up truck and climbs out.

I've seen her picture in the local papers with him, the chef. The glamorous couple at all the big local events. She's a lot better looking than her photos. Tall and lean, she's wearing jeans and a t-shirt, with her light brown hair hanging loose to her shoulders. The photos online always show them both in white chef's uniforms with tall paper hats, or in black tie evening wear at some charity event they've catered. I like her better this way. She's avoiding meeting my eye and I can tell from her body language that's she's nervous.

I walk toward her, my boots crunching on the gravel.

"I'm Detective Constable Wright," I say. "You're the owner. Rose Ellis." It isn't a question.

"Detective?" She looks at my car, a vintage Mustang Selby, fully restored down to the last screw.

"This is one of the new police service vehicles you've probably been reading about in the paper," I smile. "Just kidding. I thought it might be better to come in my own vehicle. In case your customers feel uncomfortable seeing a police cruiser in the lot."

"That's good of you." Her voice is flat and she avoids looking at me. Clearly she's timid or she's hiding something. "How can I help you?" Her eyes flicker anxiously toward the restaurant.

"We've had a report of a missing person," I say, motioning toward the restaurant sign. "The chef. Raymond Ellis."

"The chef is my husband," she says, crossing her arms and her eyes flicking up to meet mine. "He's not missing."

I'm not surprised. "The person making the report indicated you'd say that," I say and wait for her to respond, watching for her response.

She doesn't say anything. Then a movement in the kitchen window catches her eye. Someone is watching.

TWO

Rose

I MOTION FOR Detective Wright to walk with me and we move away
from the restaurant window. I need to preserve a bit of privacy—
and my dignity. It's probably Lotte or Montana spying through the
window, the *sister wives*. Chef's kitchen apostles, they both hang
on his every word. Doe-eyed and delicate Montana is his current
favorite, not that it does her any favours with the rest of the staff.
They tease her constantly, calling her Virginia, Dakota, Georgia—
any US state they can think of, as well as a few international gems
like Serbia and Latvia. I pretend not to notice.

"When is the last time you saw your husband?" Wright asks,
getting out his little notebook and a pen. He smiles. It's the easy
grin of man used to getting his way with women. A charmer with
a killer smile, just like my husband.

A wave of anxiety washes over me. It's always hard to know
how honest to be. "A few weeks ago," I answer. "Late July sometime." His eyebrows shoot up.

"You don't remember the exact day?" I shrug. "Do you know
where he is?" I shake my head. He's making me nervous, and
embarrassed. This isn't something I want to talk about.

"Not exactly." He nods. I can read his mind. "My husband

didn't leave me, if that's what you're thinking." I try not to sound defensive. "He's gone on a *stage*."

"A *stage*?"

"He goes to work in other restaurants, under famous chefs, to learn new techniques, and to improve his craft."

"And he doesn't tell you where he's going?" I shrug again.

"To be honest with you," I say. "He doesn't always know where he's going himself until he arrives." I pause, trying to think of what to say. "He gets restless. He's a creative guy, always looking for inspiration. And, the restaurant is quiet now," I lie. In fact it's the busiest summer we've ever had at the Thorny Rose. The Shaw Festival is having a great season and the theatre crowd is filling the restaurant most evenings. Not to mention that tourism in general is doing well, with all the Niagara region wineries hosting successful tastings and events. I've had to bring in extra staff just to manage the catering.

"So this isn't unusual?"

"Not for him." I try not to sound bitter. From his expression I can guess Wright doesn't believe me. "He's not here, but he's not *missing*. He took his knives. He'd have taken them to work on a *stage*," I insist. "I didn't hide him away in the wine cellar." We don't even have a wine cellar.

"Has he gone away like this before?"

"Last year he was in Copenhagen. At Noma." I glance at him for any sign of recognition. "And he even went to El Bulli before it closed. In Spain? It was voted one of the best restaurants in the world?" Wright does not look impressed.

"Are you a chef here too?" he asks. I almost laugh out loud thinking of chef's face if he heard that. He barely thinks I can cook soup from a tin. And for a while, that was true. But I've been working hard since we've opened the restaurant, and I've learned a lot more than he'd ever acknowledge.

"No. There can only be one chef in a kitchen," I attempt a smile. "I do help out with the service a bit. But mostly I'm the gardener. I supply the restaurant with herbs, flowers and vegetables."

"Look. I'm sorry to be doing this." He hesitates a moment. "It feels like a prank. We don't normally even follow up unless the missing person is high risk, or the immediate family makes the report. But we've had several calls on this."

"Several?" He looks uncomfortable. But not as uncomfortable as I feel so I don't feel sorry for him. I think for a second then make a decision I hope I won't regret. But I need to make sure he never comes back.

"I assume you'll want to speak to some of the staff," I say. "Can I offer you a coffee?

"Sure," he says with that killer smile. "I've always wanted to come here. For dinner I mean," he clarifies.

We step up the wide back porch that runs the length of the restaurant and I hold open the screen door for him. The instant we enter every one of the staff gets busy doing something very important. Maggie the sous chef is mincing shallots for a veal *demi glace*, the saucier is doing *mis en place* for the dinner service and Lotte is pretending to stir some *creme fraiche*. Montana is nowhere to be seen.

"Maggie," I call. She turns, puts down her knife and wipes her red hands on a kitchen towel. "This is Detective Constable Wright. He's here about a missing chef." I notice that Lotte flushes red before she turns to another task and pretends not to eavesdrop.

"Missing chef?" Maggie grins. She walks over, her expression both amused and intrigued. "We've got one I'd be happy to give you." Maggie shakes Wright's hand, revealing her forearm, strong and muscled from years of cooking on the line. She's a big woman, but her face is slack and drawn, showing her recent loss of weight. She wears a red bandana, both to stop the sweat from pouring off her brow and to hide the effects of chemotherapy.

"Maggie is our sous chef," I say to Wright. "She's in charge of the kitchen when chef isn't here. She runs the line, does the ordering, trains the staff…"

"…and chef gets all the glory," Maggie interrupts with a laugh. Her face is shiny with steam and perspiration. The kitchen isn't air-conditioned and the main exhaust fans aren't used until the cooking begins with service. That's the kind of compromise you have to make when you transform a century farmhouse into a gourmet restaurant. The air conditioning is for the customers, and during a heat wave like the one we've been having the temperature in the kitchen never drops to anything close to tolerable.

The phone rings and I excuse myself. While I'm taking the dinner reservation I keep one ear on their conversation and take a closer look at Wright. He's lean and fit and I can see his biceps bulging through his shirt. The guy clearly works out a lot to get that kind of definition. He's good looking but something about his heavy brow and especially his jaw gives him a brutal look, one that tells me he's used to getting what he wants. I'm glad we don't owe him money. He doesn't look like a patient man.

"Typical of him," Maggie is saying. "Taking off again."

"He's done this before?"

"Yes," she sneers. "He goes off on some *stage* at Fat Duck or Alinea or wherever."

"And he doesn't he tell you? Or tell his wife?"

Maggie crosses her arms and leans against the pass through. "He doesn't think anyone else exists."

The phone rings again and I reluctantly answer, straining to hear Wright and Maggie over the noise of the hood fans.

"The food's just as good—probably better if you ask me—when he's not here," I hear Maggie snap. Wright's expression is surprised and I catch his glance at me as I take down the dinner reservation.

"Let's be honest," Maggie interrupts before Wright can say anything. "He's always trying to micromanage the line," she glances an apology at me but continues muttering. "Thinks he can do everyone's job better than they can."

"He is the chef, Maggie," I interject, with my hand over the receiver. "And actually, he can." She glares at me, eyes narrowed, then turns back to her *demi glace* reduction.

There's an awkward silence. Finally Wright says, "I wonder if I might have a word with Montana Lambert before I go? Is she here today?"

Maggie cackles. "I saw her duck into the walk-in cooler to hide when you first arrived. She's probably got hypothermia right about now." She then strides over to the cooler, yanks open the heavy door and yells inside, "Hey Alabama! Someone's here to see you."

I hang up the phone and go into the dining room where I pretend to set a table. I don't trust myself to be close enough to hear what Montana says.

I can see her and Wright talking. She stands with her arms folded tightly across her chest, her face flushed and her eyes red from crying. He's asking her a lot of questions, and as she answers she becomes more and more agitated.

"I know he's dead," I finally hear her blurt, her voice loud. "There's no way he'd just leave. She killed him."

THREE

Rose

A FEW MINUTES later, I glance up and see Wright enter the dining room. His expression is carefully neutral.

"Is that offer of coffee still valid?" he asks. I pull out my best smile, the one I use for a busy Saturday night when we're over-booked and in the weeds.

"Sure thing," I say and lead him to a table next to window, over-looking the *parterre* garden. I ask Maggie to have coffee brought in.

We sit in silence and he studies the elegant garden, taking in the carefully sheared boxwood hedges and cones, the gravel paths and clipped trees, all set in a symmetrical pattern that's best viewed from the dining room. I designed this view to look good year round, especially in winter. There's no point having a garden view that looks like sticks and mud for six months of the year.

The Thorny Rose sign sits at the edge of the garden, next to the driveway. It's beautifully hand carved in wood and painted so the rose and its thorns look real. In the summer months it's covered with fragrant climbing roses, but in winter the canes are bare, their sharp thorns mingling with the carved ones on the sign.

"You don't seem that prickly," Wright says, breaking the silence. I look at him in confusion. "The sign?" he clarifies. "The name of your restaurant? Thorny Rose."

"Sorry. Right," I shake my head then smile. "It was a joke. Between my husband and me." He is about to ask something else, but Lotte arrives with a French press of coffee and a plate of pastries. I notice she has changed her apron for a fresh one and smile my thanks. Appearances are important; I always keep reminding the staff of that. How things look matters more than how they really are.

"To answer your question honestly," I begin once she is out of earshot. "Business has fallen off a bit since he's been away. Our food and service are absolutely the same—maybe better, as Maggie said, but…" I'm not sure how to finish my thought. He raises his eyebrows, waiting for me to continue.

"Chef might be demanding or difficult in the kitchen, but customers love the attention he gives them—touching tables, flirting, recommending dishes. I guess they've noticed he's not here… but it's not like I advertised he's gone." I'm no substitute for him in the front of the house. He has charisma and knows exactly how to handle people. I'm too awkward and shy. And I'm usually dirty, with muddy boots and broken fingernails. I'm the gardener not a *maitre'd*.

Wright nods and goes for a pastry.

"What's this one?"

"It's a *bichon au citron*. Basically a lemon curd turnover made with puff pastry." He takes a bite and nods in approval.

"Your pastry chef is good," he remarks casually. But he watches me for a reaction.

"Chef has an eye for talent," I say. If Wright catches my tone he doesn't let on.

"Why do you call him *chef*?" he asks, through a mouthful of pastry. "He's your husband, isn't he?"

"It's tradition. Respect. And it helps keep a professional tone in the restaurant with the staff, more so than using his name."

"What does he call you?" I hesitate, unsure how to answer.

At that moment the dishwasher is bringing tray of clean water glasses in to stock the service area. Catching sight of Wright he almost drops them all, then he quickly unloads the tray and slips back into the kitchen. Wright makes notes as I speak, but I don't look at what he's writing down. I notice he has a large gold signet ring on his hand, set with some diamonds. Pretty flashy for a police detective. After a minute he stops, then meets my eye.

"How long has he worked for you?" he asks.

"Paul?" I feel a flash of irritation when I understand where this is going. "Ages. Why?" I read his expression. "He's a good kid," I say, defending Paul. "And a very hard worker."

Wright raises his eyebrow, says nothing. "What?" I'm irritated. "So he was maybe in a bit of trouble once…"

"…or twice," Wright interrupts. "His brother runs the grow op up the road."

"It's not a *grow op*. It's a legitimate business…he's licensed by the government to grow medical cannabis. It's all perfectly legal." Wright doesn't reply. "Does this have anything to do with my husband?"

"No. You're right." He closes his notebook and puts it into his pocket. "Why do you suppose your business has fallen off recently?" Wright returns to his earlier question. "Would he have told the regulars he was going away?"

"And not told me. Which is what you are really asking," I reply. I don't have an answer to that.

The screen door to the back porch opens and I hear a shriek from Maggie. I turn and see a tall, lean man standing in the doorway, holding a large gathering basket in each arm. He nods gravely in response to Maggie's welcoming smile. I see his hungry eyes searching the restaurant for me.

"Excuse me," I say to Wright as I get up to leave the table.

"That's my forager Yuri. I'll be a while," I add, hoping he'd take the hint and leave.

"No problem," he says. "I can wait. The coffee's great." Note to self, I think as I make my way to the kitchen: Don't offer coffee to people you would prefer not to linger.

Maggie is already plating up a meal for Yuri, urging him to sit and eat at the little table next to the kitchen phone extension. It's covered with invoices and half-completed orders, with the reservation book laying across it all, where I'd left it. I quickly clear it away so he can sit.

"You look half starved!" Maggie says, placing a large earthenware bowl of *cassoulet* on the table, with a chunk of bread. It's true. Yuri's cheeks are sunken and his eyes are lost in dark shadows. He eyes the food like a feral dog, tempted but wary, but he won't sit until he has properly greeted me with an embrace and a kiss on both cheeks. Then, handing off the baskets to Maggie he sits down and begins to eat like a hungry wolf.

I squeeze Yuri's shoulder as I set down a glass of beer for him. He doesn't much enjoy human contact and that's enough to let him know I've missed him. A touch is more than enough contact for a man who lives alone in the forest, venturing into civilization as seldom as possible.

Yuri's hands are earth stained and nails dirty and hard-bitten. He looks much older than when I last saw him in the spring, which worries me. The summer should be an easier time for him, with warm weather and plenty to eat and gather. But Yuri looks like he's just survived another Siberian winter.

The last time I saw him was in late April, when he came through the door bringing with him the intense scent of fresh ferns and the moist earth after the thaw.

"How was the winter?" I'd asked once he'd had something to eat.

"Not so bad," he'd shrugged. "Not like Russia." Which was his standard response. Nothing was like Russia—not the cold, the snow, the heat, the mushrooms, the garlic, the dill. Nothing he could find or nothing we could cook would ever be like his homeland. Yuri's *toska*, his intense melancholy and nostalgia for Russia, was profound and immeasurable, the loss inconsolable.

I have no way of reaching him or knowing when to expect him, or what he'll bring me when he shows up. In the spring he brings heaps of ramps—the delicate wild leeks, and the tightly curled green spirals of fiddleheads. Wild berries and mushrooms in summer and autumn. Yuri just shows up a few times a year, bearing his offerings, like a boreal forest version of Saint Nick.

While he's eating I turn my attention to the baskets, inhaling the delicious earthy aroma that's already filling the kitchen.

One basket holds five giant white puffballs.

"Maggie, look! These will be great on the grill with some garlic and rosemary. Maybe as a side with the lamb chops?" Maggie looks as excited as I feel. We get pretty worked up over these things.

The second basket is even better. It's full of crinkled golden chanterelles and beautiful marbled and whorled black morels.

"Oh, my beauties!" I inhale their earthy loamy scent. "These are exactly what I need for the Festival pairing for the weekend. Maggie—we can do the wild mushroom bruschetta, with *burrata*." Maggie nods her approval and I turn back to Yuri.

"They are beautiful. And earlier than last year."

He shrugs and keeps eating. "Warm summer. Lots of rain up north."

"Thank you." He nods then sips his beer.

"How much do I owe you?" Yuri looks over the baskets, his lips pursed in thought.

"One hundred fifty." I start toward the office but he puts his hand on my arm. "You pay next time I come, okay? I have to go."

Then his eyes narrow as he looks over my shoulder. Wright has come up behind me. I guess he got bored sitting alone in the dining room.

"This is Detective Constable Wright." Yuri stands, looks him over then dismisses him. Then he holds up his bent finger, and pulls a crumpled brown paper bag from inside his pocket and hands it to me with a wink. Inside is a plastic bag full of spruce tips, the tender bright green new growth from the ends of the spruce branches.

"I freeze for you. They don't keep fresh after picking in May." I press the bag to my chest and smile at Yuri.

"*Spasibo*." I say. Yuri smiles.

"He's here because someone reported chef missing," Maggie tells him with a smirk. She's raised her voice loud enough so the sister wives could hear. Yuri snorts his lack of interest and walks out, his hand raised in farewell. Through the window I watch as he gets into his beaten up red pickup and drives off.

"He doesn't seem particularly concerned," Wright observes. Maggie rolls her eyes.

"Why should he be?" she says, then turns her attention back to the baskets of mushrooms.

"Thank you for the coffee." Wright fumbles in his breast pocket for a card. "Let me give you my number." Unable to find one he scribbles on a page torn from his notebook and hands it to me. "Please let me know when you hear from your husband."

I finally feel myself relax as I watch him drive off. Maggie turns to me. "Are we sure he's even a cop? No card." She shakes her head in disapproval. "Aren't they supposed to show you a badge or ID or something?"

"He's definitely a cop," a low voice mutters behind us. "We've met a few times." It's Paul the dishwasher. He stares out the window until the full throaty roar of Wright's classic muscle car disappears down the road, his face expressionless.

I take a deep breath and reach for my apron. "Okay everybody," I raise my voice. "Fun's over. It's time to get to work."

The staff reluctantly return to their tasks as I pretend to study my clipboard. The visit from Wright has really disturbed me, though I'm doing my best to not show it. *How will it look now that the police have been around looking for my husband? Who else knows about it? What can I do now? Will Thorny Rose's business fall off?* Maggie puts her hand on my shoulder.

"It's going to be all right," she whispers.

"I'm not sure how." Out of the corner of my eye I watch Montana as she works, rolling pastry and keeping an eye on the thermometer clipped in the caramel sauce. "I can't even fire her for that stunt. She'd probably sue for unfair dismissal. And win." Maggie squeezes my shoulder. "It was bad enough when I could pretend there was nothing going on. When I could turn a blind eye and wait for it to end."

"You'll figure it out. Like you always do," Maggie says, then she returns to her station. Thank God for Maggie. She believes in me when nobody else does, not my husband, and not even me. I wish I had her faith.

I'm not even sure I can make it through the wine festival. It starts tomorrow and will run weekends for the next month, with local vineyards offering VQA wine and culinary pairings. I'm already exhausted and overwhelmed with the work that needs to be done, by the reality that I'm doing it alone for the first time, and by the fact that I don't think I can pull it off and make it look like I know what I'm doing—both to the customers and even more importantly, to the staff. They already haven't got much respect for me, and I feel their judgement as they watch me struggle to keep it together in chef's absence. I understand they're concerned about their jobs, but I'm doing the best I can to keep the restaurant going. I just hope it's enough.

Lotte has her back to me as she stands chopping parsley, the nine-inch chef's knife looking like a toy in her big hands. From the back she could have been one of her four brothers. They're all from the same Dutch farming stock, tall and broad shouldered. Sadly she's the least attractive of the litter, and she knows it. Her face is broad and flat, like a *saute* pan. Completely without grace, she lumbers around the kitchen like an ox and everyone tries their best to steer clear of her during service.

Montana is her opposite. Pale and lightly freckled, with her auburn hair long and naturally curly, she's like a Botticelli maiden. Slender and light, she moves quickly through her tasks without apparent effort. She's a talented pastry chef, true. But how can I keep her around, after her accusation? And then I'll have to find her replacement, which is a challenge without chef around to interview the candidates.

I watch as she tucks her hair behind her ear. Then Montana raises her head and meets my eye. She doesn't flinch and I look away first. She has the face of a fox—pointy little chin, wide set eyes, appraising me.

I remember last summer, when she first arrived at Thorny Rose. Seeing her in her pristine kitchen whites, unruffled and competent even after a tough service spent in the weeds. She was always cool under pressure. Chef liked that.

I observed as she timed her early morning strolls through the flower garden, when the light would show her at her languid and beguiling best. She'd just happen to come across chef in the garden, who naturally had just happened to be there. He taught her how to select the freshest herbs, the blue borage and orange nasturtium blossoms, the delicate pea tendrils and fresh shoots to garnish the plates. How to pick the lavender blossoms to garnish the special honey I made, that we served in its comb alongside a scoop of lavender ice cream.

And I remember the morning I saw him, feeding her a tiny taste of my honey, her face held up to his, his hand cupping her delicate chin, just as I came into the kitchen. I'd quickly dropped a glass then bent to clear it away so no one would see my tears.

FOUR

Wright

WELL THAT WAS a waste of time. At least the coffee and pastry were good. And that little pastry chef was sweet too. But there's nothing here. The guy is gone, and nobody knows where. Seems like nobody even cares, except for the girlfriend. His wife isn't concerned; she's just embarrassed that I'm asking questions.

Must be nice to have a wife who'll look after things so he can go off on a *stage*, or run around with a young pastry chef. He's like some tomcat, going wherever he wants all night, but the wife knows he'll be back in the morning looking for a meal and a warm bed.

But the girlfriend just wouldn't give up.

"Look," I told her. "I have nothing to go on here. Nobody else seems to think there's a problem. They all say that he's just gone off on a *stage*, which he's done before."

"He would never just go off like this without telling me," she kept saying. But clearly the guy did just that. "We're in love. He tells me everything." Except where he went. I think she's just pissed that he left without telling her.

"We have plans," she'd said. "We're working on a project…he wouldn't just go. Not now."

"What kind of project?" She looked like she'd already said too much, and didn't answer.

"Have you heard anything from him?" I asked. She said nothing and I was getting impatient. "It's a yes or no question."

"He's texted," she finally admitted. "But something is wrong."

"So, then he's not *missing,* is he?" I told her. "He's not dead. He's just gone off somewhere—-on this *stage.*" She wouldn't even look at me. I'd say the chef was just a typical married guy who got into something deeper than he was prepared for and he split. The girlfriend is hot, but maybe she had expectations, like they all do.

He's run off, that's what I think. I feel it in my gut and I'm not happy about it. Where's he run to? That's the real question.

Now the wife, she interests me. She's so calm and self-contained it's tough to read her. Her grey eyes give nothing away. She admits she doesn't know where he is, but denies he's missing. That feels off. A wife always knows where her husband is, in my experience. She's a quiet one; maybe she doesn't have a lot of self-confidence. Maybe he bullied her and she lost whatever she'd started out with. I guess whatever happened in their marriage is a secret. Everyone's got secrets, and this chef is no different. I know it.

FIVE

Rose

I WAKE UP this morning with my wedding ring on my right hand. What do you suppose that means? I don't remember changing it. Now I can trace the faint pale line on my finger where it's been for six years.

My hands aren't elegant or manicured. They are working hands, worn and stained with dirt under my nails. Strong hands. Capable. I like to think of myself that way, as the reliable one who gets things done. But I'm not sure it's true. I just hope I can manage the situation I now find myself in, with a missing husband and a restaurant to run. Most days I feel out of my depth and I fear it's all going to come crashing down around me. But I can't let it show. I've got people depending on me.

I drag myself out of bed and into the shower, planning my day as I go through the motions of getting dressed. Staff will be coming in soon to start prep for dinner service. I have to visit my mother at some point, not looking forward to that. I've got a quick stop to make before I take Maggie's shift at the farmers market for a few hours. She's supposed to be working the Womyn's Collective stall, to help her daughter out. But Maggie had looked so tired after service last night I thought she needed to relax this morning, so I offered to step into her shoes. She's always pushing herself to do more, to act as if she were her old self, as if nothing has changed. But it has. Everything is different now.

I run a comb through my wet hair and head downstairs. With the truck windows down my hair will dry quickly enough. I don't really have the time or the interest to do more than comb it and tie it back to keep it out of the way when I'm working anyway.

It's only just after eight o'clock and already the temperature is almost thirty degrees Celsius and it will definitely climb higher during the day. With the humidity it feels like it's in the low forties and the temperature barely drops overnight. It's been like this for weeks now, with no end in sight. There's still no rain in the forecast.

I step out onto the back porch into the heavy, still morning air. The punishing humidity hasn't let up overnight and I'm instantly covered in a moist film. I do a quick tour of the gardens and make a list of chores and of what to harvest for the staff, and leave it in its usual spot on the porch under a stone. The birds are sitting in the trees, as if it's too even hot for them to fly to the feeders. Even the bees seem lazy and slow to wake from their beds in the cosmos and dahlia blossoms. Everything is scorched from the relentless sun beating down. With no rain for weeks I've needed to irrigate the gardens daily and the depth of the reservoir is lower than I've ever seen it.

I get into my stifling truck and drive along the escarpment, with the deep blue of the lake and the town below me in the distance. The road winds through mature maple and beech forests, interspersed with open areas of farmland and pasture. Bales of fresh cut hay stand stacked in fields, the rough bristles of the remaining stems visible against the soil like a day old beard.

I pass century farms with handmade signs for maple syrup and brown eggs, next to newly built country estate homes on acres of green lawns. These are playgrounds of the newly rich: the brokers, investment bankers and hedge fund managers who've built weekend getaways here in wine country. Some of them call themselves gentlemen farmers, which is a joke around here. They aren't even gentlemen, let alone farmers.

The egg farmer next door probably makes a bit of money every week cutting the rich man's lawn with his riding mower, since the guy in the new house won't be wanting to spend his precious weekend doing it. Not when he could be out on the golf course. That's the way it is around here, with the old making room for the new. And making allowances for them. And making money off them. That's certainly how Thorny Rose stays in business.

As much as I may not like a lot of the new rich arrivals, I can't deny I need them to keep going. Chef used to defend our prices, talking about the high level of gastronomy we offer, and how it's not just for anyone and everyone. *It's for those with cultivated palates,* he'd say and *it's not about the money.* But it is, obviously. Only certain people can afford it, or care enough. And it's tough to care when the decision between tuna casserole and fish fingers for dinner is based on the coupons you can find in the evening paper.

I turn off the Concession at the tenth Side Road and onto an unmarked driveway, then drive in past a rusty farm gate that's hanging off its hinges with the posts long rotted out. The long driveway is nothing more than a pair of ruts through some grass, whatever gravel had been laid down years ago now long grown over. Red cones of Sumach flowers and Elderberry branches brush the sides of my car on either side as I creep along, trying to avoid the deep ruts and potholes. Soon there will be no driveway at all, which is likely how Jay wants it: Isolated, unwelcoming and impenetrable.

A hundred yards through thick brush the driveway ends in an open field of rough cut grass surrounding a typical old Ontario red brick farmhouse, a large barn, several ramshackle outbuildings and broken down hoop greenhouses, their plastic flapping in the breeze.

The house is three stories tall, with flaking paint on what remains of the gingerbread trim. Most of that has rotted and fallen away like missing teeth in an old man's smile. But I notice that, like the barn, the house has a brand new metal roof with solar lighting panels arrayed on the south facing side.

The farm is completely fenced, apart from the driveway entrance, and three large Dobermans run alongside my car barking as I approach the house. Jay is very security conscious. The risk of gangs or even local kids breaking in and stealing his crop is always top of mind.

I get out of the car as soon as the dogs are called off and make my way toward the decrepit barn, waving at couple of big guys who sit on the wraparound porch pretending not to watch me. Several rusty cars, a tractor and an abandoned trailer are parked along the side, making the farm look like a hillbilly palace, as Jay means it to. The last thing he wants to do is draw attention to what he's doing. But in a quick glance back toward the house I catch a glimpse of a brand new Dodge Hemi and a Tesla Model X tucked in next to the back porch. Clearly Jay is doing all right for himself.

I push open the barn door, which opens into a small reception space, with a desk and a couple of worn upholstered chairs. It looks a lot like a cut rate travel agency, but instead of signs for deals on vacations, there are posters for award winning cannabis strains: White Widow, Sour Diesel, and Bubba Kush—along with a vintage movie poster for Reefer Madness.

The steel security door behind the desk opens and a smiling Jay sticks his head through. His buddies on the porch have obviously given him the head's up, as they're paid to do.

"Sorry, I totally forgot you were coming today," he rubs what's left of his hair and looks sheepish. "I think I've got Hempenheimers." Jay is short and wiry, and wears his long hair tied back in a ponytail. He's pretty much bald on top, and I wonder why he doesn't just cut it all short. Jay has worn a ponytail since I knew him in high school, back when he actually had some hair. He dresses the same as well: jeans and t-shirts, with a plaid shirt or down vest over that in winter. With his wire-rimmed glasses he looks like a typical graduate student or teaching assistant, in something esoteric like Old Church Slavonic or Hegelian Dialectical Materialism. Not like a successful cannabis grower and semi-reformed drug dealer. Not that any of us know what that actually looks like, I think with a smile.

In fact Jay looks exactly like his brothers Paul and Jim, if you overlook Jim's hillbilly beard and Jay's glasses, even though they are many years apart. You'd have a hard time telling them apart in a lineup, which I realize they've all probably been in at one time or another.

"Not a problem," I reply. "I'm in no rush."

"Why don't you come on back while I get your order," and he opens the door wide so I can pass through. "It'll just take a minute." Jay makes his way into a back storeroom, where he keeps the product ready for sale and for shipping to medical dispensaries across the country.

In what looks from the outside like a dilapidated old barn is a state of the art indoor grow. Most of the barn's interior, and the loft space above, has been converted into separate grow rooms, all fitted with LED lights, fans, heaters and automatic watering and ventilation systems. Each room is tented off to keep the crop clean and to mask the intense purple light given off by the grow lights that are optimized to provide the wavelength specific light his cannabis plants require to grow fastest.

After the weed is harvested and cured, which Jay does in the loft area, it's ready for trimming. The individual buds are shaped with small sharp scissors. All leaves are clipped off and the bud is shaped into a tight, compact nugget. The entire front section of the barn, directly behind the office, is given over to five long folding tables and chairs, each set up as a station for the trimmers. Each station has its own work light, a couple of pairs of sharp, pointed scissors and a bottle of rubbing alcohol for cleaning the sticky cannabis resin off the scissors.

The air in this part of the barn isn't conditioned and controlled like in the reception area and grow rooms and I start to feel beads of perspiration crawl down my spine. It's hot, stuffy and dim—apart from the bright circles of light cast over the trimmers' hands as they clip and shape the fat colas into buds.

Several Vietnamese women are bent over their work, taking no interest in me as I sit in a spare chair to wait. Officially, for immigration purposes, the women are Jay's nannies. The only question, if anyone was curious enough to ask, is why would Jay, who has a couple of grown kids living with his ex-wife, needs five nannies to look after them.

He'd first met a couple of them in a nightclub in Niagara Falls, and they brought in friends who could be trusted when there was a harvest. They'd been working in the city as manicurists. Trimming weed is perfect work for them, given their training. It's detail oriented, close work, not much different than working on nails—and you don't have to make inane small talk with clients or smell acetone all day.

It's piecework, but the money is great. Trimmers are paid by the pound, so the faster they are, the more they make and Jay pays them in cash, of course.

Some go home to Vietnam a couple of times a year and come back to work for Jay when the next harvest is ready. Or, they go back to work in the nail salon in the off-season.

One of them stops trimming for a minute to clean her scissors. She eyes me for a second while she runs the alcohol soaked cloth over the blades, then dismisses me and gets back to work. Time is money and I am of no interest.

Jay emerges from the storage room, with two small jars of buds and a vial of oil. He bags my purchase, just like in a grocery store. Then he thrusts a bulging plastic grocery bag full of leaves into my hand, with a wink. "For tea," he says. "It'll help."

My eyes well up and I thank him. He shakes his head.

"No problem. You know I'm happy to help anyway I can," he says. And he means it. Jay's an evangelist for medicinal cannabis. He has chronic back pain from a herniated disc and he medicates with weed for it, so he knows from personal experience what to recommend to his customers.

"This is ACDC," he says. "It relieves nerve pain and should help with nausea."

I slip a fat brown paper bag across the desk to him. He glances inside then nods.

"This is for the last week," I say. "We really appreciate what you're doing for us."

"It's all good," Jay says with a smile. "It's a pleasure doing business with you Rose. Say hi to Sophie and Maggie for me." Thanking him again I go back out to my truck, do a quick turn-around and head back down the driveway to the road.

Jay's a good friend. I've known him since we were kids. He'd struggled halfway through high school as a stoner, reading too much Carlos Castaneda and experimenting with peyote and mescaline. *Only organics,* he'd always say—*never synthetics. They fuck with your brain chemistry.* Then he'd dropped out after repeating most of Grade Ten and roamed around. First he went out to BC, then down to Humboldt County in California where he'd learned his trade. He spent some time in jail down there; he called it his *finishing school.* Now he's back in town, growing cannabis legally for medical patients.

I'm lost in thought as I make my way back down the overgrown driveway and turn onto the Side Road. I almost don't notice the grey car parked down a side lane. It pulls out and follows me as I drive back to the main road, and I pretend I don't see him.

SIX

Rose

I PULL OUT of the driveway, checking in my rearview mirror as Wright follows me. Then I lose him at the level crossing when he's caught waiting for a freight train to pass. I wonder if he's doing some surveillance on Jay's operation, but that doesn't seem likely in such a conspicuous car. I consider giving Jay a call and giving him a head's up. But maybe it's better if I just let him sort whatever it is out. He's dealt with cops more times than I ever have and I'm sure he knows what he's doing.

I turn left onto Ridge Road, which runs just under the top of the Niagara escarpment. I can see the wineries and villages below and, a few miles away, the deep indigo of Lake Ontario. Here in Niagara's Twenty Valley, we have a distinct microclimate that's ideal for growing high quality grapes. The ridge of the escarpment runs like a prehistoric geological spine through the region, protecting the vineyards on the slopes below from strong prevailing winds from either direction. Both Lake Ontario to the north and Lake Erie to the south provide temperature moderation and air circulation for the extended growing season.

I pass family farms and apple, pear and cherry orchards. Roadside stalls are just setting up for the day, displaying baskets of peaches, tomatoes, jars of honey and local jams and preserves. I slow past the hundreds of hectares of vineyards, with dozens of white sheep grazing among the vines. The rows are full of fat clusters of white and red grapes hanging below the carefully pruned and trained vines. Growers remove all the lower leaves in and around the fruiting zone to allow the grapes to ripen.

Sheep are allowed to graze in some vineyards for six weeks in summer, but are moved out when grapes start to mature. They eat the grape leaves but won't touch the young fruit since it's too tart. They also fertilize as they work and don't need a salary. And they are delicious, which is not something you can say for most employees.

Visiting my mother is never easy. Every week I make this same drive out to Pelham Woods, all hope extinguished. Since her diagnosis with early-onset Alzheimer's just before her seventieth birthday her decline has been so fast I never know from one week to the next what I'll find. But it's never as much as she's lost.

I return home after every visit, my heart reduced to ash. In between I move through fear and resentment through pity to grief. I'm mostly past anger. We don't get to talk about happy family memories, or look through photo albums and reminisce. My mother barely recalls most things and what little she does remember, she gets wrong. When I correct her she becomes agitated and defensive and we have to change the subject. It's exhausting trying to get her to remember things correctly.

I key in the entry code and then make my way to her room, after I don't find her in the main lounge. That's always a bad sign; it means she didn't get up for breakfast, which means she's had a bad night, which means she'll be at best irritable or at worst hysterical. If I'm lucky she's just asleep.

Her oldest friends Doreen and Anna visit her most days, which I'm grateful for since it alleviates some of my guilt. But it also makes me jealous because she usually recognizes them, whereas most days she is vague about who I might be. Unless it's a good day, and those are coming around less frequently.

Today is not my lucky day. She's being especially difficult, complaining of pain then refusing to take her medication; insisting on walking to the toilet and then falling; demanding to know where her daughter is and then not recognizing me when I hug her and pushing me away. And I know that within minutes of my leaving she'll forget I was ever there.

Not even the smiling, endlessly patient Filipina caregivers are able to distract her. Eventually they get her toileted and dressed and settled into a chair where she'll doze until they come to fetch her for lunch. The pain medication takes hold and she nods off while I sit next to her, a stranger.

I watch the clock for ten minutes then quietly creep out the door.

By the time I arrive at the farmers' market there isn't much for me to do. The members of the Womyn's Collective have already been there for over an hour and everything looks perfect. The honey, flowers, dried lavender and herb sachets, natural essences and extracts—are all beautifully displayed. And it's still hours before any large crowds are likely to show up.

They've created hundreds of beautiful hand-tied bouquets of brightly coloured zinnias and dahlias, sunflowers and gladiolus. At only ten dollars a bunch they'll be sold out by noon, like they always are. They make bouquets so beautiful you could cry. And they are always unique, using natural accents found in the forest and fields around their farm.

The Womyn sell natural honey as well their own herbal extracts and distilled essences from lavender and roses. But they make most of their money on their flowers. They are creative geniuses in flower design, creating loose, natural arrangements that flop and are beautifully uneven, full of greens and berries or fruit.

Today everyone at the Womyn booth is wearing flower crowns. They've also distributed them to all the women working at the other booths in the market to advertise that we'll be selling them at the stall. Let me tell you there is no woman on this earth who doesn't look beautiful wearing a flower crown. Young girls, elderly grannies, middle-aged moms; all looked whimsical, lovely and regal.

"Here," one of the Womyn says, placing one woven from roses, daisies and ivy on my head. "This is perfect for you." I feel embarrassed, but can't deny it makes me feel transformed somehow, into someone more feminine, more charming and loveable. It's been a while since I've felt any of those things.

I can smell a tantalizing aroma drifting over from the Green Bean Cafe stall. Their fair trade coffee is fantastic…they roast their own beans to perfection. "I need a coffee," I announce, and ignoring their offers of herbal tea, follow the delicious scent to the coffee booth.

Phil the coffee roaster set up in town a couple of years ago, and struggled for a time in competition with the several Starbucks and the Tim Hortons on every corner. But Phil offered what neither of them did—superior coffee at a reasonable price, served in a funky rustic space. His cafe has long wooden harvest tables and mis-matched chairs, lots of sunny windows and tons of houseplants. Huge Monstera philodendrons filled the windows, with tall Fiddle Leaf figs, snake plants and palms in ceramic pots on the floor. Each table has a succulent centerpiece in an antique coffee pot or espresso tin. It feels like having a coffee at a friend's place, not a chain coffee shop. And Phil is always there; a friendly knowledgeable barista, who isn't too much of a hipster that the locals shy away.

I have a sip of the coffee. It's delicious; a dark roast, organic and of course free trade. It tastes like virtue.

I sit at a picnic table and watch the early birds drift into the market, baskets and shopping bags over their arms. Pushing bikes and baby strollers, filling panniers and baskets with loaves of fresh bread and pastry, plums and preserves, fingerling potatoes and delicate peaches. I love to watch their faces as they taste the samples and fill their eyes with the colour and textures of the produce. I listen to them plan what to cook for dinner that evening with the glossy eggplant or purple beans they've just bought, happy to share their pleasure in the food.

We're a diverse little group in our local foodie culture. In the market there are the biodynamic farmers, the organic farmers and the conventional farmers. There are artisanal cheese makers—both goat and cow, and the Womyn collective with their slow flowers and honey. There are crafts people selling handmade baby clothes and booties, pottery, and hand woven tea towels. There's a local Wild Food guy who leads foraging tours, where he teaches people how to not die from eating the wrong mushrooms. There's the butcher, the baker and even the candlestick maker—Andrei the honey farmer is selling handmade beeswax candles.

The most popular stall at the market is the small petting zoo, and it already has a crowd gathered around admiring the pigs and goats and exotic chicken breeds that look like showgirls with their absurd feather plumes.

Every week there are buskers and I always look forward to the old man who plays an accordion. He always wears black dress pants and a perfectly pressed long sleeved shirt, with his shoes polished to a dazzling shine. I construct elaborate stories about him, where he's come from, who'd been the love of his life, how his heart had been broken. But I don't even know his name. His nose is enormous and beaked, far too large for his face and his eyes are so dark that they look black. Their expression is so intense it makes him look as if he is mad with grief, from his broken heart, naturally. His hair is always worn slicked back and dyed black to cover the grey and his nails are always buffed and shiny, which I can't help but notice as they dance over the accordion keys.

He's usually joined by young guitar players in impromptu, somewhat discordant, jams. These musicians are usually men with acoustic guitars who play folk ballads and singer songwriters from the seventies—which would be several decades before any of them were born. But the music is always great and they draw a large crowd.

I can see the Mill Race dairy booth is set up with a small cooler at the back of their stall, full of milk in old style glass bottles with foil tops. The necks of the whole milk bottles are thick with delicious full fat cream. The bottles are embossed with the farm's logo of cows, flowers, grass and a mill wheel. They are collector's items and look great as vases, and many shoppers are happy to pay an extra few dollars for their milk just to have one.

It occurs to me that we can use some cheese for service. It's time to refresh the cheese plate selection on the menu. But then I see Helen is at the booth. She's the owner of Mill Race Dairy and I'm not going to go over there and face her. I decide to have Maggie call in an order later instead. Soon it will be impossible to buy anything in the market without running into one of chef's conquests.

SEVEN

Rose

THE MARKET IS starting to get busy and I realize I should get back to the Womyn booth. Then I catch a glimpse of Detective Constable Wright in the crowd and my heart speeds up. Why is he here now, if he's on surveillance at Jay's? Then I know the answer: it's not Jay he's watching. I don't like it. My heart pounds with fear. Why is he following me?

He's speaking with a short young police officer. She's young and something about her red hair looks familiar, but I can't place her. Their conversation seems very heated and a bit furtive, and he keeps looking around and over his shoulder to make sure no one can hear them arguing. At one point he grabs her arm and she shakes him off, shaking her head. Then he sees me and breaks off the conversation. The police officer leaves in a hurry without looking back.

"Good morning," Wright says with a smile as he comes over to where I'm sitting at the picnic table. Any trace of whatever the argument was about is gone and he seems relaxed, his complete attention focused on me. "You look amazing." I'm taken aback by his random compliment then remember the floral crown. I'd forgotten I'm wearing it.

"Thanks. Not my usual style," I mumble. "I'm helping out at the booth today," I say, gesturing toward the Womyn Collective display. He smiles and nods his appreciation. I'm not comfortable with him looking at me.

"You on duty today?" I ask, anxious to change the subject, and to figure out what he wants.

"Nope. Day off. I'm just looking around." Maybe it's just a coincidence that I saw his car at Jay's. Or maybe he's a customer, something that just occurs to me. Jay can sell to whomever he chooses, even police, as long as they've got a prescription. In any case, it's not my business.

I stand there awkwardly with nothing to say, but he seems unperturbed. I wish he would go away. He makes me nervous, afraid I'll say the wrong thing and I don't want to talk to him.

"Well. I've got to get to the booth." I start to walk away, but he follows along. As we pass the petting zoo, someone calls out to me.

"Rose!" It's Luca, our pork supplier. He's standing inside the petting zoo fence, stroking a Large Black pig. There are several other Large Black and Tamworth pigs with him in the pen, nuzzling him for attention. "Thank you for the fantastic Amarone you gave me," he shouts. "It was delicious." I make my way over, with Wright following behind.

Luca is tall and lean, with dark hair. With his Roman nose and sharp cheekbones he looks like a younger version of my husband. They are even about the same height.

"I'm glad you enjoyed it," I say. "But really, thank you. For everything you do for us." If it wasn't for Luca I'm not sure where I'd be. "I'll see if I have a couple more bottles," I wink. "Maybe I'll bring them around tonight after service if it's not too late." Luca rubs his hands together in anticipation.

Then I remember my manners. "Luca, this is Detective Constable Wright. Detective, this is Luca Ricci, owner of Millvale Cured Meats and grower of the best heritage pork you've ever tasted."

"Detective?" Luca raises his eyebrows. "Any problems?"

"Off duty," clarifies Wright. "I'm just enjoying the market."

The pigs come up to fence and stick their noses through, asking to be petted. Wright backs off in alarm.

"Don't worry, they won't bite," says Luca. "They are just curious."

I laugh out loud. "Hell yes they will!" I say. "They can take your finger off." I reach in and stroke one who has stuck his nose through the fence, his eyes covered by his large floppy ears. "But they are very affectionate," I continue. "And as smart as a dog."

"Smarter," replies Luca. "They don't see very well, but have great sense of smell. Excellent memories. And they are very social," Luca says, all the while stroking the pig's flanks and blowing in its nose. It flops over, clearly expects a belly rub, which Luca provides.

"What do they eat?" asks Wright.

"Only the best for my pigs. Fresh barley grass pasture, whole vegetables, acorns and nuts. They're gourmets," he laughs.

"Don't listen to him," I say. "Pigs will eat anything. Literally."

"Look," Luca points toward the far side of the market. "It's my booth," he says with excitement. Luca is new to the market. I can see the sign above his table: Millvale Cured Meats. "I didn't want to have it too close to the source, so to speak." He smiles. "Didn't want to offend anyone's delicate sensibilities."

"Great sign," I say. "Who's minding the booth?" Luca looks startled.

"*Shit.* I am." He climbs out of the pen and runs over to his booth, waving goodbye.

"Now there's a man who loves his pigs," I say, giving the Large Black one last pat.

"Doesn't it seem strange to you," Wright says as we walk toward the Womyn booth, "that you're petting him now but one day soon he'll be dinner?"

I shake my head. "You get used to it. We all die. At least their deaths have meaning, providing sustenance. Not like humans."

A longhaired guy with a huge frizzy beard that has never seen a trimmer jostles my arm. He's wearing work camouflage pants and work boots. My coffee spills all over my arm. At least it isn't hot anymore.

"Hey!" I say. "Excuse me!" He barely turns to look over his shoulder and I see that it's Jim Tapper, one of the infamous local Tapper brothers. Jay the cannabis grower and Paul my dishwasher, make up the rest of the trio. Jim glares at us then moves along.

Wright turns and watches as Jim strides off. "What's your problem?" Wright yells after him. "Pretty sure that wasn't an accident," he turns to me. "What's he got against you?"

"I think he was looking at you, Detective," I say. "He bumped into me by accident." Wright's expression darkens.

"Keep walking, buddy," he mutters. I feel Wright's anger flare and I'm surprised. I'd have thought a cop would manage to control his temper better than that. Jim really had better stay well clear, if he knows what's good for him.

"That guy's trouble," Wright says. I don't like where this is going. Jim lives quietly, and keeps to himself. As a survivalist, he takes self-sufficiency to the limit.

"Jim's okay," I say. I don't really believe that, but feel the need to stand up for Paul's family. They are good people...mostly.

"The guy lives in an abandoned shack in the bush. He's not okay."

"It's a house, not a shack," I say. "He's not the Unabomber. He's a prepper. He's just...very committed to his ideals."

Wright snorts. "What's he prepping for?"

I try to stay calm, but Wright's attitude is getting on my nerves. I have no idea why's he's attached himself to me this morning, but I don't like it. "Jim's an activist. He's been fighting for compensation from the refinery for years," I say. "He's also self-sufficient and has been living sustainably off the grid for a long time. Stocking up on supplies." Jim also believes the world will run out of food any day now, and has an elaborate survival plan. But I don't need to share that with Wright.

Wright looks skeptical. "What kind of supplies? Does he have weapons?" I stare at him and don't reply.

"C'mon, I'm just making conversation," Wright laughs. "I'm not going to get a warrant and search his place."

I shrug. "I would imagine he has enough weapons to fight a zombie apocalypse and anything else that might be coming." I look at him for a minute. "But he's not bothering anybody."

We continue walking toward the buskers, who are set up just past the flower stall. The old man is there, playing his accordion. He starts with a version Dave Brubeck's Take Five which sounds quirky and odd. Then a hipster with a fuzzy red beard joins in on an acoustic guitar, which makes it sound ironic. A small crowd has gathered around, listening and clapping. Some toss bills and toonie coins into the open accordion case.

After a few minutes the accordion switches over and plays the familiar opening bars of Neil Diamond's Sweet Caroline, and the guitar player picks it up, grinning. He isn't a great singer, but he's definitely enthusiastic and he gives it all he's got. The crowd cheers and sings along to the chorus.

Moms sway to the music, babies on hips. A couple stands close, hands in each other's back jean pockets. Everyone cheers as the guitar player belts out the song.

Then a homeless looking crackhead shuffles in and starts to dance. He wears ragged clothes and has holes in his sneakers. His skin is grey and I bet he has no teeth, but I don't look that closely. People start to turn away and mothers hide their babies' heads, pushing the strollers away as quickly as they can.

It's unsettling whenever the dirty secret of our little town shows its face. For the most part we can ignore it, until we read in the local paper about another crime or drug bust there. The only time you can't avoid it is if you're heading for the beach that borders its south end, and even then that's only for the summer months.

It's just past the canal, wedged between abandoned refinery and what's left of the industrial area. We do have a constant reminder of it whenever we drive over the canal lift bridge heading east. There's a piece of graffiti sprayed on the side of the bridge: LIDSVILLE. The area is classed as a *Low Income District*, and in some kind of pride or rage or defiance the word was sprayed on in huge black letters. For years the graffiti has been removed by the bridge operators and within days it reappears, as a constant reminder. But, like most things, you stop noticing it after a while.

This is the underbelly in our little community. Being so close to the US border and between two of the Great Lakes we have heavy drug traffic through town. Ever since the nickel refinery closed down in the eighties, there have been generations of unemployment, poverty, hopelessness and now drug addiction. There are parts of town I won't visit at night. But then I have no need to. We exist on separate planes and only rarely do those planes intersect, like they are doing right now, this morning at the Farmers' Market.

Suddenly the crackhead stops dancing, bends and scoops up the money from the accordion case. Then he hitches his pants back up and runs off with the buskers' money. The music stops.

"Police!" Voices shout in the crowd. "Stop! Hey!" The guitar player is about to give chase but then realizes there is no point. The thief is long gone. Within a couple of minutes two uniformed policemen on bicycles appear. One takes a statement and the other takes off in pursuit of the thief.

I look at Wright. "Shouldn't you be doing something about that?" He thinks for a moment before he replies.

"It's my day off." He looks quite comfortable doing nothing.

EIGHT

Wright

AFTER I LEAVE her at that flower stall, I wander around the market for a while. There are lots of good looking women there, buying fresh veggies for their families. Some of them are checking me out, looking for a little something on the side. Typical women, wanting to have it all, to have whatever they could get. I make a mental note to come back next week. Maybe see what I can get too.

There are fruit and vegetable vendors, two cheese booths—in competition I guess, cider and beautiful homemade pies and tarts. Another day I might have bought a dozen tarts and taken them back to the station. But I won't be going into the station today. And I have other things to do.

I followed her this morning when she left the Thorny Rose. I was curious and had nowhere in particular I had to be. When she turned onto the Concession I knew exactly where she was going, I just didn't know why. So I parked a few hundred yards down the road behind some tall grass and waited. I had some time on my hands.

I think she's telling me the truth. She believes her husband is away on some *stage*, but she expects him back at some point. Even though there's a report about him being missing, it isn't something the police will be following up. It's just the girlfriend who'd called it in, and from what I can tell she's just another silly twat. There's no reasonable cause for suspicion. So there's no choice but to wait until he returns and everything goes back to normal.

I don't buy anything at the market. I never cook anyway, so what's the point? I'm just looking around a bit then I pass the pork guy's booth. Luca Ricci, Millvale Cured Meats. He smiles at me, so I go over to have a chat.

"Hi!" Luca says while serving a customer. "Enjoying the market?" I smile and look over his display. There are lots of salamis of all shapes and sizes hanging from poles he's set into the tent supports, and on a table in front are a few big hunks of some kind of meat. He's putting those into a meat slicer and shaving off orders for customers. I hear the customers asking for *prosciutto* or *bresaola* but I'm not sure what those are.

When the last customers leave with their meat tucked into their grocery bags, Luca comes over to me.

"What do you think?" he asks, full of pride.

"It looks good," I say, not that I have any basis for comparison. Luca grins like a kid at his birthday party.

"So, I saw those pigs of yours over at the petting zoo. It made me wonder," I begin. "Do you manage the whole process…from beginning to end?" Luca laughs.

"Yes, the whole thing. Sometimes we buy weaners—piglets that are weaned from their mother and fatten them up. But we also have piglets from our own sows and we raise them all the way to slaughter weight. Then we do that too—humanely. We butcher the meat ourselves, smoke it, cure it, season it and sell it."

"And it doesn't bother you, killing them?"

"No," he shakes his head. "They have a good life, a happy life, you know? We should be so lucky to live like they do," he says over his shoulder as he goes to serve someone. "And we need to eat. It's human nature, you gotta kill to live."

Luca bobs on the balls of his feet, like a tennis player waiting for a serve. He's smiling, chatting with his customers, glad-handing with everyone. Then he makes his way back to me again. "I'm really glad Rose convinced me to get a booth here." He rubs his hands together. "It's already been great for getting the word out, you know? Just this morning I've met all kinds of people, new customers. And I'm making good sales."

"She seems to be a real supporter of your store. What about her husband, the chef? Does he buy from you too?" Luca's face darkens, but the smile doesn't leave his face.

"Oh sure," he says. "He buys all the time." I nod, encouraging him. "He's just…well, he's a chef, you know?" As if that says it all. "They've got these big egos. Always have to be right, even when they don't know anything. Sometimes it's tough to deal with them. You know?" I nod as if I know exactly and wonder if Luca is even aware of how he says *you know* all the time.

"Before he'd place the first order with me he insisted on going through every step of my production with me," Luca says.

"Every step?"

"Oh yeah. From the butchering and breaking down the carcass, to making sausages, to curing and smoking. He even came by on a slaughter day. Cut the pig's throat himself, just to show how big his balls are."

My stomach does a little flip. "Really?"

"That's the kind of guy he is." Luca rolls his eyes. "Thinks he's a real bad boy, you know?"

"Doesn't seem much like his wife." From what I've seen of Rose she's quiet and shy, maybe introverted. She seems to lack confidence, which I guess isn't surprising if her husband is such a big noise.

"No way," Luca says. "Rose is amazing. She's the bomb. I'd do anything for her." I wonder how far that might go, and if she'd ever ask him. I definitely get what he's saying though. Rose is very attractive, in a quiet way that's tough to shake.

"Have you seen the chef lately?" I ask Luca after he's finished shaving off another order of *proscuitto* for a customer. He looks sharply at me then shakes his head.

"It's Rose I deal with." He grins at me. "Even though she doesn't eat pork any more."

"What do you mean? Since when?"

"Last couple of months, maybe," he laughs. "She just told me one day that she believed pigs were too intelligent to eat. That it was like eating a pet dog."

"No pork at all? Not even bacon?" I ask. "It's the gateway meat. Even vegetarians will eat bacon."

"That's funny," Luca bursts out laughing. "Rose used to love my charcuterie." Luca looks off into the crowd and sounds wistful. "And she still orders it for the restaurant, don't get me wrong. They go through lots of it," he adds quickly in case I get the wrong idea about his sales. "But something put her off pork."

"It's probably the petting zoo," I say. "The pigs looking so damn cute, you know?"

"Hope she'll come around again." It doesn't take a trained observer to see he has a serious thing for Rose.

"Maybe you should try bacon."

NINE

Rose

IT'S A BUSY day. We're all hands on deck prepping for the Wine Festival. Thanks to Yuri's morels we have the appetizers all set for tonight. Maggie is sweating them down with some shallots and thyme, and their rich loamy aroma is filling kitchen. We'll finish them on site—served on crostini with *burrata* cheese. The pork shoulder has marinated overnight in the *mojo* sauce, and is going into the oven to roast. We'll slice the meat and assemble the *Cubano* sliders at the winery.

I had to bring in extra staff for the night. I need Maggie here for service and I'm now short staffed since I fired Lotte. I called her yesterday and told her not to come in. Ever. I'd been thinking about it for a while, and maybe it was a rash decision, but I've had enough of her and Montana whispering behind my back. I'm not a chef, and I'm not experienced in running a kitchen, but after the visit from Detective Constable Wright the other day it was all very clear to me what I need to do: get rid of both of the *sister wives*, fast, regardless of the consequences. It's time to clean up a few things around here.

There aren't too many reservations in the book for tonight, I think because most tourists will be at the Festival, which should take some pressure off. But I also have to do some prep for the big corporate event we have coming up at Taiga. It could mean lots of new business for Thorny Rose, so I need to make sure we get everything right.

We worked late last night and I'm tired. Working all the shifts, every day since chef left, is really taking a toll on me. Yesterday after my shift at the farmers' market we'd had a busy service. The restaurant was packed and we did two full turns, thanks to all the people in town for the Festival starting today. And after clean up and driving the dishwasher home I didn't get to sleep until at least three o'clock. I'll need to keep making coffee just to get me through the morning.

I don't hear the knock on the door over the noise of the kitchen staff chatting and their music playing. Chef never allowed music in the kitchen and insisted staff work quietly. I always thought it made the kitchen feel like detention, or church. Which fit chef's whole *food as a religious experience* vibe, I guess. I'm not that controlling. Or at least not about the small stuff.

When I finally hear the knock and look up Wright is already standing in the kitchen. My heart drops. Why is he here again? Everyone pretends to keep working—chopping, stirring, whisking, but their attention is on him.

"Good morning." At least he's smiling. I wipe my hands and usher him into the dining room.

"If we talk in there someone's going to lose a finger."

Wright nods. "Actually I just have a few follow up questions for Montana."

"She's not in yet. "

"When do you expect her?"

"Forty five minutes ago." I try to keep my voice level. "We were behind before we even started this morning. And she's late."

"Okay…what about Lotte De Vries? The intern? Maybe I could speak with her in the meantime."

"I let her go yesterday," I say. He probably thinks I sound bitter but honestly, it was legitimate. I didn't really do it out of spite; at least not entirely. "It was overdue actually. Her *stage* was done and she wasn't learning anything with chef being gone. Well, except from Maggie." Out of the corner of my eye I catch a glimpse of Montana, who has slipped in the back door and is now whisking a bowl of *creme patissiere*. She is pale and her eyes are red. I indicate to Wright that she's arrived.

"Please don't take too long," I say. "You can use my office."

"Thanks. But I'd still like to speak with Lotte. Do you have an address and phone number for her?" I place the staff list on my desk for him as Wright approaches Montana. She looks terrified, which pleases me.

After thirty minutes the office door opens and Montana slinks out, her lips tight and eyes narrow. Whatever Wright has said has clearly taken her from fear to anger. She makes her way back to her station and starts to work, keeping her head down.

Wright sits at my desk for a minute longer, transcribing Lotte's address into his notebook. Then he approaches me as I'm removing my apron.

"I wonder if we can chat for a minute." I pointedly look at the clock on the wall. "It won't take long."

"I really don't have time. I have to make a pick up," I say, making a decision I hope I don't regret. "If you want to talk with me you'll need to come along." Maggie stops dicing tomatoes and looks up, her brow furrowed.

"What do you need?" she asks.

"I need to pick up some charcuterie for service."

"But we got a delivery this week. We've got tons of *pancetta, speck, bunderfliesch*. That red wine salami you like."

"I know. I need a *filetto*. I forgot it in the order." Maggie shrugs and goes back to her chopping. Wright follows me out to the truck.

"What's a *filetto*?" he asks as he climbs into the passenger seat.

"It's a pork tenderloin, cured in sea salt." I turn the key and the truck engine roars to life. "With a bit of spice. We slice it very thin. It's delicious." I turn the truck around and drive to the end of the driveway, then stop.

"I've just got a quick stop first," as I drive across the road into the neighbour Anna Kozlowski's driveway. "One second." I stop the truck and get out, then lower the tailgate. I haul out a fifty-pound sack and carry it over to the front porch. Then I collect a pile of mail from the box and bring it back with me to the truck.

"You're strong," Wright observes. "You go to the gym?"

"Nope," I say, flexing my bicep. "This is all from moving wheelbarrows of compost and manure around the garden."

"You do it all yourself?"

"Not entirely. I have help," I admit. "Brains not brawn," I laugh. "You can move a lot of weight if you have the right equipment. I've shifted tons of stone by myself, using dollies and levers."

"What was that you left on her porch?"

"Mealworms, for her chickens. We receive her deliveries because she can't sign for them," I reply. "She's blind. Well, practically. Has severe macular degeneration." I reverse the truck back down the driveway and turn onto the main road.

"And she lives alone?" He's looking back at the farmhouse as we drive away. It's dilapidated, and has holes in the rubble stone foundation walls where feral cats get in and out. A large bag of dry cat food is left torn open on porch, as an all night buffet.

"Just her and the cats."

"Must get raccoons too."

"A few I'm sure. The ones Jacob my handyman doesn't get first. He traps raccoons and drowns them in a rain barrel. Keeps telling me that KFC is the best bait."

"That doesn't bother you?"

"Pests need to be dealt with," I shrug. "It's efficient. Not how I'd want to go though."

"Drowning?"

"No. Eating KFC."

Wright laughs. "You collect her mail?" He asks, nudging the pile of envelopes on the center console.

"I go through it once every couple of weeks or so. She doesn't get much. I sort out what bills to pay, toss the junk. It helps her son with some of the burden."

"What about food? How does she manage?"

"Mostly on her own," I say. "She can see well enough to make simple meals, cups of tea. But we bring her dinner every night from the restaurant."

"Every night? Lucky her," he whistles in admiration. "That's generous of you."

"I've known her my whole life. She's like family." Which is true. Anna Kozlowski is a lifelong friend of my mother's. Their farms were across the road from each other and they shared equipment and workers when needed, helped out whenever asked. Though usually there was no need to ask.

This area of Niagara was farmed by waves of immigrants: Italians, Dutch and Eastern Europeans who all grew fruit and seasonal produce. But for decades now the market farms have been sold off one by one to developers. The rich farmland was scraped off and sold as topsoil, and the rest paved over and built up as subdivisions that were filling up with commuters taking commuter trains into the city. Some farms were being bought up by boutique vineyards and given over to hectares of vines. And some, like Anna's and mine, hung on.

"Anna's son Peter still runs her farm. He just doesn't live with her in the house. He's got a place just down the road with his partner," I glance at Wright and see that he is watching me intently, his eyes running up and down my body. I flush with embarrassment and keep talking. "They grow apples and cherries and make the organic cider that we feature on the restaurant menu."

"Her chickens are free range. They roam the orchard and help keep down pests and weeds, and their manure fertilizes the trees." I keep up my monologue partly to fill the silence and partly to make sure Wright doesn't get a chance to ask whatever questions he might have. Detective Wright makes me nervous, which I suppose is only natural. Still, I don't like how he keeps checking me out and I wish I had a jacket on over my t-shirt.

"You'll be interested in seeing Luca's place," I continue, not at all sure if Wright would have any interest at all. "It's a great operation. His pigs are free range too, with acres of pasture to graze and forage naturally and root around in. Huge wallows by the pond, large trees to shade under, tons of fresh vegetables, apples, grains and fodder."

"And that all makes a tastier pig?" Wright asks, when I finally gave him a chance to get a word in. "Or does it just make everyone feel better about slaughtering them?"

"Both, I'm sure. You've seen how happy his pigs are. He has the best *guanciale,* and his *prosciutto* is like butter. He feeds his pigs tons of acorns and pastures them on fresh grass, trying to improve the flavour of the meat. To make it more like a *jamon iberico* from Spain. Of course the best is his wild boar meat and his *boudin noir.*

"What's that?" Wright asks. His tone is wary, as if he's not sure he really wants to know.

"Blood sausage," I tell him. "Made with boar's blood and thickened with chestnut flour. It's the best thing on our charcuterie board. It's just to die for."

"Literally?" Wright looks revolted."Boar's blood?"

"Absolutely! Luca's got about two dozen wild boar in a separate pen area behind the barn. It's a natural pasture, but with heavy-duty electric fence and steel posts around it, and even under it, so they don't tunnel they way out. Those guys are great diggers, really strong. Not to mention vicious killers who destroy crops and ecosystems and kill livestock. If they manage to get out that is." I grin at him.

"And they taste good?" Wright sounds skeptical.

"They are delicious. Rich and gamey, and as long as the boar is castrated before maturity it doesn't have any taint."

"*Taint?*" He looks uncomfortable.

"You don't want to know." I make the turn onto Luca's lane, drive down his rutted driveway and park next to his truck.

I make my way toward the barn, with its sign for Millvale Cured Meats a replica of the one at his market booth. Wright follows me in.

Inside Luca has built a small wholesale supply counter. There's a big walk in cooler behind the desk, with a glass window through which you could see hanging cuts of pork and strings of sausages curing. But there is no Luca.

The room looks exactly the same as when I'd last seen it. On the table is an empty bottle of Amarone and a single glass. And on the counter lays a wrapped parcel of meat—*my filetto*, with Rose written across it in black Sharpie.

"That's weird," I say to Wright. "He's always here if the door is unlocked." Wright looks disinterested and impatient. I wait for a minute and consider just helping myself to the *filetto*, but then think better of that, given I am in the presence of a police officer. I'd have written a note, but still.

"I think I'll check around back. Maybe he just forgot to lock up." I walk along the gravel toward the back of the barn and think I can hear the boars grunting. But wild boars are nocturnal, so I was mostly likely hearing them snore.

"Luca?" I call.

I walk down the side of the barn toward the boar pen. I can see two adults standing close to the fence, one male and one female. They are huge, with powerful necks and humped backs. The male boar's upper tusks are curved and lethally sharp. Both are covered with thick coarse black hair and have long black ears. They raise their dark piggy eyes and look toward me, but don't run off.

That's weird. They always run away when people come around. The male goes back to rooting in the soil, and the female to eating a boot. Why is she eating a *boot*? There's a heavy metallic smell in the air, a sweet odor of ferment and shit and wine, so thick I could almost taste it.

I glance at Wright and he can tell from my expression something is wrong. He runs over as I approach the electric fence and look into the pen. There are several large boars fighting for something I can't see about twenty feet away. That makes no sense. They should be asleep at this time of day, or wallowing in the mud under the oak trees, especially in this heat. In the middle of the pasture about fifty feet from the barn I can see a large red mass. There are more streaks and blotches of red, and something white that looks like entrails spread across the entire yard. I see another boot. Some denim fabric, covered in red. When I understand the red is blood I realize I'm screaming.

I find myself back at the Thorny Rose. Wright has brought me away from Luca's place in the truck. I remember he drove as fast as he could to get me away from the blood soaked pasture. He said he'd called an ambulance, but I'm not sure what the point of that was. Luca is obviously dead, what's left of him.

I sit in the dining room, nursing a glass of brandy while Maggie hovers around. I look down at the table and see the *filetto*, with my name written on it in Luca's hand. I burst into tears.

Wright is standing next to the window, talking on his phone. I guess he is calling it in, since we didn't stick around for the police and ambulance.

Why didn't we? I wonder. I remember Wright was talking and talking as he drove me back here, trying to keep me calm. I feel stunned—in shock I guess.

"You've got a big event tonight, right?" he was saying. "If you stay and wait for them you'll be here for hours. Trust me. Let me call it in. There's no real need for you to tell them you were even here."

"You're in shock," he'd said. "Let me do you this favour."

I wonder now about that. Wouldn't it be the right thing to do? But I let it pass. He's probably right, and I need to be back at Thorny Rose. What good would it do for me to sit around the barn until they were ready for me to give a statement? The teams of police and attendants would arrive, do their jobs, and they could come and find me if they needed to. Let Wright be the witness. He saw exactly what I saw. He can tell them.

I keep thinking of the smell. The stink of Luca's dead body. I feel it still clings to me and I want to take a shower. And whenever I close my eyes I see the deep red of the blood-soaked grass, and the greyish white of his intestines dragged along by the boars.

I saw a ladder lying in the pen, as if it had fallen over. It looked like Luca had been working on the roof. He could have fallen off, hit his head. Those wild boars would have eaten him in just a few hours, especially if they hadn't had their morning feed and were hungry. The forensics team was probably already going through the sty looking for evidence, wearing their white overalls like I've seen on television. Would they autopsy the pigs? What would happen to them? Would they have to be sold as dog food? Or would they be slaughtered and sold as usual, for humans to eat? My stomach turns at the thought.

Wright sat beside me at the table. "I don't understand what

happened," I repeat for the hundredth time. "This is my fault," I moan. "I dropped off that Amarone yesterday, as a thank you."

"Was he a big drinker?" Wright asks after a moment. "I saw the empty wine bottle on the table." I nod. Luca enjoyed good wine. Maybe a little too much.

"Still, it doesn't make a lot of sense," he says. "To drink a bottle of wine and then to go up a ladder. What could be so important that he had to do that?"

TEN

Wright

THE WOMYN'S COLLECTIVE Flower and Herb farm looks like an advertisement for country living, with the white farmhouse sitting up on a rise above fields of flowers. A small creek lined with trees runs along one side, with a rope swing hanging from a large limb arching over the water. Colourful scarecrows, all wearing dresses, are scattered through the fields. Some of them have crows sitting right on them, so I wonder how effective they are. Dozens of white geese wander around the property. I bet they're probably all females too.

At the end of the driveway there's a large wooden sign with a large sun, a field of flowers and some massive bees. It looks like a child painted it. There's a holder nailed to the signpost, stuffed full of pamphlets. I help myself to one and leaf through it.

Welcome to Womyn's Collective Flower and Herb Farm!

We are committed to ethical food production, organic gardening and whole food cooking. From our small farm in the beautiful Niagara Region, we are proud to offer you the best flowers, honey, jams, jellies, vinegars and cordials.

Plan a visit to our gardens, enjoy a meditative

*walk through our flower labyrinth, or shop for our
unique jams and jellies, made in our kitchen.*

*Sample our herb-infused liqueurs and cordials,
distilled on the premises, and bound to make
your cocktails even more intoxicating.*

*Try our soothing lotions, soaps and balms, made daily in small
batches from the herbs and flowers we grow on the farm.*

*Please visit our flower farm, where you can
pick your own blossoms and create the bouquets
of your dreams. We also do weddings.*

I toss the pamphlet onto the passenger seat and drive up the lane. The roadside verge is lined with wild goldenrod coming into bloom. Beyond that I can see rows of sunflowers in all shapes and colours. I can see several women out in the field cutting flowers and placing them into deep buckets that are then loaded onto wagons.

At the far and of the driveway sits a row of doublewide trailers. They look well cared for and most have folding lawn chairs and umbrellas set up in front. One has a small child's wading pool and a collection of toys piled up next to the steps.

There's a flower stand by the parking lot, but the shelves are empty. It's probably too late in the day and they are picked clean. I park alongside the barn and follow the sign with arrow that reads Shop.

The interior of the barn has been completely renovated. A large commercial kitchen takes up most of the building and I can smell the aroma of something sweet and fruity cooking. A smaller area near the door is given over to a retail store, and I guess there's probably storage behind it. The rustic shelves in the shop are filled with jars and bottles of their advertised lotions, jellies and vinegars.

I can see at least a dozen women sitting behind the counter laughing and talking when I come in. They are all working on something: knitting, quilting, crochet. When they see me enter they stop talking and pretend to ignore me. I can feel their hostility. They start whispering about me and I can see their expressions, narrow eyes and lips pressed together. After a minute one stands to greet me while the others keep working. She's overweight and not very attractive; not my type at all.

"I'm Detective Constable Wright, with the Niagara Regional Police," I say. "I'd like to speak with Lotte De Vries. I understand she lives at this address." Two of the women behind the counter glare at me, then get up and go into the back kitchen, closing the door behind them.

"I don't know who that is," she says. "I'm only part-time." She turns to her companions for help. One of them, a blonde woman of around thirty-five, approaches me, her expression serious. She has dark blue eyes and wears her hair in a long braid pinned up on her head like a crown. She's beautiful, and from what I can tell under the baggy smock she wears, she has a nice shape.

"Can I help you?" She catches me checking her out and her tone is cold. Another uptight woman. "I'm Sophie Tuinstra, the owner of the farm." Her last name is familiar, but it takes me a minute to recall why.

"Any relation to Maggie Tuinstra? From the Thorny Rose?"

"She's my mother."

"The staff directory at the restaurant has this as Lotte De Vries' address. Is she here?"

Sophie shakes her head. "She left last month."

"Any idea of where she went?"

"No. It was my mother who gave her a place to stay here. Lotte isn't part of our collective. We just did her a favour."

"You have a lot of women staying here?" She looks at me

and blinks. It seems like a simple question so I don't understand her hesitation.

"Detective," she says, her tone clipped. "You really should have called before you came."

"The police don't usually do that," I laugh. "Any reason why you'd expect me to?"

"*Yeees*." She slowly draws out the word. "Because that's the agreement we have with the department. They call ahead, so we can take appropriate security measures."

She studies me for a minute, her eyes narrow. I'm getting irritated with her attitude.

"Detective…" she begins in a more conciliatory tone. "I'm guessing you don't know very much," she hesitates a moment "… about us." I nod, indicating she should go on. "Many of our collective members come from abusive situations. They are here for their protection."

"So you're like a women's shelter," I interrupt. "I get it. But I don't understand the hostility," I say, indicating the women behind the counter. "We're the good guys."

Sophie's eyebrows rise in surprise. "If you say so. Police never helped a lot of them when they needed it." I feel my temper rise. I'm tired of that same damn story, women blaming the cops because they got themselves into a bad relationship.

"We do the best we can." I'm careful not to roll my eyes.

"Do better." She folds her arms across her chest.

This is not going well. Most women find me charming. I decide to change the subject.

"You keep referring to your *collective*. What is it, like a commune?" I ask. Probably a bunch of feminists and socialists.

I can tell Sophie doesn't like my tone. "Not exactly," she says, her eyes cold. "We provide employment to our collective. And we offer an alternative to mass production and consumerism by offering handmade artisanal products, produced in traditional ways, on a human scale."

I nod, not understanding a word. Doesn't seem to me like they'd have much employment or money in that. I guess this Sophie doesn't have much of a head for business.

"You do crafts? Make jams?" Sophie stares at me for a moment.

"Yeah," she finally says. "We make jams." I can't tell if she's mocking me. She keeps looking at me, saying nothing. Usually women make an effort to chat with me, to be friendly. Or at least smile.

I notice a familiar odor now drifting through the barn, a bit like burned skunk. "What is that?" I ask. "It smells like cannabis." Sophie just looks at me then shakes her head.

"It's one of our herb mixes. We use it for our liqueurs. It doesn't smell great, which is why we cook with it after hours, when customers won't be around." She gives me a look that clearly means she'd like me to leave.

An old woman with waist length grey hair comes over and rescues me. She's very overweight and wears what looks like three dresses layered on top of one another, five sets of beads and a shawl. Her huge hoop earrings are hung with beads and feathers and she wears silver and turquoise rings on every finger.

"Hello officer," she says with a nice smile. "I'll help this gentleman." Sophie throws up her hands and backs off. The old lady then takes my arm and walks me outside. It was just like being escorted off the premises by my grandmother.

"Lotte is a good kid," she says, answering my earlier question. "But she had to go." I see that Sophie shoots her a look as we leave, but the old lady ignores her. "I think she has a boyfriend. Pretty sure she moved in with him, maybe somewhere in town?" She continues all the way toward the flower stand, her arm looped through mine, talking as she walks me to my car.

"Any idea where she went?" I ask. She shakes her head. "Or who this boyfriend is?"

She shakes her head again. "He looked older then her. Good looking though, what I could see of him. Dark hair, nice bone structure. He was around a fair bit, picking her up in his car, driving her home late at night."

"He ever stay overnight?"

"Not allowed," she laughs. "No men here." A light bulb goes on over my head.

"Are you all…*lesbians*?" I ask, thinking of the beautiful Sophie. That's disappointing, but at least her hostility makes sense to me now.

"Now why would you think we're all lesbians?" she asks, batting her eyes at me.

"Oh! Sorry…" This suddenly got awkward.

"…Just because we don't shave our legs," she interrupts me. "Or have sex with men." Then she bursts out laughing so hard I think she'll fall over. Lucky she has her arm through mine.

She finally catches her breath and extends her hand. "I'm Rachel, by the way. Sorry, I just like to have a bit of fun."

She looks over her shoulder toward the store. "By the way, Sophie's not gay," she continues. "You should ask her out," she says. "I saw you look her over."

"She's really attractive," I say. "But she'd look a lot prettier if she smiled." Rachel's bright eyes are on me, considering.

"Is Sophie the manager here?" I ask, changing the subject.

"You could say that," she says. "Sophie started the collective, after she finished her PhD."

"I'm impressed," I say, and I mean it.

"You don't think you're smart enough for her," she chuckles. "Oh go on! Some women like their men a little…dim." I'm not sure how to respond to that. "You're a good looking man. You seem fit…" She checks me out and I reflexively suck in my stomach. "Give it a shot." She laughs again and I begin to think she's making fun of me.

"What's she doing here, with a PhD?"

"Sophie came back home to look after her mother when Maggie first got sick," Rachel says. "Then Maggie signed over the family farm to Sophie and moved into a trailer out back."

I put what she said together with the bandana Maggie wore. "Is Maggie going to be okay?" I ask.

Rachel is silent for a moment and I know what that means. "We try to keep her comfortable. I give her some homeopathic treatments."

"Like what?" Rachel studies me before she answers. I'm pretty sure she thinks I might be too *dim* to understand.

"Bee venom therapy. Laetrile. Both are effective against pain and studies have shown they fight cancer."

"Sounds really painful. Do the bees have to sting Maggie?"

"They could…but that's not necessary. We collect the venom from our bees and inject her."

"You must go through a lot of bees. Don't they die after they sting?"

"No, we milk our bees." I stare at her. "Not literally of course," she says. "It's a method that uses an electric current to irritate the bees so they sting a piece of glass, and we collect and dry the venom. Since they are stinging glass and not soft flesh, their stingers don't get pulled out." She pats my arm. "Don't worry Detective, they live to sting another day."

It seems ridiculous to me, but then I'm not dying of cancer. "Isn't Laetrile illegal? It's cyanide isn't it?" It occurs to me to ask.

"Yeeees… Sort of. We extract it from bitter apricot kernels. It's been proven to shrink cancerous tumors." When she sees the skeptical expression on my face she stops talking and shrugs.

"Going to arrest me?" She asks. I shake my head. "Good. Because I also grow a most excellent weed," she laughs. "It's great for pain relief and managing the side effects of chemo."

She looks at me, her expression serious. "I wouldn't want to get raided by the cops. It's bad enough I get kids hopping the fence at night to steal it. I don't need you cops helping yourselves too."

"So, you don't have an address for Lotte," I say changing the subject. "Or know anything about this mystery man she was seeing?" Rachel shakes her head.

"You could try Oak Ridges Winery," she suggests. "I know she used to work there part time. Maybe they'd know more."

I thank her and watch as the women in the fields continue cutting flowers. Others are pouring buckets of liquid along the outside rows.

"What is that? Some kind of organic fertilizer?"

"Sort of," she laughs. "You know how you can buy coyote urine online, as a deterrent to deer and rabbits?" I shake my head, but Rachel continues anyway. "You spray it around your garden to scare off critters who might eat your crops." I nod, wondering where this is going. "Humans are predators—maybe the most dangerous ones on earth. Our urine should do the trick, I figured. So, we use it in the fields to protect the flower crops."

"Those are buckets of urine?" My mind is blown at the thought of the collective saving their piss. "They spray urine on the flowers?!"

"Not the *flowers*," she looks at me like I'm the crazy one. "On the paths and around the perimeter. That does a great job of helping keep the pests out, along with the deer fence and hardware cloth buried along the fence line to keep them from burrowing under."

"Seems like a lot of trouble to go to for some flowers." Not to mention disgusting.

"Guess that depends on what *some flowers* are worth to you.

The farm nets over three quarters of a million dollars a year from cut flowers and weddings alone. Mostly cash."

Oak Ridges is off the main highway bisecting the escarpment. It's a small new winery built on what I guess used to be pasture. Their Wine Festival tasting event is being held in a large steel barn on the property. It looks brand new and out of place, compared to the original century farmhouse down by the road. From the outside it looks like a typical agricultural building, sitting in the middle of a gravel parking lot. And from the inside it doesn't look much better, I realize once I enter. The place has no atmosphere and feels like what it is: a steel barn. The huge space is high ceilinged and it echoes. I imagine that if there were any music tonight the acoustics would sound terrible bouncing off the metal walls and ceiling. Luckily I'll be gone by then.

There are two bars set up at either end of the space, with a few sofas and sectionals set up in the corners. The large open area in the center of the room is being set up with folding tables covered with white cloths. Catering staff are laying out stacks of plates and cutlery rolled in white napkins.

A few early birds are milling around the barn, holding glasses of wine and waiting for the food to be put out. I approach a guy who's working behind the bar, setting up for the night.

"I'm looking for Lotte De Vries."

"Lotte? She's not here yet. She's working the evening shift, seven to close." I look at my watch. That's a couple of hours away yet. No way I can wait around until she shows up. "Why don't you have a drink," he offers. "Wait as long as you like."

"That would be great, thanks." I pull up a seat at the bar.

"What would you like?" he asks. "Tonight we're got an excellent Riesling and a Gamay Noir. What do you feel like?"

"Gamay," I say, but what I mean is a beer. He pours me a small glass then busies himself arranging glasses and bottles behind the bar.

"Are you the manager here?"

He nods then extends his hand. "I'm Joel Trudel, manager, bartender, chief cook and bottle washer. Oak Ridges is my winery."

"Are you the chef too?"

"No way. That I can't do," he says. "We don't actually have a restaurant here, not yet at least. I'd like to open one in the next couple of years, once I can build something to house it."

"So where does your food come from, Joel? Like for the Wine Festival this weekend?" I know the answer but I'm fishing.

"I have a partnership with Thorny Rose, a restaurant that supplies me with the food pairings for special events, like tonight."

"Thorny Rose," I nod. "I've heard good things."

He gives me a tight smile. "The food is excellent." He clearly isn't saying everything he'd like to.

I lean in and meet his eye. "I wonder if I could ask you a few questions."

"Questions?" he asks. "Are you a journalist?" He looks hopeful, like he thinks I'm covering the event and he'll get some publicity out of it.

"No. I'm a Detective, with the Niagara Regional Police." He looks around, making sure no one is listening. But he doesn't ask to see my ID, probably hoping that I don't flash it around in front of his patrons.

"Uh...okay. What kind of questions?"

"About Raymond Ellis. The chef at Thorny Rose," I say. "Do you know him?"

"Yeah, I know him." The tone of his voice speaks loud and clear. "Not well. He's not a friend." I'm beginning to think chef doesn't have any friends at all.

"He came by quite a bit," he says. "Or at least he used to.

And I would see him around town, at other restaurants or pubs. He'd always make a point of talking to me, once he knew who I was." Joel looks uncomfortable and I nod at him, encouraging him to continue.

"The guy drove me crazy to be honest. He'd ask a million questions about growing wine, grape varieties, climate and whatever. Then he turns it around and starts telling me how to run my winery, as if he's the vintner. Guy was like a sponge, sucking up everything, then dripping it back all over you." He pauses for a minute then goes over to pour a few glasses of wine out for a server. He helps her place them on the tray before he comes back to me. When he returns he's worked himself into a righteous anger.

"He was so full of shit about the *terroir*. Always going on about the soil and drainage and the gravel and the damn whatever.

"In January when it was almost time to harvest grapes for ice wine, that was absolutely the worst. He'd be calling me every night with the fucking weather report—it's the third night of below eight degrees Celsius. I think you need to be harvesting today."

"Then when I did decide to harvest, he makes it seem like it was all his idea," Joel says, shaking his head. "He wanted to take credit for everything."

"Did he come along for the harvest?"

"Yeah." He looks embarrassed. "In the end I let him come. He showed up with this photographer for fuck's sake, poses for a few shots of himself with the harvest and the frozen grapes. Then he leaves!"

"A user." I know the type.

"Whatever," he says. "I let him use me I guess. It was good publicity for us too in the end. Famous local chef and all that."

"Have you seen him lately?"

"Not since January, maybe eight months ago? Honestly, I avoid the guy."

I sip my wine and think about it. Chef goes away and nobody except his girlfriend seems to even notice he's gone, much less care. Where is he? I intend to find out.

ELEVEN

Rose

I AWAKE IN a panic, my heart racing, unable to breathe. Guilt and shame wash over me and I don't know how I'll get through the day. This is how I've lived every since my husband disappeared and it's not getting any easier to deal with. I'm exhausted trying to make it look like I know what I'm doing, and trying to make sure the staff don't see through me. I'm dancing as fast as I can and I'm just so very tired.

Our big corporate event is in two days and I'm nervous. We booked it months ago, and chef had created the menu with the clients. Taiga is the large corporate cannabis producer, with huge state of the art grow facilities in the region. They are contracted by the Federal government to grow and supply medical cannabis across the country. They've got a big budget and this event could be the start of a profitable relationship with them for Thorny Rose.

We managed to pull off the Wine Festival event last night. It had been hell, especially after the shock of finding Luca's body, torn apart by wild boars and spread across his pasture. That was something I could never un-see, and will never forget.

At least the restaurant hadn't been as busy as I'd thought, since most fine dining customers were at the Festival. Maybe that's not so great for business, but we can only stretch so far. With chef missing, and Lotte now gone we're short handed, even if I hadn't been in shock and barely able to keep up on the line.

Tonight should be even slower, based on reservations. If we can just get our *mis en place* done early, and all the appetizers for the tasting menu delivered to the winery for the second night of the Festival, we'd be in good shape to do the catering for Taiga on Sunday.

Rage and frustration rise up my throat. Chef should be here. This is our biggest weekend ever. It's a huge deal for Thorny Rose. You'd think he would have wanted to. But clearly whatever else he chose was more important to him, regardless of the consequences. He made his bed. I hope he's happy in it.

I quickly get dressed and run downstairs to the restaurant. It's only six in the morning, but I need to have a coffee and triple-check the prep list. This catering opportunity could make the restaurant and I do not want to have a single thing go any more wrong than it already has.

We aren't actually preparing any food with cannabis. There are no edibles or oils containing weed on the menu. What we've created is a menu that pairs food, wine and cannabis in combinations that best showed off their unique flavours. The guests could smoke cannabis if they chose. The producer will have experts available at the event to describe the various strains and their flavour profiles.

It's already so intricate and complex trying to find a balance of flavours and textures, with a visual appeal and harmony between all the elements on the plate. And with this tasting menu, adding the complicating factors of wine…mouthfeel, acidity, texture and now cannabis…it's multiplying my anxiety a hundred times.

We all know the five flavour categories: salt, sweet, bitter, sour and umami. All of our culinary efforts go to working to serve and balance these in a sort of alchemy. I think there's also a sixth flavour category: emotion. What are the feelings and memories the fragrances and flavours evoke in you, and how does that affect the total experience of eating? Of course everyone's emotional landscape is unique and I can only hope that whatever feelings we help the guests recall is a positive one. I also pray my current emotions of dread and anxiety won't come through into the courses I've created for Taiga, though that's unlikely. It's not that magical.

The menu we created is fairly simple, though I'm afraid it will be difficult to execute since the main course has to be cooked to order. The appetizer is easy: *ceviche*, using fresh caught local perch, is already marinating in the cooler. It will be paired with Chemdawg, a cannabis strain with a sharp, citrus-pine flavour, thanks to its main terpenes of pinene and limonene. We've chosen a minerally, grassy Sauvignon Blanc to serve with it.

The desserts are also easy: coconut mango sorbet, mango lime cheesecake and grilled pineapple shortcake with *dulce de leche* cream. They're paired with a local award-winning ice wine and Pineapple Kush. The cannabis strain's main terpene was the earthy and fruity myrcene, which gives Kush a quality that pairs well with tropical fruit.

What worries me is the main course. We've decided to pair Durban Poison with a big Syrah. The cannabis' earthy, woody aroma really demands to be paired with a red meat, and I was able to source grass fed beef locally. We've set up a BBQ since the venue's kitchen doesn't have an adequate grill. Steaks absolutely need to be grilled to order, and I'm nervous about doing that properly. I'm not a trained chef and everything I've ever done in the kitchen was just as back up or to help out on the line when we were in the weeds. Maggie is our best person to grill the steaks, but I need her for service at the restaurant. That means I'm grilling tonight at the venue.

As if I don't have enough to worry about.

TWELVE

Wright

I TURN INTO the driveway of the restaurant and drive past a pickup that's stopped and parked off to the side, its hood up. Two people are bent over the engine and I can only see their backsides, covered in blue denim. Then the one with the nicest butt straightens and I recognize Rose, with her hair tucked into a baseball cap. She wears work gloves and holds a wrench in her hand. She waves and gives me a shy smile and I get out of my car to have a look.

The other pair of jeans belongs to some guy who is working on the truck. A mechanic, I guess. He doesn't stop what he's doing and keeps his head down.

"Funny place to work on your engine," I say to Rose.

"It just stopped dead when I was on my way to pick up some wine," she says.

The guy looks up and sighs. "It's the alternator." He seems pissed off. I would be too if I had to come out here and work on a truck by the side of the road in this heat.

Rose looks worried. "But we just replaced it last month," she says to the mechanic. "It doesn't make sense that it would go so soon."

He nods. "I remember. We used a reconditioned part to save a bit of money."

"Buy cheap, buy twice," Rose mutters, pulling off her gloves and getting her cellphone out of her pocket. "It's still under warranty, isn't it?" she asks him, looking through the phone for a number.

"Better be," he grunts in reply.

"You work on your own truck?" I ask in surprise. Rose blushes and shakes her head.

"It's not like I have a choice," she shrugs. "I'm broke. Steve's been teaching me about engine maintenance and minor repairs so I can look after my truck and the tractor myself. And he lets me pay him in food."

I leave them to it and continue up the drive, parking my car at the only free space in the Thorny Rose's parking lot. Weird that it's already full, since the restaurant isn't even open yet. When I step into the kitchen I can see why. The place is packed with staff. Everyone is cooking: chopping, poaching, frying or running into and out of the walk-in coolers. It's controlled mayhem. I recognize the *sous chef* Maggie by her red bandana and make my way over to her.

I know Maggie's type. I'll bet she's a local woman, who'd grown up around here. Not much education, likely she learned her trade from years on the job—probably at diners and family style restaurants before she moved up to this kind of fine dining. She's probably divorced. And from what I can see she wasn't very attractive, even before the chemotherapy. She's heavy and older, and looks nothing like her beautiful daughter Sophie. I guess the chef didn't come onto Maggie like he did the young women in the kitchen. Did that make her bitter? It's clear she didn't like chef much. And she's fiercely loyal to Rose. One thing for sure, I know Maggie sees everything that goes on in that kitchen. I need to have a private conversation with her at some point.

"I need a quick word with Montana," I ask her. "Please."

"C'mon. I'll take you out," Maggie says. "She's out in the

garden." I follow her back out into the blinding sunlight as she navigates the path in her kitchen clogs, under an arbor and through a gate in a trellis fence until we're in a large garden made up of dozens of raised beds all overflowing with herbs, vegetables and flowers. I recognize only a few of the vegetables—tomatoes and beans on trellises.

"Hey! Kansas!?" Maggie calls. I hear a faint response, somewhere at the distant back of the garden. I follow Maggie as she makes her way there. The air is stifling and there's no breeze. I can see a haze rising above the vegetables, as if steam is coming off the leaves from the heat of the sun. It's moving like the waves of a mirage.

Beyond the tomatoes and peppers and several rows of beds packed with some kind of green leaves, we come up to a large section full of flowers in bloom, growing around at least a dozen beehives. Montana is there, looking as cool and unruffled as if it was a spring day, despite the sweltering heat. She holds a basket over her arm and is cutting some tiny blue flowers with an equally tiny pair of snippers. There are hundreds of bees flying around the blossoms, and around Montana. They make me uncomfortable, but she doesn't seem at all concerned.

"Yes?" she asks, her voice bored.

"Detective Wright needs to speak with you," Maggie says, her voice flat. Montana looks up in surprise.

"Sorry. I didn't realize..." she blushes. Clearly she'd thought it was just Maggie looking for her, nobody important. This girl is a piece of work. I bet the only person at the restaurant she listens to is the chef. Which is what happens when you're sleeping with the boss.

"I won't take much of your time," I begin. Some bees fly past me, and one lands on my shirt. "I...I wonder if we could speak somewhere else? These bees..."

"Are you allergic?" Maggie asks.

"No. I just don't want to get stung."

Montana smiles. "I'm very allergic. But chef taught me that they don't bother you if you don't bother them. And they don't." She speaks in a blissed-out, childlike voice.

"You're very allergic and you work in an organic garden, cutting flowers? Using honey?" She shrugs.

"I go out and pick at off-times, when the bees are quiet. I have an EpiPen. I manage."

"That's Montana. Loves the honey, but can't take the sting," Maggie scoffs as she heads back to the kitchen. Montana bends to pick up her stainless steel water bottle. She takes several big swallows as she glares at Maggie's retreating back. *If looks could kill,* I think.

"Anyway," Montana continues. "If you get stung a few times your body learns how to combat the bee sting. It's venom immunotherapy. Chef told me about it." Sounds crazy to me, but I bet Montana would believe anything chef told her. "I drink honey water too," she says shaking her steel bottle at me. "It helps with the therapy…"

I couldn't be less interested and cut her off. "I just wonder if you can tell me how to reach Lotte?" I say. "I understand you're friends."

"There's a staff list…"

"It's out of date," I interrupt her. "She's moved—which I'm sure you know." Montana looks away for a moment, then reaches into her pocket and gets out her phone.

"She's staying with me," she admits. "Please keep that to yourself." She pulls up the contact list on her phone and shows it to me so I can take a picture. When she does I notice some scarring on her arm.

"Did you burn yourself?" I ask. "I guess that's an occupational hazard for a chef." She stares at me.

"No. I didn't burn myself," the disdain in her voice is unmistakeable. "Someone put hogweed sap into my sunscreen. I ended up in hospital with second degree burns."

"What's hogweed?"

"It's a plant that she grows in the pond garden. It's got big leaves and white flowers," she sounds bored. "Apparently it's *architectural*. It's also phyotophototoxic—if you get the sap on your skin then it's exposed to sun it'll burn."

"Do you know who did it?" I'm not sure I believe her. It seems like the kind of thing a certain type of person might do to get attention.

Montana smirks. "Someone who wanted to make a point I guess."

"Are you saying Rose did it? I find that hard to believe."

She curls her lip. "I see she's got you fooled already." Montana turns back to her flowers. "You don't know her." I can't deny that. But Rose doesn't seem like the kind of woman who'd do something so spiteful.

"Anyway, it was probably that bitch Maggie. She'd do anything for Rose."

"It's strange that such a dangerous plant would be grown here, isn't it?"

"She grows lots of strange stuff." Montana sees my curiosity is piqued and she motions for me to follow her to a raised bed on the far side of the garden. From what I can tell it's full of weeds.

"There's purlsane, nettles and dandelions in here," she says.

"Dandelions?"

She nods. "They're very nutritional and high in iron. Some even taste okay if you cook them properly. If not they're pretty bitter."

"They're on the menu?" I'm surprised a high-end restaurant served weeds, cooked properly or not.

"Sure. Chef likes them because they are true locovore eating, and growing them here ensures they're organic. Better than if we looked for them along the side of the road or wherever, right? All that exhaust and salt and road runoff tainting the soil." She makes a face.

"Do you grow anything poisonous?"

"A lot of poisonous plants are often medicinal. It just depends on how you use them. We grow lots of medicinal plants, like goldenseal and ginseng," she says. "The forager sometimes brings some in, but growing gives you a reliable source."

I reach out and touch one of the tall plants with notched leaves. Instantly my hand begins to burn.

"You shouldn't have done that," she says, a little too late. "That's stinging nettle. It's covered with tiny needles that are full of acids and histamines that burn skin." She doesn't have to tell me. The pain is intense.

"What do I do?" I start to panic. "How long does it last?"

"Relax," she says, as she pulls a big leaf off another plant. She takes hold of my hand and strokes it with the big leaf. Almost immediately the pain stops.

"What is that? Magic?" I'm so relieved I can barely think straight.

"It's burdock. The leaf texture will pull out the tiny nettle spines. Nature is so interesting," she says in that breathy voice. "These two plants grow together in the same conditions, almost as if the universe knows the one is the antidote for the other. Chef taught me that." I wonder who'd taught him. It sounds just like the kind of thing he'd take credit for.

I turn to go but she calls me back. "You won't find Lotte at my place," she says. "She picked up some shifts at the Wine Festival. She'll be at Oak Ridges tonight." I wave my thanks and head back to the kitchen. No point letting her know I've already been there.

THIRTEEN

Rose

I LEAVE STEVE working on the alternator when I see Maggie lead Wright out to the kitchen garden and rush over to the restaurant, then stand and watch him and Montana from the back porch. From my vantage point I can see him waving his hands to shoo away the bees, and then see that he's taken some information from her phone.

The kitchen garden is very sheltered and enclosed at ground level, thanks to the fences and trellises that surround it. But if you are up just a few steps, like I am here, you can see everything that goes on inside it. I've spent more time on this spot than I care to admit to, watching chef and Montana in the garden. She's beautiful and captivating with her long hair flowing, her wide eyes enticing and full of admiration for him. I hate her.

I first met chef when I was supplying fresh organic herbs to the restaurant where he was chef in the city. I'm very aware of how he is with the young women who work in the kitchen. I was one of them, once.

He seduced me, completely, with his charm, his presence, and his passion. The way he inhaled the fresh picked dill, tasted the peppery nasturtium flowers and spicy Thai basil leaves. I swooned at his obvious, unembarrassed sensual pleasure in the aroma and the taste of what I brought him every week. He'd close his eyes and inhale deeply, as if he were trying to find the very essence of the flower or herb. He was transported and I fell in love with him, hard.

I'd search for the finest and best of everything for him, presenting it with pleasure and pride and he never disappointed. Tiny wild violets, with a scent unlike anything you'd ever find in cultivated varieties, that he would candy and use on desserts. *Fraise de bois*, a mere half pint—not enough for him to put on the menu. But they were a gift for him. The ripest berries, the most tender micro greens, delicate rose petals redolent with essential oils. I only grew Rosa damascena and centifolia, the most fragrant species, perfect for a rose sorbet or rose petal ice cream. And in the end I seduced him right back.

I watch as Montana turns away and goes back to gathering borage flowers. Wright watches her for a moment then makes his way back toward the kitchen. I quickly go inside and get busy chopping something, then glance up and meet his eye when he enters. I can tell that he knows I've been watching.

"She doesn't like you very much," he says. I pick up the cutting board and scrape the herbs into a bowl with the knife.

"The feeling is mutual," I mutter, my temper flaring but I keep it under control. It won't do any good to let him know how I feel. Wright looks embarrassed, as he should. What's he even doing here, coming around, still asking questions? I take a deep breath before I speak.

"I'm sorry," I say. "It's very stressful. This accusation…"

"I didn't accuse you," Wright interrupts.

"I'm not talking about you. The *sister wives*—Lotte and Montana. It's intolerable. I can't stand having her here—and I can't fire her. I've called the Labour Board, and apparently her accusing me of murdering my husband isn't sufficient grounds for firing her ass. She could sue me for unfair dismissal, unless I give her a nice severance package," I laugh. "I can barely afford to pay her salary, let alone a severance package!"

"Maybe she'll leave on her own. She can't feel very comfortable here, what with chef gone, and you and Maggie…"

"…hating her?" I finish his sentence for him. "She won't leave until she has another job to go to. And honestly, she's not that good a pastry chef. She's adequate. Apart from the whole accusation thing I don't think I could give her a good reference—not in good conscience."

"At least Lotte is gone."

"Yes. That was more straightforward. She was just an intern, not an employee, so I could get rid of her with no legal repercussions."

"And you didn't waste any time doing so."

"Damn right." I smile. Getting rid of Lotte had felt good. But this pressure is getting to be too intense for me. I'm tired and it's all too much.

"Excuse me for a minute," I say. "I've got to make a call." I go into the office as the tears stream down my face. I've got to get a hold of myself and stay in control. I need to maintain my composure, especially in front of the police.

When I come back into the kitchen a few minutes later, Maggie is chatting with Wright. I pause behind the door and eavesdrop.

"These girls come and go, always a new one," she says. "He was always looking for something. Looking, looking, never finding. Never realized what he had here."

"That's a tough spot to be in," Wright says and I flush with shame at his pity. "I guess they fought a lot?"

Maggie shakes her head. "She'd never say a word against him. She'd turn a blind eye. Hold her tongue. Pretend to listen as he pontificated to the interns or sister wives or whoever would listen. *Mansplained* everything." Maggie snorts and makes a face.

"The guy was such an ass. He thought he was such a great genius with food. Truth is, Rose has forgotten more than he ever knew. She's got a naturally gifted palate."

"Was?" Wright interrupts. "You said *was*. Past tense. Do you think he's dead?" Maggie looks uncomfortable.

"Yeah," she admits. "I do." She wipes her hands on her towel and gets back to work. "There's no way he'd miss the Wine Festival, or the event tonight. That's the sort of thing he'd be all over, micromanaging everything, taking the credit, basking in the glory."

I enter the room and they stop talking. Maggie returns to her work and Wright comes over to me.

"I've just got a few more questions." I nod and he continues. "Who might have spoken with your husband the day he left? Maybe they'll have a better idea..."

"Of where he's gone? And why?" Wright tries not to look embarrassed for me.

"I've thought about this, believe me," I say. "And honestly I don't know for sure. Any one of the kitchen staff? A supplier dropping off a delivery? Maybe even Jacob, if he'd been in the kitchen garden."

"Jacob?"

"My garden helper and handyman. He's worked on this farm since my grandparents' day."

"Is he here today? Could I speak with him?"

"Sure. He's out back somewhere. Maybe in the shed or the barn. I'll take you."

The storage shed is across the gravel driveway. It's ancient and if we tried to move it I'm sure it would fall down, so I've done my best to disguise it with lots of planting. It's covered with blue morning glory vine that I've trained up the sides on wire mesh. The wood has long ago faded to a light grey and whatever paint colour it was is forgotten. I've planted a large group of pollinator-friendly plants on both sides and behind it all the way to the fence line. It's at its best now, in late summer, when the grasses and perennials reach their peak of bloom you could barely see the shed at all.

As we approach the shed the sun beats down and the noise of cicadas fills the air. I can see dozens of hoverflies and carpenter bees flying around the blossoms and several Monarch butterflies sitting on the cosmos and milkweed, flapping their wings in the sun.

"Are you sure there's anything in here?" Wright jokes.

"When the sunflowers tower over the shed, it's incredibly beautiful. It's a favourite spot for weddings. We get a lot of couples taking their photos there," I say. "But this drought has taken a lot of the blossom early, especially the milkweed." I break off a blossom for him to smell. He nods in appreciation. "It smells great and feeds the monarchs."

The shed door is open and we can see Maggie inside, gathering wood chips into a basket. There are several large sacks of corn and grain, and the different types of wood we use in the restaurant, depending on what was being smoked: apple, cedar, and maple.

"Just getting some apple wood for the salmon," she says. She doesn't seem in any hurry to get back to the kitchen and turns to admire the view. "Beautiful, isn't it?"

"It used to be," I mutter. Now it breaks my heart. The ground slopes away behind the shed to a small gully that should have contained a creek, a creek that had been there since before I was born. In the spring it was wet from snowmelt and if we had a heavy rainfall the water would naturally drain from the farmland and seep in, overflowing the banks.

But the creek no longer exists, thanks to the house being built next door. The ten-acre parcel of land that used to be part of Herridge's farm had been stripped and re-graded, so all that surface water no longer feeds the creek. The stream died, along with all the wildlife it had supported. The toads, spring peepers, turtles, snakes, weasels, and countless birds, are all gone.

Just beyond the creek a huge new partially built house is just barely visible through the trees. It's clear that construction has been stalled for months. It stands abandoned, the house wrap shredded and flapping in the wind, and its plywood blackened by exposure to rain and mould. Piles of scaffolding lay rusting in a heap on a heap of gravel.

"Nice big house," Wright says.

"If you like that sort of thing."

"Looks expensive." He sounds impressed. "Construction is just abandoned like that?"

"It was a property developer and his wife. They were building their dream home last year."

"What happened?" Wright asks. "Did they lose all their money? How did the dream die?"

"Not likely," Maggie sneers. "They have more money than God. You should have seen their car."

"What was it?" Wright is suddenly interested. He obviously liked cars. "A Porsche? Ferrari?"

"Something obscenely expensive," I say. "It was bright orange. The name sounded Scottish...it started with an M."

"A McLaren?" Wright suggests.

"Yes!" Maggie says. "With the doors that open up like bird's wings, right?"

Wright whistles in admiration.

"And they just...went away?" he asks. "They just stopped working on it?"

Maggie gives him a sharp glance. "They disappeared. Lauren and Steven Monk. It was in all the papers," she says. "Surprised you don't remember..."

"We never saw them again," I interrupt her. There's no need to go into that story now.

"And it's not sold?" Wright persists. "They're just letting it sit there, disintegrating?"

"They disappeared. It was in the news," Maggie says. "No sign of foul play…they just vanished."

"I couldn't tell you what happened to them. And I really don't care," I say. "He was probably just another rich, crooked businessman whose bad deals had finally caught up with him. Developers are all the same." I point to a row of pine and spruce trees along the fence line. "I planted those when they first started building, as a screen to hide their McMansion. They pretty much do the job so I don't give it any more thought."

Maggie says nothing, but gives Wright a look and continues to the restaurant with her wood chips.

If Wright wants to find out more he can read the paper. He can visit Town hall. They would tell him the story of the several complaints we'd made about the build, the stop work orders that had been issued, the appeals we'd made to the Ministry of the Environment and the Conservation Authority. It's all public information. It's not my job to tell him. The whole situation was upsetting and I don't want to discuss it.

"How big is your farm?" Wright asks, changing the subject.

"I own fifty acres, with a stream and big pond we use for irrigation. But only ten acres are given over to Thorny Rose, for the restaurant and the gardens. The rest are leased to the farmer next door as pasture."

"*Only* ten acres?"

"I guess is sounds like a lot, but it's not really. The house, parking lot, barn and outbuildings use a big part. I've only taken up about three acres so far with the various gardens. But I've got plans for a lot more."

We head toward the barn, looking for Jacob. Past the shed, all along the length of the driveway are a series of garden rooms, each with their own theme and unique plantings. They are separated from one another by hedges or stone walls. One is formal Italian in style, with swept gravel and evergreens arranged around a lion's head wall fountain. The next is an overgrown English cottage garden, with roses cascading down over the arbours and the borders overflowing with flowers.

I stop short next to the Casablanca lilies, which are just fully in bloom. Their scent is amazing and I stoop to inhale deeply. Then I catch sight of a red lily beetle, sitting on a leaf. I quickly catch it and crush it between my nails. Then I look through the planting and find a few more, and enjoy the satisfying crunch when I crush them as well.

"You're not squeamish?" Wright asks, looking disgusted.

"No," I say. "Lily beetles are voracious and destructive, and I love my lilies." Wright leans in for a sniff then nods in appreciation.

"And there's no spray you can use to get rid of them?"

"Not organically, and not as effective. I prefer the hands-on method."

"And you can't just let them fight it out? Maybe some other predator will take care of the problem for you."

"There's no predator as effective as a human," I say. "If something is a pest, if it can't be controlled, it has to be killed. That's life."

"That's death, you mean."

I shrug. "Two sides of the same coin."

Wright changes the subject. "How many different gardens do you have?"

"Six so far." I point each one out as I list them off. "Formal, cottage, shade, Asian, pond, prairie…and of course the vegetable gardens for the restaurant."

"We've got chicken runs and compost heaps, a small pasture for goats, a dozen beehives, cutting gardens and greenhouses where the real work is done for the restaurant. But those are hidden away.

I want people to take away perfect memories of their Thorny Rose experience, so we offer them great spaces for photo-ops and selfies. People need a great setting for their captured moments."

"You're very aware of how to make things look good."

"Of course. How else can you make sure they remember things the way you want?" That's something I can't ever allow myself to forget. We need to make sure appearances are kept up, and we have to tell the story so people remember it in the best possible light.

"Here we're trying to create an experience, a sense of place. We encourage guests to wander the gardens. We give them lots of hidden nooks, and spots to sit and enjoy the flowers. We've had guests arrive two hours early or stay three hours late. We only know they're even here because of their cars are still in the parking lot."

"And at closing time you have to go looking for them?"

I nod." It can be a bit awkward. Finding couples making out. Last week Maggie found a guy fast asleep on a bench," I say. "He'd had too much wine and a rich meal. We had to give him a strong coffee so he'd wake up enough to drive home safely. That switchback on the hill as you go down the escarpment is tricky to navigate if you aren't alert."

Wright nods. "There have been lots of accidents at that spot. It's steep and there's a tight bend in the road there," he says. "And a sheer drop off the cliff. Lucky you sobered him up before you sent him on his way."

We come to the end of the finished garden rooms and stand next to a huge pile of limestone boulders. A bobcat with a chain sits parked next to the heap. Beyond it stretches a newly planted *allee* of oak trees, extending a hundred meters towards the back of the property. They are planted with precision, twenty feet apart and exactly parallel, forming a straight path that ends in another pile of stone, just barely visible from where we stand.

"What's all this for?" Wright asks.

"It's my *allee*. In time it will form a kind of an avenue, leading guests to the far end of the garden to a seating area—to a memorial garden. I'm having the stones engraved with poetry. Prayers."

"In memory of anyone in particular?" he asks.

"Not really," I shrug. "We've all lost someone we'd like to remember."

"I've got lots I'd like to forget."

"Then you'll love this," I point to the *allee*. "I was doing some research and I learned about soul ensnaring trees that pagans once planted. Trees were planted on the spot were a body was buried, so the soul-entangling and ensnaring roots of the tree would keep the spirit of the dead from haunting you." I glance at Wright. "That would make it easier to forget them," I say with a smile. "Of course, they'd have to be dead first."

"Anyone haunting you?"

I evade his question. "Right now it's kind of a pet cemetery."

"Who's buried there?"

"Cats, mostly. A dog. Quite a few chipmunks, or at least parts of them, whatever the cats leave behind."

He changes the subject. "When will it be complete?"

I laugh. "Now that's a good question. The bobcat guy is coming again this week. He can only work for me when he's got time between jobs."

I notice Wright's attention is caught by some movement at the far end of the *allee*. I see a dog on a lead is snuffling around the base of one of the oak trees, very interested in something it smells.

"Who's that?" Wright asks.

"That's Roland. He's training his truffle hounds."

"You're kidding me."

"Nope. All of those oaks were inoculated with truffle spores when I planted them. But it'll be years before they start producing."

"That dog looks like he'll be good at it. He already seems pretty interested in whatever's buried there."

There's a squeal from behind the stones. I go over to investigate and find a rabbit, caught in one of the humane traps Jacob has set. It sits huddled in the corner of the cage, fur fluffing up in the breeze, bright eyes blinking, and nose quivering.

"He's a cute little guy," Wright says as I tip the trap up and reach in, grabbing the rabbit by it back legs, holding it firmly in my arms as we walk to the barn. "He's not afraid of you. Is he a pet?"

"Not a pet, no," I say as I reached into the barn for a broom. "And he's definitely afraid. You should feel his little heart beating." I lay the rabbit on the ground and place the broomstick across its neck, holding it in place with my foot. Then I quickly pull up on the back legs until I hear the rabbit's neck break. Wright freezes, his mouth open in shock.

"They do a lot of damage in the garden," I say as I placed the broom back in the barn and pull a knife and some string out of my pocket. I cut off the rabbit's head so it can bleed out. "But they are tasty."

I'm tying its back legs together as Jacob comes out of the barn. He looks from the pale Wright to the dead rabbit and smiles.

"Jacob," I say. "This is Detective Constable Wright. He's got some questions for you." I turn to Wright. "Excuse me. I've got to go wash up."

"Aren't you a cop?" Jacob says. "Would have thought killing was something you're more comfortable with."

FOURTEEN

Wright

I IGNORE THE old man's taunt taunt and follow him into the barn. He's short and sturdy, with a rolling gait that tells me he's overdue for a hip replacement. He has a full head of silvery hair, with lots more coming out of his ears and nostrils. He hasn't shaved in a while, and his chin and cheeks are covered with patches of stubble, but I'm not sure it was enough to call a beard. I guess he could be anywhere between seventy and a hundred years old.

He hangs the rabbit next to another couple they must have caught earlier. While Jacob ties and re-ties the string until it's just right I look around the barn. There are the usual tools you'd expect to find in any barn: rakes and shovels and hoes; a small tractor and a couple of wagons; huge sacks of grain and corn. And a few bags of fertilizers: seaweed and blood meal and large bags of lime.

"What's the lime for?" I ask. All I remember from my student summer jobs in construction is that it's used in cement mix. Jacob turns his attention to me as I smile and tried to win him over. "Getting rid of any bodies?" I joke. "It's corrosive and eats flesh."

Jacob cackles. "True. It's also used to sweeten the soil. We're pretty acid in spots around here, especially down by the pond. Acid soil is great for blueberries, but it's crap for asparagus and cabbage." As he speaks I detect an accent. Slavic maybe, or possibly Dutch.

Then he turns and walks out of the barn, leaving me no choice but to follow him.

"You're looking for the chef." I'm about to confirm when he cuts me off. "Why waste your time?" He snaps. I didn't expect that.

The old man picks up his garden fork, lays it into a wheelbarrow and starts walking, forcing me to follow along behind him. I notice for the first time that he's wearing hip waders. Is he going fishing? He pushes the wheelbarrow along a shady path marked Private, toward an enclosed garden with a pond. It's surrounded by tall clipped cedar hedges, which cut off most of the sound from the rest of the garden. It's quiet, apart from the trickle of a small fountain. The space feels cooler than the blistering heat in the rest of the garden and the pond looks refreshing enough for a swim.

Jacob stops the wheelbarrow at the edge of the pond, picks up the garden fork and lowers himself into the water. He wades in and stands there, looking like a derelict Poseidon with his trident.

"I have to follow up on a report…" I say, as I get out my notebook. He cuts me off again.

"The guy left. It's a free country." He looks at my notebook. "Anyway, good riddance." Jacob starts gathering some long stringy green algae with the fork and dumping it into the wheelbarrow. It looks like long green hair.

"What is that?" I ask.

"Algae and blanket weed."

"What causes it?"

He stops what he's doing and looks at me before answering. "The sun. Too much decaying organic matter and dead things in the water."

"What kind of dead things?" He shrugs and continues gathering algae.

"When's the last time you saw him?" I ask. "Did he tell you he was going away?"

"Don't really remember." Jacob sounds evasive. "I saw him most days. It's my job to pick up the trimmings from kitchen, for the compost. They'd leave them in pails by the door. And I leave fresh vegetables on the back porch—whatever's on the list they leave me in the morning to pick. That's about it."

"That's it? No conversation?" He chuckles.

"Not if I can help it. I'd see him go out and wander around the garden. I stayed as far away from him as I could."

"Was he alone? With his wife?"

He shakes his head. "He liked to parade around with one of his *interns*—always tearing off bits of herbs and telling her to smell this and describe that."

"Where do you suppose he is?"

Jacob thinks for a minute. "He could be under this pond liner—that's where I'd put him," he laughs. "His body would be under four feet of water, some stones, plants and fish. Nobody's ever going to find that."

I play along. "I imagine that pond is a few years old. You'd have to put a body under the liner when you're building the pond, right?"

"True," Jacob nods and scratches his beard. "He could be in the vegetable garden. If you just buried him three feet or so deep, we're never going to find him." He's giving the idea some serious thought. "You never go down more than eighteen inches in a vegetable garden, even digging potatoes. You just add more compost to build it up on top. A body could be there forever."

"Or maybe he's under the pile of stones in that memorial garden." Jacob is enjoying himself. I bet he could go on for hours.

I put my notebook away. "Where do you really think he is?"

"Hell, I hope."

FIFTEEN

Rose

I WAIT ON the front porch as Wright makes his way back to the house.

"Here," I hand him a postcard. "This came in the mail today." It was a typical touristy postcard with a picture of the Hollywood sign on the front. The postmark is smudged so the date stamp is illegible.

Wright turns it over and reads the back aloud. "Glad you're not here. Love me." He looks up at me in surprise. "Wow. That's harsh."

I'd like to tell him that it was just a joke. That it was banter. That we always signed off that way, instead of *Wish you were here.* But whatever I told him would only be half true. That comma between the last two words isn't missing. He'd meant as an instruction, as an order. My husband always demanded love.

"Is this his writing?" I nod. "And you received it today? It's Saturday—there's no mail delivery today."

"It was in with Anna Kozlowski's mail. The pile I picked up yesterday. I was so upset after finding Luca I didn't look through it until just now."

"Delivered to the wrong address," Wright nods. "So you think he's in Los Angeles? Or was?" I shrug.

"The postmark is smudged but maybe we can get a better look

at it. May I take this?" He puts it into his pocket without waiting for a reply.

"Any particular restaurants in Los Angeles he might be doing this *stage* at?" The way he says the word shows his disdain for the idea. I find I can't be honest with him. To tell him the truth—that I don't really know my husband anymore, and that maybe he should ask one of the *sister wives*, is too embarrassing.

"Paramount?" I venture. "I know he's a big admirer of Ludo Lefebvre at Trois Mec." It's a shot in the dark. He writes it into his notebook.

"I really don't understand why he's not back," I say. "Even if he did go on a *stage*. The Wine Festival is a big deal for us." He should be here. Even if we did have a big fight, I think. Even if he was thinking of leaving me. He shouldn't be gone.

Jacob steps up onto the porch. It's lunchtime.

"It's almost ready," I tell him. "Have a seat." Jacob nods and sits at a bistro table on the porch, ignoring Wright.

"I've got to get his lunch," I say to Wright and turn to go, hoping he'll leave. But he follows me into the kitchen.

I place a bologna sandwich made with Wonder Bread and a bowl of Kraft Dinner on a tray. As I start to pour Jacob a glass of fluorescent pink liquid, Wright speaks.

"What the hell is that?!" His outburst surprises Jacob, who turns to look.

"Fruit Punch. Colourful, isn't it?" I laugh. "It has no nutritional value, zero added vitamins and is one hundred per cent artificial colours and flavours. Jacob loves it. He used to prefer Tang, but I'm not even sure they make it anymore."

I take the tray out to Jacob and serve him lunch while Wright watches, astonished.

"He eats like an astronaut, right Jacob? Everything's dehydrated or processed." Jacob smiles and nods. "And with all the important food groups: sodium, MSG, preservatives—everything a man needs to live a long life."

"Especially preservatives," Jacob jokes, his mouth full.

"Jacob doesn't eat with the rest of the staff?" Wright asks when I come back into the kitchen. He can see through to the dining room where the staff are all seated together at a large table, eating something Maggie has made. This was the family meal, where the entire team ate and relaxed before service, after *mis en* place was complete. It's a restaurant tradition around the world.

"No. He doesn't like fancy food," I say. "As Jacob likes to say, *That crap would choke a pig.* So I make him a grilled cheese sandwich or something from my stash."

"Your stash?"

"I have a special cupboard for contraband stuff, just for Jacob." I open the door and reveal the boxes of Kraft Dinner, Hamburger Helper, Instant Noodles, plastic bottles of ketchup and neon fruit punches, packages of Jello and Kool-Aid.

"Why do you call it contraband?"

"It's a joke. Sort of," I explain. "Chef hates it. He makes a big deal of my even having it in his kitchen, so I have to keep it out of sight." Wright shakes his head.

"Jacob lives on this stuff. And Velveeta cheese and condensed milk. And Twinkies." I lower my voice. "Everything has to be soft. He has no teeth."

"How old is Jacob?"

"Not sure," I say. "A hundred? He came with the farm."

"Seriously?"

"Yes. He grew up around here somewhere, and worked for my grandparents. I inherited the farm from them, along with Jacob."

"I thought you'd bought it with your husband."

I laugh. "No way—it's worth a lot. A lot more than we ever could afford—which is nothing." I serve myself a helping of Kraft Dinner.

"You eat that stuff?" Wright looks shocked.

"Yes, I eat it," I laugh. "I enjoy it—and I don't mean that ironically. It's comfort food and I'm not going to apologize for it." I did enough of that to my husband. I run through the list in my mind of things I no longer have to pretend to like, just because he did, or because as a restaurateur I *should*: Marzipan. Pumpkin pie. *Foie gras*. Organ meats. Wright shakes his head in disbelief.

"Not timbale of…Not reduction of…deglazed with…"

"Nope. Just straight KD. Original."

"I'm afraid you're going to tell me you like Velveeta too."

"Hell no. I hate that stuff," I grimace. "It really would choke a pig."

There's a spray of gravel as a truck roars into the parking lot, swings around and stops. I can hear an argument, and can see the driver slamming his fist against the steering wheel. Then the passenger door opens and Paul climbs out. The driver keeps on swearing and yelling in the cab, but he keeps the window rolled up so I can't hear what he is saying. It isn't tough to guess.

Paul storms up the porch steps and stops dead in his tracks when he sees Wright. He drops his eyes and it looks as if he wishes he could disappear.

"Sorry I'm late," he mumbles as he slips past us, heading into the small staff change room.

"What do you suppose that's about?" Wright smirks, cocking his head toward the truck in the parking lot. The driver has stopped yelling and is staring out the window at the restaurant, his face unreadable. After a moment he guns the engine and tears down the driveway.

"That's Jim Tapper," I say. "Paul's brother, from the market."

"I didn't recognize him. He's shaved his beard," Wright says. "And his head." Jim's normally long, unkempt beard is gone, and under his cap it's clear he now had a buzz cut.

"I think he probably has to be in court," I say. Wright raises his eyebrows. "There was a situation a few months ago." I regret saying anything the moment the words are out of my mouth.

"Situation?"

I probably shouldn't have said anything. "It was nothing really. It all got blown out of proportion," I say. Wright waits for me to continue.

"Jim's a good guy. I rely on him for lots of things around here. There's nothing he can't do. He's the plumber, the electrician, the gas fitter, welder, he fixes the well...you name it."

"He's trained to do all that?" Wright looks skeptical.

"Self-trained," I explain. "I told you he's a prepper. He's taught himself everything he'll need to know how to survive, post-collapse. Jim is the ultimate in self-sufficiency." Jim has told me a lot about his SHTF plans, for when the Shit Hits The Fan. He's got food and water stored in his farmhouse and barn, as well as in several root cellars he's dug around his property, that will last years. He rations everything and keeps a strict inventory of all his goods, rotating the stock to avoid spoilage just like we do in the restaurant.

He's got his home entirely off the grid, with solar panels and a newly dug well, heat sinks and a septic system. He's building three large aquaponic ponds where he'll raise fish in tanks under hydroponic vegetables. And he's invested in weapons, mostly illegal, to keep others away from his supplies when it becomes necessary.

Wright nods. "So what was this *situation*?"

"Jim got into it with chef, at the organic market last summer," I say. "Chef was selecting produce, and he rejected some pears because they weren't perfect. Jim went a bit nuts, shouting at chef about his food vanity, his ego, his unsustainability." All of which was true, but chef still pressed charges. And the local police had nothing better to do that afternoon. But I didn't say that last part aloud, even though it was also true.

"Really?" Wright is surprised. "You seem pretty sustainable to me. You grow your own produce, have the big garden out back and all that."

"Don't believe everything you see, Detective," I say. "We buy in a lot of our produce and certainly our meat, fish and dairy products. I don't grow any of that."

"And to be perfectly honest, a lot of this," I gesture to the kitchen garden," is for show. It's part of the Thorny Rose brand."

"How does Jim feel about Thorny Rose?" Wright asks.

"I've never asked him, but I'd think that he despises us," I say. "This frivolity, this obsession with foodie culture, and the trivial minutia of haute cuisine. He's a very serious young man."

Jim is working on becoming the *grey man*, the man who doesn't stand out, who you don't notice. He has lots of clothes from thrift store, bought a couple of sizes too big, so when he's wearing them it looks as though he's lost weight and is starving, like everyone else who didn't prep once the inevitable collapse he's anticipating happens. Even though he's got plenty of food stored he doesn't want others to know. They might steal it from him or make him share.

But wouldn't you want to share with your neighbors in a crisis? I'd asked him. *Not if it means my family starves,* he'd said. *My job is to protect my family.* Jim really is a very serious, earnest and resolute young man. One who'd do anything to protect what matters to him. I admire that. But I don't need to tell any of that to Wright.

I place my empty bowl in the bus pan by the dishwasher and tie on my apron. It's time to get to work. "Jim hates that Paul works here," I continue. "That's probably what the shouting in the truck was all about."

"And about chef?" Wright asks. "How does Jim feel about him?"

"He threatened to kill him," I shrug. "That's why he ended up in court."

SIXTEEN

Rose

"**Dammit!**" **Maggie yells** from inside the walk-in cooler. "What idiot left this *gravlax* on the bottom shelf?" Then I hear a crash as something falls over, followed by more swearing.

After a busy weekend like the one we've just managed to get through, with regular service and catering and a special event, it wasn't a surprise that I hear Maggie swearing first thing this morning. There's always some catch up and confusion, trying to identify things that have been put away in a rush at the end of service, making sure the stock is properly rotated with the freshest to the back so the older gets used first. Clearly Maggie isn't pleased with the state of the walk in but since she was on duty when it ended up that way she can blame herself.

Maggie is running behind today and the rest of the kitchen staff are already doing their prep work when she arrives. It isn't like her to ever be late, so I'm concerned. I'd watched her carefully out of the corner of my eye as she came in this morning, trying to assess her wellbeing. But the swearing and yelling sets my mind at ease. She's probably fine.

Maggie is like family, all I really have left. It's amazing that she's able to continue working like she has, all through her treatments. Through remission and then through the oncologists finding the cancer had metastasized. It's only a matter of time now. We all know that. Any time she looks tired, or is late like this morning, I'm overcome with dread. Not yet, I pray. It's too soon. Please not yet.

I sip my coffee and go over the produce order. Then I have to find a new supplier for our *charcuterie*. We have enough cured meat to last a couple of weeks, but then Luca's supply will be gone. It's possible someone will take over his business. Maybe he has family who'll step in. But I haven't heard anything about it and I can't be left with nothing in the meantime.

Maggie is standing over the new *saucier* Will's station as he struggles with a recipe.

"What's the problem?" she snaps.

"I'm trying to figure out a vegan substitute for butter in this dessert I'm making for Montana," Will says. Maggie rolls her eyes.

She places a pound of butter in front of him. "Use this." He's shocked. "Nothing else will produce the same texture."

"You can't do that!" he gasps. "It's for vegans!"

"Oh really," Maggie looks him in the eye, making her point clear. "Vegans make the decision to be lied to every time they eat in a restaurant," she walks back to her station. "Anyway, Montana isn't a legit vegan. I saw her eating a goat cheese *gougere* the other day. So fuck her." I smile. Maggie is feeling like her old self after all.

I look up and see Jacob standing over me. Jacob, who never comes into the kitchen. Something is wrong. The expression on his face makes me leap up and follow him outside. He walks quickly through the kitchen garden toward the beehives, with me following behind. Then he stops and steps aside so I can see.

Montana lies in the cutting garden. Her russet hair has come loose from its usual tidy ponytail and spills across the mulch path. Part of her tongue sticks out between her teeth. Her face and lips look swollen and I can see hives on her hands and neck. Her skin is blue, especially around her ears and lips. I can see broken blood vessels in her eyes, which are bulging wide open, unseeing. She isn't pretty anymore.

I hustle Jacob away to call 911 then kneel by her body. A basket lies by her side, holding some nasturtium blossoms and spikes of pineapple sage flowers. Her water bottle is tipped over and bees fly in and out of the opening, looking for nectar. Even more bees fly around her body, settling on her pristine kitchen whites.

I take one last look around before joining Jacob. We wait on the driveway for the ambulance to arrive. It's only when the siren and flashing lights pull into the parking lot that the rest of the staff realize something is wrong. They spill out onto the porch to see what's going on as I tell the paramedics where to find the body. I feel nothing, which surprises me. You'd think I'd feel relief that she's dead, or sorrow that a young woman had to die. But I don't.

I meet Maggie on the steps. "It's Montana. She's dead," I say. Maggie looks grim.

"How?"

"Anaphylactic shock?" I guess. "She was in the cutting garden. It looks like she was stung."

"Didn't she have her EpiPen?"

"I didn't see one. I guess not."

Within a few minutes the police arrive. Wright isn't with them. I can hear the crackle of their radios as they speak with the dispatcher. They ignore us and walk into the garden. I know they'll be speaking to me soon enough. I can wait.

I can already anticipate their questions: *Didn't she have an EpiPen? How allergic was she? Why would she be out near the beehives? Why would the bees attack her?*

I just hope they won't ask any of the questions that cut close to the bone. *Was she sleeping with your husband? How long have you known about it? Are you glad she's dead?* It's unlikely they'd even know about those, unless Wright has said something. Where is

Wright anyway? I'd have thought he'd the first one here, the way he's been hanging around lately.

I recognize one of the officers who stands barring the entrance to the kitchen garden as the short red haired woman Wright was arguing with at the farmers market last week. She gives me a big smile, as if we know one another, but I don't think we've met. I approach her.

"Excuse me," I ask. "Will Detective Constable Wright be coming by?" She looks at me, brow furrowed.

"No," she replies, looking confused and I immediately regret approaching her. Maybe I'd just stepped in the middle of a workplace romance gone wrong. That might have been why they were arguing at the market. "Is he a friend of yours?"

"No." I shake my head. "He's just been here this week, asking about my husband. I just assumed he'd show up." I start to back away. "It's not important."

When I look back over my shoulder I see that she's talking with some other officers. They keep glancing in my direction.

I retreat to the back porch and sit next to Jacob. We watch as the police and ambulance attendants mill around Montana's body. She lies in the same position Jacob found her. Clearly she's dead so there is nothing they can do for her. I wonder why they aren't removing the body, then, as a woman carrying a medical bag arrives I understand they're waiting for the coroner.

I watch as the coroner checks over Montana's body and looks around the garden. One of the police officers approaches us with his notebook open as they cover the body and begin to load it onto a stretcher. The show is over.

He introduces himself and asks Jacob and me to describe again how we'd found her that morning. He takes Montana's personal details and emergency contact, which Maggie has already printed off from the staff list. Then he closes his notebook and leaves. Within an hour they're all gone and it's as if nothing has happened.

There isn't even any police tape left at the scene, like you see in the movies. Jacob goes to retrieve her basket and her water bottle.

The mood in the kitchen is somber. Everyone is working quietly, focused on their tasks. We don't open until five o'clock and our first reservation tonight is at seven, so there's plenty of time to get ready. And to grieve I suppose, for those who feel the need. I go into my office to discreetly call a wholesale pastry supplier. We'll need some dessert to get us through the week. I also make some calls to people I know in the industry to see if they have anyone they could recommend, even as a temporary replacement until I can fill Montana's position.

I'm on my third call when there is a knock on my door. It's Wright.

"I just heard. I was out on another call," he seems worried. "Got here as fast as I could."

I'm surprised and don't know what to make of his concern. Why did he feel the need to rush over, if this wasn't his call? He's investigating my husband's supposed disappearance. What's that got to do with what happened here this morning?

"Thanks," I reply. He looks uncomfortable and I can understand why. There's not much point offering his sympathy when he knows what Montana has done, and how much I disliked her. Still, a young woman died. It was a terrible accident.

"She didn't use her EpiPen?" he asks. I reach under my desk and pull out Montana's Herschel backpack and place it on a chair. Wright looks at it.

"Look for yourself. It's still in there," I say. "I brought this in here for safekeeping. Normally she keeps it in her station, tucked under the salad prep table." What's the protocol for personal effects in the case of a workplace death? Presumably someone from her family will want it.

Thorpe unbuckles the backpack and looks inside. As I already know, there's the usual stuff in there: hairbrush, makeup, wallet, and her EpiPen and cell phone.

"I'm surprised she didn't bring it out with her."

"I'm more surprised she didn't take her cell phone. She spent an awful lot of time out there making calls," I say. Then I realize how unkind that sounds. "I'm sorry. It's been…surreal." He smiles then takes a closer look at the EpiPen.

"Huh. This is expired," he says. "Almost eighteen months ago."

"I'm pretty sure they work fine for a few years after expiry," I say. "I read that somewhere."

I watch as he picks up the cell phone and swipes the face. It lights up. The screensaver is a selfie of her and chef, smiling in some restaurant I don't recognize. Wright does his best to hide the image from me, but I've already seen it. In fact, I've looked through the phone already, checking all her texts and calls. But I'd been careful and didn't delete anything.

"No password?" He's surprised. I shrug and feign disinterest as he goes to the texts and scrolls through them. He stops and reads a few carefully.

"There are texts here from your husband," he says. I nod. "They were sent recently, after he left." I turn to Wright. "One is here from last week." This is not news to me.

As he holds out the phone to show me, it rings. The screen flashes up Mom. My heart goes out to Montana's mother. Too soon she'll have a visit from her local police, giving her the worst possible news. Until then she has a few hours to believe her daughter is still alive. Wright mutes the ringer and lets it go to message.

"So you think he's around somewhere?" I ask. "Why isn't he coming in to work then? Why has no-one seen him?"

"Why would Montana accuse you of killing him," Wright asks as he scrolls through the texts, "when he texted her the same day she reported him missing?"

SEVENTEEN

Rose

THANK GOD IT'S Monday. That's the opposite of how almost everyone else in the working world feels, but in the restaurant industry Mondays are sacred. Thorny Rose is closed.

I get up early as usual, and don't have to face anyone else in the kitchen when I go downstairs. There's no staff here, prepping and cleaning. No one I need to put on a smile for. No music is playing. I never allow deliveries to be scheduled for Mondays and I always made sure to hang the Closed Mondays sign at end of service on Sunday. Not even Jacob works on Mondays. There's never anyone here to disturb me and I can do whatever I want.

I make coffee and look through the fridges for something to eat. Then I sit on the porch in the shade, hidden by the large planters of ferns and coleus. It's still early enough that the heat hasn't started to build, but the humidity has lingered overnight. It's blissfully quiet. The farm cats bask on the paths, savouring the peace. I'm sure they love Mondays too, when they can roam at will, and sleep wherever they please, with no threat of humans interrupting their business.

Last night's private party at Taiga had gone perfectly and I finally start to feel my shoulders relax from the tension I've been holding. It feels like my shoulders have been up around my ears for days. Every course was served on time, and the steaks were perfectly grilled to order. The client was very happy and I'm sure it will mean more business for us, both from the corporation and from private clients who'd attended.

Large sliding doors were open from the dining room onto an enclosed courtyard, where guests could go to smoke between courses. Specialists in cannabis spoke throughout the meal, describing the flavour pairings and the various cannabis strains, what they were good for and how they'd been hybridized. And over dessert there had been a brief pitch for investment, so discreet one might easily have missed it. Billions of dollars are now being invested in the cannabis industry, and many billions more are being made.

The event was held inside Taiga's grow facility, which is on a gravel Concession right in the middle of nowhere. It's next to a small family run winery and around the corner from a derelict RV repair shop, not the kind of spot where you'd expect to go for a high end evening out with an elaborate gourmet tasting menu.

The contrast struck me as typical of how things have changed in the region. The old town is full of new money, and sometimes the two don't sit together very comfortably. At the event last night the guests were resplendent in very expensive clothes and jewels, being served the finest cuisine the region has to offer, in a repurposed greenhouse where for decades people have worked for less than what they now paid their babysitters or dog walkers.

Agricultural workers make less than minimum wage and are often migrants who come up for the fruit season. If they're lucky enough to live locally, it's in one of the rundown houses in the East Village. The irony that the guests last night were paying over five hundred dollars a plate for a gourmet dinner that included all the weed they could smoke wasn't lost on me either. It was sure a step up from hash brownies and a keg of beer.

One of the guests was Amit Joshi, a regular customer at Thorny

Rose. He's a very large man, thanks to his taste for food and wine. And, thanks to his fat bank account he's able to indulge his tastes in everything. Amit always dresses in colourful custom tailored shirts, which he needs to accommodate both his size and his love of attention. Like the peacocks he has roaming on his estate, he struts around in turquoise, emerald green or fuchsia silk, with brilliant pocket squares, ties or ascots, depending on his mood. He wears large jeweled rings on most fingers and a thick gold watch and chain around his wrist. As usual, he removed his tie and jacket the minute he sat down; I've never seen him in a jacket for more than a few minutes in all the years I've known him. His vibrant orange shirt is visible from across the room, which is what he wants. People will definitely notice him, but he reminds me of a school bus.

Amit Joshi is one of our best customers and is always the first we'll call to invite to one of chef's special tasting menus or seasonal celebrations. He's the perfect guest; he always raves about the food and never questions the price. He'd dined at Thorny Rose just last month when we'd served a special menu to an intimate gathering of local *gastronomes*. The menu had featured extreme-aged steak that chef had been resting in the restaurant's aging room, a specially built cooler in the former root cellar under the farmhouse. Typically the steak we serve is aged between forty to sixty days. Chef had aged this grain-fed loin of beef for a full year—three hundred and sixty-five days in the dark, cool and dry aging locker.

Slivers were sliced off the end and served as a *carpaccio* appetizer, and everyone at the table moaned with pleasure as they took their first bite of the musky, dense meat. Then small steaks were cut and grilled, simply sprinkled with sea salt. No other condiments were served. They would only mask the extraordinarily complex flavours of the beef. The steak tasted of aged blue cheese, of truffles, of *umami* and brown butter. It was a fantastic gastronomical experience and Amit couldn't stop talking about it for weeks. When could we do it again? But it would be at least another year before we could hold another tasting like that, since we needed to age the meat. And with chef gone it might be even longer than that.

Amit saw me at the grill and came over after the perch *ceviche* had been served, while several guests were outside partaking of some Chemdawg.

"Where is chef tonight?" He got right to the point, as usual. "I'm surprised to see you here."

"Hi Amit," I smiled and avoided the question. "How are you enjoying the evening?"

"It's brilliant," he said. "People are going to get very rich." Amit is a local entrepreneur who'd made his money in software and cyber security. He'd sold his shares when his startup was acquired and he's now bored and looking for something interesting to do.

I laughed. "You're already very rich, Amit."

"That is true," he nodded. "But this is giving me ideas."

"For your own grow?" Amit has the idea of a boutique operation, growing organic, artisanal cannabis. He would discuss it over cognac with chef for hours after most of the other guests had left the restaurant.

"Exactly, yes." Amit is an *aficionado* who believes in treating cannabis with respect, like a vintage wine. He wants to develop some kind of place that offers tastings, like what was offered at our local Niagara wineries. He and chef had spoken many times about having a restaurant attached to his operation where food and weed pairings could be offered, now that it's legalized. They'd talk for hours about *terroir*, about our local climate, and how this or that particular strain would do well in the Twenty Valley's climate. I'd hover in the background, refilling their glasses and making sure the rest of restaurant service ran smoothly, listening in when I had a chance.

"What you are doing here this evening is exactly what we've been talking about. What I'd like to provide, the food, the wine, the weed—all together in an experience that is unique, exciting, and unparalleled."

I smiled my thanks. "It is exciting to be part of this," I said my scripted line, repeated several times already that evening. "There are so many new creative culinary opportunities."

Amit rubbed his hands together and surveyed the room. "Are you thinking of investing?" I asked.

His eyes danced with excitement. "This has the potential to become much bigger in the Niagara region than the wine industry," he said. "The amount of money that can be made from the same size plot of farmland is astonishing, with fewer inputs." He leaned closer to make his point, counting off on his fingers as he spoke.

"There's no need to press grapes, to cask, or bottle, or label, or age, or store millions of bottles of wine. All you have to do is grow weed, harvest, cure and sell." He laughed with glee. "Some people are gonna get so rich!" I bet he'd be repeating that all night.

Weed has already made lots of people rich, I thought. And there has always been opportunity there for those who know how to take advantage of it. It just takes courage and a disregard for the small thing called the law.

EIGHTEEN

Rose

THE SUN HAS made its way around the house and I'm now sitting on the far end of the back terrace, in the last bit of shade. The sultry air shimmers with heat and cicadas buzz in the trees. A slow breeze barely whispers, rustling the leaves of the maples that over- hang the drive. It's a beautiful lazy late summer afternoon with just a trace of autumn in the air. I feel that deep nostalgia that overwhelms me when I smell the phlox, the ripe wheat, see the first leaves fall. Summer is over.

I've spent the morning in the kitchen garden taking a series of photos of artfully displayed tomatoes, heaped on an antique board with some herbs. Then later, on the back porch, using a weathered table with flaking periwinkle blue paint, I placed some quail eggs in a wooden bowl filled with straw, next to a glass cloche and some potted herbs. The arrangement wasn't quite working and I fiddled with it until I gave up in frustration.

From where I now sit hiding from the sun I can just see the front facade of the abandoned house next door. I remember the day the new owner came over on her duty call to meet the neigh- bours, plans and elevation drawings rolled up under her arm. I watched as she'd first checked out the Thorny Rose sign, the gar- dens and barn, the house and wisteria-draped porch. Her eyes were narrow and her disdain clear. I could almost hear her thinking *We'll see about this.* I knew instantly it would only be a matter of time before the complaints about the restaurant would start: Too much noise. Too much traffic. Wedding music too loud. Deliveries too early. They'd ruin Thorny Rose as soon as they moved in. I had to stop them.

She'd unrolled the plans on this very same periwinkle blue table and asked me what I thought. She didn't really care about my opinion of course. She was expecting me to lavish praise.

What I thought? A faux French manor house surfaced in cultured stone. It looked like an expensive bunker.

What I thought? She didn't want to know. I thought it was extravagant, grotesque, pretentious, wasteful and ugly.

What I thought? That there was no way I'd allow that to be built if I could help it.

And it hadn't been. Funny how sometimes things just work out.

I sit with my lunch: a glass of wine, some walnuts and olives and a nice piece of Manchego cheese, savouring the view of the mature maple trees in the woodlot across the road. The leaves on the tops of many of trees are turning to red, weeks early. I feel another pang of sorrow, realizing that summer is passing quickly. Soon it will be autumn, too soon. How is it that every year it feels like summer is over so much faster? I remember the long days when I was a child, the endless sense of time, stretching in front of me. I was often bored, hours and days with nothing to do but play and read, and I longed for school to start so I could see my friends again. Now summer is over in a blink, like life.

Then Wright drives up, interrupting my morose thoughts, his classic muscle car's engine throbbing. My heart sinks even further. What the hell is he doing here? Can't he read? The sign says Closed Mondays.

He gets out of his car and as he walks up to the porch I force my face into a smile.

"Good afternoon," he says as he sits down, a little too comfortably, on the porch swing. What the hell is he doing here?

"Can I offer you a glass of wine?" I reflexively say, as if he were a guest. "Or are you on duty?"

Wright shrugs then accepts. "Sure, why not?" I go into the kitchen and bring out a second glass and the bottle.

"What's that for?" he asks when I hand him the glass. He points at my set up.

"My blog. I'm staging a few vignettes that I can use at some point. This one with the tomatoes is current, obviously. But the egg one is more for spring I think. That's the feeling I'm going for."

"Spring is six months away."

"Readers don't know when I wrote it or when the photo was taken. It's illusion. They love glimpses into the life behind the scenes at the restaurant."

"So nothing is real?"

"Reality is overrated," I laugh. "This..." I gesture wide, taking in the entire farm, garden and Thorny Rose, "...is a story we made up. One we get to live in every day, one that people enjoy. They get to read about it, see the pictures and the videos on our website. And maybe buy our products and eat here in the restaurant."

"Thorny Rose is an *Idea,*" I continue. "It's this beautiful, chaotic, fertile Eden, bursting with goats, chickens, tomatoes, giant sunflowers, homemade bread, hand-churned butter, home-smoked meat. It's charming, nostalgic, romantic, rustic beautiful...and real." I pick up my camera and take a few more shots of the quail eggs. Then I look through the images and I'm still not satisfied. "People love real. They pay more for it."

"You sound cynical," says Wright. I have an idea and quickly substitute the straw under the eggs with some moss I tear out of the garden at the foot of the steps.

"Yeah. Sorry," I reply as I rearrange the setup. "It's been a rough time." I fire off a series of shots. Then, glancing through them I smile. They look perfect. The fresh green moss sets off the tiny mottled quail eggs. The image looks just like spring. Satisfied, I sit back down and take another sip of my wine.

Wright goes over to the vignette and picks up the glass cloche. "Didn't I see a lot of those inside? In the restaurant?"

"Sure. Chef uses them all the time, to capture smoke."

"Capture smoke?"

"For the presentation," I explain. "Dining is all about anticipation. About the moment when the customer sees the food, smells the food—even before they taste the food. It's the unveiling of the story. The intrigue, the mystery, the excitement." Wright looks confused.

"You really don't eat out often, do you?" I observe. "It's been around for ages. All the foodies go nuts for it. We did a great smoked watermelon salad in the summer."

"Smoked watermelon?" Wright looks revolted.

"*Mmm.* Delicious. Cold smoked using apple and cherry wood chips."

"That doesn't help," he says, shaking his head. Clearly he's a meat and potatoes kind of guy.

"In autumn chef would scorch root vegetables with a smoking gun, then serve them smouldering under a cloche. It's a dramatic way to serve a few simple carrots, beets and rutabaga."

"You get to charge more too, I'm sure."

"Now who's cynical?" I say. "We've got a prix fixe menu. No choices. All in." Wright laughs.

"On the current menu we serve quail eggs on a bed of smoking dried ferns and hay. The aroma of the smoke evokes memories and emotions." Wright looks skeptical. "We make a little pile of juniper twigs, with the eggs nestled into them. Then we set fire to the juniper and quickly blow it out so it's just the embers smoking. Then we put the lid on and present it to the diner, who is curious about what's inside the smoke-filled cloche. It's unveiled at table, revealing the beautiful plate. The smoke permeates the dish adding flavour, but mostly it's a fantastic presentation. Very dramatic and theatrical."

"I bet people Instagram the shit out of all that," he says. "But it seems like a lot of work, for a bit of drama."

"Any good drama takes effort—so much behind the scenes that the diner never knows. But that makes the story."

"Shouldn't it just be about how the food tastes?"

"Anyone can cook well and serve good food. It's the romance, the drama, the story that lures peoples, entices them. Seduces them. And then they come back for more." I look away for a moment. "Chef was good at that…the story." *At the seduction too.*

"You're not so bad yourself," says Wright. "That's a good story."

"I just realized," I say, laughing at the absurdity of what I was about to say. "We have a smoking gun. Just like in the detective stories."

Wright smiles, joining in. "Who killed Colonel Mustard with the candlestick?"

"Who's got the rope in the library?" I continue. "Who's holding the smoking gun?"

"Who is?" he asks.

"Maggie. Usually."

I sip my wine then ask the obvious question. "What brings you here today Detective Wright?" He looks relaxed, sitting on the porch swing with a glass of wine as if he's a guest, not a cop.

He reaches into his pocket and takes out the postcard.

"The postmark is too smudged to get any information about when this was sent," he says. "Or who sent it."

"But it's obviously from Los Angeles," I interrupt. "It's my husband's handwriting."

"I called those restaurants you mentioned, the ones the he might go to on this *stage*," Wright continues. I stare at him, afraid of what he's found out.

"At one of them the chef had a good laugh. Said it was a joke. Said he'd been asked to send a postcard by your husband. Said it would *amuse his wife*." I stare at Wright, not comprehending what he'd just said. "But he says he didn't send one."

"Well someone clearly did," I snap, pointing to the postcard. "You're telling me you think that he never went to Los Angeles. That this is all some stunt, some *joke* to *amuse* me?" I gulp my wine. "I'm not laughing."

"Are you sure it's his handwriting?" Wright asks.

"Of course I am. You think I don't know my husband's hand-writing?" Wright doesn't reply.

"I don't actually understand why you're here," I began. "I've told you chef isn't missing. He's on a *stage*. You've spoken with all the staff, none of whom are concerned. Apart from Montana, who, by the way I'm sure was the one who made the ridiculous report in the first place." He watches me as I speak, my frustration obvious.

"We just need to be satisfied about a few things," he replies. "The fact that he's been away so long. That's he not back for these big events, as he clearly should have been." He looks at me for a moment. "To be honest, I'm surprised you aren't more concerned yourself." He's irritating me and I'm getting angry. And afraid.

I take a sip of wine and I think hard about what to say before I speak. How much I should reveal. What I can say to make this situation better, and to make Wright leave and never come back.

"He's been siphoning cash out of our bank account."

Wright looks very interested. "What do you mean?"

"I went to the bank and saw some of our retirement funds have been cashed out." I glance at Wright's expression. "And I went through the books for the restaurant and found some discrepancies. Some money unaccounted for."

"That's rough," he says. "A lot of money?"

I sip my wine. "When you are as broke as we are anything is a lot. But, yes, it was everything we have." Wright nods, thinking over what I've told him.

"I also think he was doing some side jobs," I add. "Cash jobs that never went through the books."

"What kind of cash jobs?"

"I don't know. There have been orders for supplies that I don't think have actually been used in the restaurant. Chocolate, sugar, butter, nuts…in large quantities we don't normally go through. I think maybe he was making something for private clients, something he never told me about."

"And pocketing the cash," Wright concludes.

I nod. "He was hiding this money so he could leave me." There. I'd given Wright the story: My husband has left me. He's taken the money and left me high and dry. There was nothing mysterious about it. Just another sad broken marriage. Now what will he do?

He sits for a moment, saying nothing. He looks out over the gardens, considering what I've told him. I drink my wine and eat an olive.

At the base of the porch a chipmunk is digging a tunnel that leads somewhere under the limestone path at the base of the steps. His little paws dug furiously at the soil and he flings it behind him in a pile as he burrows deeper into the ground. As he works, the limestone slab rocks. He's undermining it with his efforts and it's clear the stone will fall and seal off the tunnel, possibly crushing him underneath.

Wright and I both watch in fascination as the little guy works feverishly, oblivious to the danger.

"I feel like I need to let him know somehow," Wright says. "His tunnel isn't structurally sound."

"He's a chipmunk, not an engineer," I say. "He's just doing what his nature compels him to."

"Shouldn't he move? Or be told his house is falling down around him?" Wright says.

"It's his home," I say. "Even if it's unstable. People don't want to move or change. Or even know about it."

"I thought we were talking about a chipmunk."

"We all have to let things fall as they must." I give him a smile.

Wright pours himself another glass of wine and I slide the dish of olives over to him. "So, what's your story?" he asks. I don't reply at first. "How is it that you run a restaurant? I'd have thought you'd be a garden designer or something like that."

"My story," I repeat, and I think about it for a moment. "I did start out as a garden designer—you're right. I had a little business, did some nice small gardens for clients. I had an allotment garden and I grew food for myself. I ate what I grew. I preserved some things, and I gave an awful lot of squash to the food bank. And I supplied a couple of small trendy cafes downtown."

"Which is where I met Raymond. Chef." I sip my wine. "And the rest, as they say, is history." Chef had been working at one of the top restaurants in the city. He was a rising star chef and had even been approached to do a pilot for his own cooking show for television. But then he'd left in search of his own style.

"We opened a small restaurant together," I say. He wanted to do something unique, not like every other high end, contemporary restaurant. *Anyone can order passion fruit and ahi tuna*, he'd said. *I want to be unique.*

"Was it a success?"

I laugh. "Definitely. We were full most nights, on the list of top ten restaurants in the city, critics' choice. They were heady times."

Wright looks impressed.

"But all I dreamt about was being back here, on the farm." I'd longed to wake in the morning to the call of the cardinal, the screech of the blue jay, and the liquid song of the redwing blackbird. I missed the haunting coo of mourning dove. I wanted to hear crickets and frogs, not sirens and streetcars.

"Well you got what you wanted," Wright says. "You made the move and the restaurant is doing well."

"It took a while, but I did it," I nod. "I made it back home."

Wright stands and makes his way down the stairs, taking care to avoid the misguided chipmunk.

I follow him and pause at one of the planters next to the drive. The chipmunk has clearly tried digging in there as well. There are several holes and the plants are uprooted. Planter soil spills down the side of the container and is mounded in a heap. I dig into the soil with my bare hands, replanting the flowers.

"You really are tied to this place," Wright observes.

I grab a handful of soil then let it trickle through my fingers. "I feel like I'm made of it," I say. "Like I was moulded from this." Wright looks surprised.

"That sounds ridiculous I know. But this place is in my bones. In my blood. There's nothing I wouldn't do to preserve it."

"Nothing lasts forever," he remarks and walks to his car with a wave.

His offhand remark irritates me. The flippant carelessness, pretending to be somehow philosophical. *Nothing lasts forever. Change is inevitable. What can you do?* It's intolerable. There is always something to be done.

NINETEEN

Wright

JUST AFTER SEVEN thirty I pick up a call from the Thorny Rose. It's Maggie.

"I just found Rose locked in the walk-in freezer. You need to come here, now."

"Is she...okay?" I mean alive.

"She asked me to call you. So yeah, she's okay."

On the way over to the restaurant I wonder why they've called me and not 911. Probably don't want another visit from emergency services. It wouldn't be good for the Thorny Rose's reputation.

I find Rose sitting in a chair in her robe and slippers, drinking a cup of tea. There's an empty brandy snifter next to her on the counter.

"Typical." Maggie opens the door to let me in. "Do you always arrive when the show's over?"

"What can I say? I hate all the paperwork."

"Can you tell me what happened?" I ask. Rose thinks for a minute, trying to remember, to get her story straight.

"It was just after three this morning," she says. "I know because I looked at my bedside clock. I heard a noise." She swallows a sip of tea and thinks for a moment.

"I came downstairs to the kitchen and I saw the freezer door was open, which was weird."

"Were there any lights on?" I ask.

Rose shakes her head. "Just the exit sign over the door. And the lights from the pastry case." She points to the glass fronted dessert fridge.

"I couldn't figure out why the freezer would have been left open like that. I was angry and I went over to close it. Someone shoved me inside and closed the door."

"Did you see who it was?" Stupid question, but I have to ask. She shakes her head. "And this is what you were wearing? Just your pajamas?"

"And my robe and slippers." Maggie and I exchange a look. We are both thinking the same thing—that Rose is lucky to have survived. From the look on her face it's clear she knows it.

"You're lucky Maggie found you," I say. "What time was that?"

"I came in just before seven," Maggie answers. "I made coffee and did some prep. Didn't even think to look in the freezer until I needed to get some beef stock. Lucky I was making a *demi glace* or it might have been another hour before I found her."

"I tried the emergency latch release, but it was jammed." Maggie looks uncomfortable.

"I had a look at it, but I couldn't see anything wrong," she says quietly.

"It was jammed!" Rose insists. "I kept hitting it and it wouldn't open." She rakes her fingers through her hair.

"We keep the freezer at zero Celsius, so I knew I didn't have a lot of time before I froze to death. We keep a parka, hat and gloves in the walk-in. So I put those on. I thought about calling for help, but I didn't have my cell phone with me."

"It wouldn't have worked anyway," Maggie says. "Can't get a

signal in there. The walls are two layers of stainless steel over a four inch foam core."

"I tried not to panic. But I knew the staff weren't due back into work for about four hours."

"I thought if I jammed the condenser fan it would stop blowing freezing cold air. I used a box cutter," she says pointing to the ruined fan with the tool jammed into the blades. "But it only stopped the one fan. And I didn't have another tool. I tried a frozen filet of haddock, but the fan just shredded it."

"I knew I had to keep moving or I'd end up with hypothermia. Or frostbite. If I survived."

"Then I stacked all the boxes of frozen stuff up to block the blast of air. I figured if the fan was disabled the condenser would stop working and the temperature would start to rise."

"It worked." Maggie smiles and pats her on the back. "The freezer is toast. Good thinking…except now we have to get it fixed."

"Yeah." Rose tries to return the smile. "We need to get a lot of fish and seafood on the menu this week. Before we lose it all."

Maggie nods. "I'll make bouillabaisse." She goes into the freezer and starts to remove boxes of seafood. Fish, salmon, scallops and shrimp all got moved into the walk-in cooler.

"See what we can salvage," Rose instructs. "I hope we can save some of the stock. Maybe the veal stock and fish *fumee*? The sorbets and ice creams are garbage."

"You seem pretty calm for someone who's just survived a near-death experience," I say. Rose pulls her bathrobe closer.

"I don't understand what happened," she says quietly. "How did the door jamb? Maggie said there was nothing wrong…but I couldn't get it open." I think about it, but don't respond. Maybe it was frozen. Or maybe someone had jammed it, and removed the evidence before Maggie got there.

"I think the real question is why you got shoved in there in the first place. Someone doesn't like you very much." Rose's lips twist in a bitter smile.

"Rose," I cut straight to the point. "Why would anyone want you dead?"

She looks hurt by the question, but not surprised. "Nobody. Why would they?"

"Money. Revenge," I say. "Who inherits the farm?"

"My husband."

I look at her, holding her gaze. She shakes her head slowly in denial, her lip trembling.

"What was the nature of your relationship with Luca Ricci?" I ask. Her head snaps up and she stares at me. Maggie sputters and starts to speak and I hold my hand up to silence her. She turns and starts to busy herself in the prep area, looking into the coolers and making notes on a pad. I have no doubt she's still listening to everything we say.

"What do you mean?" Rose asks, her voice low. "We were friends."

"I got the impression you were more than just friends." Rose says nothing.

"It's just interesting that Luca dies...."

"That was an accident!" She interrupts.

"...and now someone has tried to kill you." I let that sink in for a moment.

"And Montana?" Rose mumbles. "Was that an accident? Or did *someone* kill her too?"

"I don't know," I say. "That may have been an accident. So might Luca's death and even your getting stuck in the freezer. But that's a lot of *accidents* happening around you, don't you think?"

Rose sits, staring out the window for a minute before she speaks. "No way. You're suggesting my husband is still here, somewhere? That he tried to kill me. To inherit the farm?" I don't say anything. The answer is obvious. I can see Rose sink into thought.

"Do you have life insurance?" She shakes her head. "Does your husband?"

"No. We both used to have insurance but I stopped paying the premiums when we couldn't make payroll." No insurance on Rose means less motive for chef to kill her, I think. But he'll still inherit the farm, and that's worth a lot. Maybe this disappearing act of his is to set up an alibi for when Rose is killed.

"How is he supposed to do all this when he's in Los Angeles?" She asks miserably.

"Maybe he's back," I say. "Or he never went in the first place."

Rose retreats into thought, considering what I suggested. I glance over at Maggie, who is staring into the walk in freezer, frowning.

"We can investigate this. There are passenger records of flights, passport control coming and going out of the country. He took his car I assume?"

Rose nods.

"And it's registered in his name?" I take a few minutes to note down her husband's full legal name, make and model of his car. "I don't suppose you have his passport number?"

Rose shakes her head. "He has two passports, Canadian and US. He's got dual citizenship." That complicates things. "There may be something on his laptop," she says after a moment.

"He didn't take it with him?"

"No. He just mostly uses his phone." Rose stands. "I'll go get it. I want to change, before the rest of the staff come in." Her expression pleads with me. "Please don't say anything about what happened here."

She comes back within a few minutes, dressed in her kitchen whites, looking as if nothing was wrong. She has a laptop under her arm, which she lays on the butcher block. She flips it open, punches in the password, and spins it round for me to look through while she goes over to talk with Maggie. There might have just been a threat to her life, but Rose still has a business to run. She's tough, I have to hand it to her.

I first check his search history, starting three months ago. There isn't a lot there, apart from searches for trips to Costa Rica and other Caribbean vacation spots. The odd search for wine suppliers, cheese importers—the kinds of things you'd expect a chef to be looking at. Then I come across a few searches for topics like "how to get a fake passport". I laugh. *Amateur.* As if you can find that online. But still, he may have eventually found someone who could get him some fake documents. Or maybe he has some criminal connections who'd helped him out. So, it looks like chef started planning to run away months ago. *Interesting.*

His email turns up nothing, nor do his deleted emails or the trash. But he could easily have emptied that. Funny that a guy empties his trash but doesn't clear his history though. I guess he never thought anyone would be looking. The IT team at the station could mine the trash but I don't have that skill. For now I think I have what I need. Confirmation that he'd planned on running, months ago. So, was he back, or did he never leave? And why?

I close the laptop as Rose comes up. Two more of the staff have come in and the workday is beginning. I can tell she wants me to leave, before they start asking questions.

"I should probably file a missing person's report now," Rose says. "Officially."

"I'll take care of it for you," I tell her. "Don't worry."

As she turns to get to work I thought of something. "It might be helpful if you go into your online banking and see if there have been withdrawals from your account or other credit card purchases," I suggest.

"Can't the police just do that?" she asks.

"It's faster if you do it," I say. "No need for the damn paperwork."

"Excuse me, Rose?" a young guy in kitchen whites calls out. "There are a couple of guys to see you outside." Rose sighs and goes out the back door. I follow her, since I'm leaving anyway.

Standing at the foot of the steps is Yuri, the forager I met the first day I came, and some other guy who looks like a miniature version of him. They both wear work overalls and boots, and both of them look very serious.

"Yuri? Andrei?" Rose says when she sees them. "What's going on?"

"I hear about the girl who died," Yuri says. "I bring my brother to tell the bees."

"Tell the bees?" Rose echoes. "Okay... sure." She doesn't sound sure.

"They have to be told," Andrei says. Yuri nods.

"Told?"

"About the death," Maggie says. She's come out of the kitchen and stands behind us on the porch. "It's bad luck if you don't tell the bees about a death in the family." I figure they already know, since they are the ones who'd stung Montana to death, but who am I to argue with two eccentric Russians?

"Oh. Right," Rose says. "Let's go." She leads the way out through the kitchen garden, followed first by Andrei, then Yuri and Maggie. I'm the last in line as we make our way along the center path of the raised beds, past the trellises of beans and the tall tomato cages to the large patch of flowers that surround the beehives.

Just like the day I'd spoken to Montana out here, the bees fly around and land on my shirt. I brush one away and Andrei grabs my arm. He scowls at me.

"You must never strike a bee," he says, raising his finger, bent with arthritis. "It will bring bad luck." I wonder if Montana had made that mistake.

We all stand back as Andrei goes up to the first hive and knocks on it gently. The he bends and quietly says something in Russian to the bees inside. Then he does the same thing at each of the hives in turn.

"What's he saying?" I ask Rose, who is standing closest to me. She leans in and whispers in my ear.

"*Montana is dead.*"

After Andrei visits each of hives he stands for a moment in silence, observing them. Then he turns and walks back out of the garden, and we follow behind. Rose continues up the steps and returns to the kitchen, but Maggie stays for a minute chatting with Yuri.

Andrei stands next to them, saying nothing. I approach him.

"Are they your bees?" I ask.

He shakes his head. "I have my own bees, on my property."

"Do you make honey?" I ask.

He looks at me like I'm an idiot. "No. The bees do." Then he laughs. "I am thief. I take their honey from them, like a bear in the forest."

"My brother has many hives," Yuri says. "He sells combs and honey, and bee pollen."

"And beeswax candles," Andrei adds with pride. "At the market."

"Andrei is a bee-whisperer," Maggie says before giving Andrei and Yuri each a big a kiss and heading back into the kitchen. Yuri follows her inside.

"Now I try to understand them," Andrei says. "Before I was killing them."

"You were killing bees?"

"My greed was. I made lots of money renting bees for pollination, but they work too hard, they make bad honey, and it kills them. Now I will only rent hives to Niagara organic fruit growers."

"I don't understand."

"I would truck bees for almonds in February, then go up to Washington State for apples, cherries and pears. Sometimes to Maine for blueberries."

"That's a lot of driving," I say. "It must have been hard on you. And the bees."

"Very." He sounds sad. "But bees are *geroi*—heroes. They are immune to even cyanide."

"Cyanide?"

"Yes. Bitter almond blossom is full of cyanide, enough to kill any mammal. But bees...they just fly from flower to flower, eating it all day," he says in admiration. "They are attracted to it."

"But almond honey they make from it is no good. Bitter," he says, making a face.

"Does the honey contain cyanide?" I wonder. "Would it kill a person?"

"Who knows?" Andrei shrugs. "Life is full of surprises."

Yuri comes out of the kitchen, folding some cash and slipping it into his pocket. That's probably payment for the mushrooms he'd dropped off. As he comes down the steps and stands next to Andrei, the two look so alike it's impossible to not know at first glance they are brothers. Yuri is tall and lean, with a dreamy, haunted look. Andrei is a smaller version of him, with the same sharp cheekbones and bright blue eyes. But where Yuri is mournful, Andrei feels electric and positively charged.

"So, did chef take any interest in the bees?" I ask. Andrei's intense eyes meet mine. He stares for a moment, and I'm about to repeat my question, thinking he doesn't understand. Then suddenly both he and Yuri burst out laughing.

"*Interest?*" Andrei repeats. "Oh yes, he was very *interested.*" I shake my head in confusion. Maggie emerges from the kitchen, wiping her hands on a towel.

"He was asshole," Andrei says. "He reads a book about bee-keeping and thinks he know something. *Oh I must only have clover honey.*" Andrei spits in disgust.

"Chef didn't know from shit," Maggie joins in. "His great palate couldn't tell the difference in honey. I used to call him a Wannabee." The three of them laugh again, and I can't help but notice Maggie still used the past tense.

Yuri nods. "Yeah, he's big expert on everything. He ask me to take him out looking for mushrooms. I refuse. Why should I? I have nothing to prove to him. Then Rose ask me…" he shrugs as if to say *What could I do?*

"So you took him out foraging?"

"*Da*, I took him out all right," he smiles at the memory. "For hours in the deep woods up north."

"Did chef like it?"

Yuri shakes his head. "For whole day he never stops talking. Telling me what he knows about mushrooms. So I test him. I say *Look there is King Bolete…so tasty*. It was Deadly Galerina. Very poisonous. He would have eaten it, *durak*."

"But you stopped him." They both look at me and grin.

"I should have left him in the forest."

"You should have let him eat it," says Andrei. They both nod.

TWENTY

Rose

SMOKE BILLOWS OFF the charcoal grill as the cornhusks catch fire. I run over to spray them with water and the flames subside, then I'm able to use my tongs and move the cobs of corn off to the side of the grill. The worst of them go right into the compost bucket, but most aren't too badly charred. That's the whole point of BBQ corn anyway, that char adds the flavour.

The real problem is, where the hell is Maggie? She's supposed to be working the grill and she's nowhere to be seen. Irritated, I look around and see no sign of her. The driveway of the Womyn Collective is filled with a steady stream of cars and trucks, and they raise clouds of dust from the dry gravel as they drive past looking for a place to park. Groups of people are milling around the farm and flower fields, going into and out of the shop, but none of them wear the familiar white jacket and black-and-white houndstooth patterned pants of a chef. None of them are Maggie.

Today is the annual Farm Crawl, a day when the local farms open their doors to guests who get to see the inside workings of a real farm. The local CSA started the Farm Crawl ten years ago, and it's grown ever since, with people travelling a hundred miles to enjoy the day. For a modest fee of ten dollars, guests get to self-tour the various suppliers in the region. They could see the farms in whatever order they chose, and leave some farms out if they weren't interested, or stay longer at ones they were curious about.

The promotion in general is to promote the local food movement and showcase farms that support sustainable food systems and use green technology. This year the farms participating are the organic CSA farm, Millvale Dairy so they can show off their water buffalo, a lavender farm, a goat farm that made an award-winning cheese, an alpaca farm, an ostrich farm, and of course the Womyn Collective.

The Womyn are celebrating corn today, even though they don't grow any. They've created a large painting depicting several corn goddesses from various cultural traditions: Demeter, Yellow Woman, Xilonen, and the Zuni Corn Maidens. Each of the goddesses is holding ears of corn or bushels of corn, or wears a gown decorated with corn, or has a headdress made of corn. It's definitely colourful and clearly art created by committee. Or by a commune, in this case.

I've set up the BBQ grills and tables under a small pop up tent in front of the painting. The tent provides a bit of shade from the relentless sun, but the heat's inescapable. It's another day of extreme heat warnings for the region, and another day of zero precipitation. Add to that the heat from the grills and it will be a really difficult day to get through.

We are serving corn on the cob, grilled in the husk, with either chili-lime butter or honey-herb butter. Customers can buy a cob, peel back the husk and roll the corn in their favourite butter. We're also selling grilled polenta with roasted peppers and plum tomatoes and paper bags of homemade caramel corn with bacon.

The Womyn farm guests today are going to pick their own flower bouquets, for an additional modest fee of a dollar per stem. They are also selling honey, jams and preserves in the shop. And, with what they are charging for the food, it looks like they'll make a nice profit from the day, given how busy it's already getting.

I pull more cobs out of the tub of water where they've been soaking all morning and place them on the grill. Once the first few carloads of guests have made their way through the flower farm and seen the labyrinth and beehives, they'll be lining up for something to eat, and I'd better be ready.

Then I catch a glimpse of white out of the corner of my eye. I'm relieved to see it's Maggie, sitting on an upturned bucket behind the barn. Her head is bowed and I can see a fine ribbon of smoke rising from her hand. I push the cobs to the side of the grill and run over to see what's going on.

"Maggie," I ask. "Are you okay?" I know she isn't. I can smell the cannabis she is smoking. Maggie only does that when her pain is intolerable, for the fast hit of relief. That means the usual medications aren't effective any longer. The morphine, the fentanyl pain patches, even the CBD distillate under her tongue aren't helping any more. My heart goes out to her and I kneel on the ground, putting my arm around her shoulder. There's nothing more I can say or do.

"I don't like it Rose," she whispers. "You could have died."

"What do you mean Maggie?"

"The freezer," she mumbles. "What were you thinking?"

"It'll be fine. I'll manage the situation, like you say I always do," I say, squeezing her shoulder. "Everything is under control."

She raises her head and looks out over the flower fields. "Is it?" I don't reply.

After a moment, she shudders and stubs out the joint. "I'll be okay," she says. "Just give me a minute." I get to my feet and head back to the grill, where there is already a line forming. The aroma of grilled corn is bringing customers from all over the farm and it's all I can do to keep up with the cooking, taking the money, giving

LIZA DROZDOV

change and instructing people to make sure all the waste goes into the compost bins.

Then suddenly Maggie is at my side. She's tossing more corn onto the grill, putting out bags of caramel corn and dishes of grilled polenta with roast vegetables. I deal with the customers and she makes sure we have enough food ready to keep them happy. Working in harmony like a pair of draft horses in harness we get through the day, each of us knowing what's needed before it runs out, anticipating questions before they are asked, and putting out the fires that keep flaming up on the grills. Finally it's four o'clock and the day is over.

The last carload of customers is pulling out of the driveway as I'm packing away the tubs of herb butter and salt and pepper. We ran out of corn and polenta an hour ago so there isn't much left to load into the truck. The table, pop up tent and BBQ grill belong to the Womyn Collective, so they'll deal with putting it away at some point themselves. Maggie has gone into the air-conditioned shop for a rest. Working out in the intense heat all day couldn't have been easy for her; I could barely stand it and can't even imagine how she did. She's got a will of iron and simply refuses to lie down and die.

Once I've locked up the truck I go into the shop to find her. I'm not sure she should be coming into the restaurant for service tonight and I'm going to let her know we can manage without her. She's done more than enough already today.

The shop is cool and quiet. The last of the customers have gone and any remaining staff must be back in the kitchen, cooking preserves or preparing for the next day. I find Maggie sitting with Sophie at a table behind the counter, drinking a cup of tea. I sink into one the chairs across from her, grateful for the cool air, and look around the shop. The shelves are still well stocked, but it's clear that certain items have been big sellers. There are very few of the lotions and balms left, and the shelves of liqueurs and cordials are mostly empty. It must have been a good day.

Maggie watches me for a while before she finally speaks. "What were you doing drinking wine with that cop?" she says. "That was reckless and dangerous." I glance quickly at Sophie to see how much she knows. From her angry expression I guess Maggie must have just told her and she knows everything. Her blue eyes are like ice. Sophie folds her arms and leans back in her chair, waiting for my reply.

"It's not like I invited him over," I say. "He just came by to tell me about his investigation. Relax."

"Relax?" Sophie snaps. "You're joking, right? We can't afford to relax."

"He's not interested in what's going on here," I say.

"Then what's he after? Sophie demands. "Why is this cop asking questions?"

"Missing chef," Maggie answers for me. "Or so he says."

Sophie snorts. "You believe that?" It is obvious she doesn't.

"He showed up last week because Montana reported him missing. So he's following up." I say. "What else could it be?"

"Are you kidding?" she snaps. "*What else could it be*?" She stands up in frustration, her chair scraping against the concrete floor. "Look around Rose!" She starts pacing in agitation. She has a lot at stake, and has absolutely no trust in the police. I say nothing and wait for her to calm down.

"He was here the other day," Sophie finally says, her voice bitter. "Asking about Lotte."

"Why?" Now I'm alarmed. "What's Lotte got to do with anything?" Why would Wright be speaking to her? Surely he'd asked her whatever he needed to the first day he arrived.

"She and Montana were friends," Maggie says. "Maybe he thought she'd told Lotte something? After all Montana and chef were *close.*" We sit in silence for a moment, thinking over the possibilities.

"Let's hope chef is all he asks her about," Sophie says.

"C'mon," Maggie says. "Lotte's a good kid. She's not going to say anything."

I roll my eyes. "*Good kid?* You know what those two were like Maggie. They were toxic."

Maggie isn't going to agree with me. "Maybe," she shrugs. "But I think that was just the bitch Montana influencing her."

"So you say," Sophie mutters. "But who knows what she could tell him?"

Sophie is right to be concerned. Lotte had stayed at Womyn Collective and Maggie had helped her out, so she owed them her silence. But Sophie doesn't need anyone knowing her business. And if Lotte was a friend of Montana's, who knows what she'd have shared.

"She's a good kid," Maggie insists. "And now she's got no job and she needs the money."

I think I know where this is going, but there's no way I will ever bring Lotte back to Thorny Rose. "Maggie, she had to go. You understand that," I say, trying to be patient. "I couldn't keep her in the restaurant." I can tell Maggie is disappointed. She likes Lotte, has taken her under her wing. But it isn't her call.

"Okay, I get it," Maggie finally agrees. "But we could use her skills in the kitchen here. She's learned a lot and could be valuable." Sophie meets my eye and shrugs. I feel pushed into a corner so I give up without a fight. But I'm not happy about it.

"If you want to bring her back here, if you want to risk having her back, that's your decision. But I don't want my name mentioned." Maggie smiles her thanks.

"It'll be fine," Sophie says, but I'm not so sure.

"Make sure she stays quiet or I will," I say and I mean it.

Maggie reaches across the table and squeezes my hand. Her face is drawn with pain and tension. The argument has taken whatever energy she has left after the hot day in the sun.

"I could really use a smoke," she says. Sophie gets up and closes the shop door, first making sure to put up the closed sign. Then she goes into the back room and brings out a glass pipe, already filled with water. She quickly prepares the glass bong and lets the smoke fill the bowl while Maggie waits patiently. Then she is able to inhale deeply and within a minute I could see relief on her face.

I glance at Sophie who's watching her mother's face and patting her hand. Lines crease her forehead and she has dark circles under her eyes. She's probably spending many late nights looking after Maggie once she leaves work and goes back to her trailer.

I used to join them for a drink several times a week for a drink, and we'd watch some television together until it was late and Maggie was ready to go to sleep. Sophie or I would first make sure she had all her pain relief so she would sleep through the night, then we'd leave her and head home; Sophie to her room in the farmhouse, me back to Thorny Rose. But since chef has been gone I haven't been doing as much. I have to be on hand to shut down the restaurant every night, which means I haven't been around to help out like I used to. I feel sorrow and shame, realizing I've let them both down.

"It's funny," Maggie says, her voice quiet. "That postcard from Los Angeles." The back of my neck prickles with anxiety.

"What about it?" I ask. Maggie is lost in thought, her eyes focused on some spot across the room. She inhales deeply from the pipe again before she speaks.

"The Hollywood Sign. It looks exactly like one he sent a couple of years ago," she says. "When he went to work at The NoMad." Her eyes are already at half-mast and it is obvious the smoke has taken away her pain.

"Really?" I glance at Sophie and we exchange a look. "You know how he is. Maybe he forgot he sent that one before," I say. This was familiar territory. Maggie gets high and will talk for hours about anything and nothing, until she falls asleep.

We help Maggie to stand and we hold her, one on each side, and walk her back to her trailer. I think about getting my truck and driving her there, but it would have taken longer and Sophie wouldn't have been able to hold Maggie up on her own. It takes us about ten minutes, but we get her inside and sitting in her favourite chair. We leave her dozing in front of some situation comedy and Sophie walks me back to the shop so she can finish closing up.

By the time we're done we're both dripping in sweat from the exertion and the oppressive heat. I drive back to the Thorny Rose to shower and get ready for tonight's service. I've got a lot to think about.

TWENTY ONE

Wright

A SECOND FATAL accident within a few days, and then someone tries to kill Rose. This can't be a coincidence. I climb the stairs to the address Montana gave me for Lotte. I need to ask her a few questions, and I might as well take a look around Montana's place, since she isn't in a position to stop me.

The address is a rundown apartment over a shoe store in downtown Port Colborne, just bordering on the East Village. I'm surprised she lives in such a bad neighbourhood and as I get out of the car I instinctively look over my shoulder. It's a rough part of town. Lots of street crime and poverty, people on social assistance, some with mental health issues.

I'd been involved in lots of drug busts around here, more than I can count. Just last year we dismantled Project Perseus, a six-month investigation into a large trafficking ring we'd done with the assistance of the RCMP, the Provincial Police and the Border Services Patrol. Two of the arrests were right around the corner from here. We'd seized a large quantity of crystal meth, methadone and cocaine along with scales, baggies, prohibited weapons and almost half a million dollars in cash.

This area, only a few blocks between the canal and the abandoned refinery and the disused railway tracks, has the highest crime rate in the region. Most of the homes are neglected and full of toxins from the refinery's smokestacks. At a glance they all just looked like rundown houses, most with rotted front porches and long overdue for new shingles on the roof. But look closely and you'll see some are heavily fortified, with steel doors and video surveillance in place. Doesn't take a trained cop to know where the dealers live.

The exterior stairs to Montana's ran up from the parking lot behind the building, next to the dumpster. Private, I think, which is helpful if she's entertaining a married man in a small town.

Lotte answers on the first knock and looks surprised to see me. She recognizes me from my first visit to the restaurant last week and lets me in without hesitation. She's tall girl, with a strong athletic build, wide shoulders and big hands. She looks like she'd be a good basketball player. Her frizzy blonde hair is held back off her face with clips shaped like butterflies; it's the only girlish thing about her. Her broad, flat face is expressionless. I decide to not mention Montana's death. It isn't my job and I have another agenda. She'll find out soon enough, if she doesn't already know.

"I need to ask you some questions about the chef at Thorny Rose," I begin. She nods and motions for me to take a seat. My choice is a futon folded into a sofa, or an IKEA chair that looks like it would be difficult to get out of. I take my chances on the futon. It's as hard and lumpy as I expected.

Lotte sits across from me. "I don't know anything," she says. "I was only an intern there for a few months."

"How did you get the job?" I ask. "Did you know the chef?" She shakes her head.

"I studied at Niagara College, in the culinary program. And I was working part-time at one of the local wineries. He used to come in sometimes. We'd talk. When I needed to do my internship I asked him if I could work at Thorny Rose. But I don't really know him." It sounds as if she's rehearsed the answer.

"What are you planning on doing when you graduate? Work in a restaurant? Open one yourself?" She wrings her hands and looks away. I wonder what she's hiding.

"How long have you lived here?"

"Just over a month."

"Chef ever come around here?" She looks down at her big hands and shakes her head. "This is Montana's apartment, isn't it? I understand she and he were close." Lotte shrugs. She's clearly afraid. But of what?

"So you don't know whether he spent time here. Okay," I press. "Think if we maybe did some testing…took some finger-prints, DNA, we'd find evidence he was here? Recent evidence?" A moment passes then she nods.

"Why'd you lie?"

"I didn't know anyone knew about chef and Montana," she mumbles.

"From what I've heard I'd be surprised if anyone didn't know." She keeps staring at her hands. Was Lotte that naive? Or maybe not. I take a shot.

"You used to live out at the flower farm, right?" She looks up, surprised at the change of subject. She nods warily. "I'm told a guy used to come out to see you often. Drove you home late at night." She flushes and looks down. "I'm thinking that was the chef." Her eyes fill with tears. Bingo. So chef was involved with both of them.

"It's not what you think," she begins. "We weren't seeing each other. Not like that." I wait for her to continue. "He and I were cooking together."

"*Cooking?* Is that what the kids are calling it now?" I cross my arms and lean back, waiting for a better story.

She looks around, as if trying to figure out where to begin. "I used to work at Taiga," she says. "After I graduated horticultural school. They hire recent grads like me. The work is tough. It's repetitive; Cutting and training plants, maintaining drip irrigation lines. Typical agricultural labour."

"Okay…" I prompt her, hoping she'll get back on track.

"But they do pay above agricultural salary, which was good. I need money. I have lots of student loans." She looks me in the eye for the first time. "That's where I first met chef."

"At the cannabis producer."

She nods. "He and I got to talking, mostly about cannabis, and how it had helped my Oma when she got sick from cancer."

She looks uncomfortable and wrings her hands. "My family is strict Dutch Reform. We don't drink or…"

"…dance?" She smiles a bit.

"…or do drugs. But when my Oma got sick I tried to cook with cannabis for her, things I learned off the internet. But they tasted terrible."

"So chef was teaching you how to cook? To help your Oma?" I can almost picture Lotte as Little Red Riding Hood, in a red kerchief bringing cannabis to her sick grandmother. She nods miserably. It seems just weird enough to be true.

"And that was all there was between you two?"

Lotte nods again. "Yes. That was all."

"So it was chef who was driving you back to the farm, late at night?"

"I don't have a car. If we worked late he'd bring me home."

"Not Rose? She never offered to drive you?" Lotte shakes her head.

"She wasn't ever around when we were cooking. It was just chef. She was always out somewhere"

"Out? Any idea where?"

"She'd go out late, after service. I don't know when she came back. I'm pretty sure she had a thing going on with Luca Ricci… the pork supplier. He'd be coming around all the time…her giving him wine and whatever...at all hours of the night." Now that was not entirely a surprise. I remember how he'd talked about Rose at the farmers market.

Lotte is still talking. "Chef might have something going on with Montana, but it was no wonder. He clearly wasn't getting any love at home," she says.

I must have looked skeptical. "If you don't believe me," she insists. "Ask the old lady across the road. She'd have seen Luca coming around, or Rose coming back late at night. She sees everything."

"Anna Kozlowski? I thought she was blind."

Lotte's eyes widen in surprise. "She's got eyes like a hawk! I should know, I brought her dinner over to her every night and she saw me coming even before I left the restaurant. Who told you she was blind?"

"Rose did," I admit.

"Rose lies," Lotte snorts. "She's all show. Acts like she's so kind and helpful and is friends with all the neighbouring farmers. Not a chance."

"Chef was the nice guy," she continues. "He was the one with the close relationships with all the local organic suppliers. She just squeezed them all for discounts and whatever she could barter."

"He even visited her mother at the nursing home," she says. "Every week."

"Why would he do that?"

"Because he's a good person, that's why," Lotte insists. "Which is more than I can say for her." That sounds like sour grapes to me, given that Rose just fired her from her job at the restaurant.

TWENTY TWO

Rose

IT'S ANOTHER FARMERS market, and the intense heat still hasn't broken. The edges of all the trees are scorched from heat stress and drought, and the maples are dropping their leaves early. They litter the sidewalks and roads like it's October. But instead of the welcome fragrance of wood smoke and the cool fresh air of autumn we swelter in humidity and record breaking high temperatures.

Maggie is feeling good, so she's over at the Womyn's Collective farm booth. I can see Sophie is there with her, keeping an eye over her mother. Sophie watches Maggie like a hawk for any sign of weakness, and I'm sure it's at least partly due to her intensity and her strength of will that Maggie has hung on this long.

Sophie and I met in elementary school and we've been like sisters ever since. Because Maggie was always working evenings Sophie would come over to my place after school every day and we'd hang out. She'd stay for dinner, stay overnight, and stay weekends. My mother used to joke that she had three daughters: Rose, Lily and Sophie. She loved having the house full of kids; it filled the empty space after my father died.

In high school we were the stereotypical book smart good girls who ran with the bad boys. And there was never a shortage of bad boys in our town, all with big attitude, long hair and fast cars.

Most with big plans and no patience, so they were good at taking shortcuts to get what they wanted. Illegal ones. But that made them all the more exciting and we learned a lot we'd never get out of a book. It's a small miracle we all finished high school and didn't end up pregnant.

My mother was so surprised that Sophie, a latchkey kid with a single mother who worked in restaurant kitchens to barely get by, went off to university on a full scholarship. I left town as fast as I could after high school and moved to the city, and eventually made my way back home. And Lily never left.

Now Sophie is back too, running the farm and the business with Maggie. We're all back together, almost. The missing piece is Lily.

Maggie raises her hand to me in greeting. She's wearing a flower crown that hides her headscarf. Her face is drawn with fatigue and pain, in stark contrast to the fresh dewy blossoms she wears. Tears spring to my eyes and I turn away before she can see my grief. It's impossible to watch someone you love die before your eyes. To see them cling to life, fiercely clutching at whatever shreds they can hold onto before the darkness takes over. Maggie is holding on as long as she can. She's my hero.

Today I'm staffing the Craft Cider Association booth, a stall that showcases the craft hard ciders of several local producers. Each of them individually is too small an operation to have their own booth, so it makes sense for them to pool their resources and set up a stall together that offers samples of all their products and promotes the local cider sustainable industry overall.

We're big fans of craft cider at Thorny Rose and we serve lots of it, and cook with it, so they asked me to be here to offer samples and explain the various flavour profiles. Cider is really versatile—both to serve as a beverage and to cook with. Our autumn menu will feature pork with Calvados and cider, and I'm thinking about adding rabbit braised with cider, mustard and thyme. Maybe some cider *gelee* with poached apples and cream for dessert. So I get to talk about cider and promote about the restaurant. It's win-win.

The buskers are setting up again. This week the old accordion player is there, already perched on his stool. As usual, he wears a freshly pressed long sleeved shirt and tailored black dress pants. The same hipster guitar player is with him, drinking a coffee, with his case sitting at his feet unopened. I think he's wearing the same shirt as last week, and his jeans are rolled up at the hem. A lanky young woman in a flowered sundress and lace-up Doc Martins is setting up a small drum kit just behind the accordion player. She has jet black hair cut in an angled bob and both her arms are covered with complicated full sleeve tattoos. The three of them make an interesting combo. I wonder if they do weddings.

The back of the Cider Association booth is lined with large beautiful posters of apples heaped in bushels and hanging from trees. I set up several quart baskets of apples on the table among the pamphlets and brochures I've laid out. These are for sampling and I'll cut a slice for anyone who wants one.

Most people make a face when they taste a slice of a real cider apple; they are as unlike an eating apple as you can get. Cider apples are sour and acidic—which is what you need to make a good cider. The perfect cider apples like Kingston Black, Bulmer's Norma and Foxwhelp are full of tannins, but they aren't ripe until next month at the earliest, so we have some Ida Reds, Empire and Northern Spy at the booth. They are good cider apples, but not the best. I also set out some early eating apples, like McIntosh and Paula Red, for the kids. Those are too sweet and don't have enough character to make a good cider, but kids don't care.

In the Styrofoam coolers behind me I have chilled bottles of five different hard ciders and a perry—a fermented pear cider. I arrange the various bottles on the table, with small plastic cups for sampling. Then I sit on my stool and wait for people to start coming by.

The drummer has finished setting up her kit and is now using brushes on the skins, creating a cool mellow sound while they discuss the play list. Then the accordion player stands and drags his empty case up much closer to them than it was last week. No damn crackhead is going to steal their money again, that much is clear. The guitar player stands next to it, on guard as they start to play The Commodores *Easy Like a Sunday Morning*, which has the right vibe, even if it isn't Sunday. I relax on my stool and prepare to enjoy the morning.

"What the hell are you doing here?" a loud voice demands. My head spins around and I see Tom Lacey standing next to me, his face red with anger.

"What do you mean?" I sputter. "I'm working the booth today."

"Who asked you to? You're not needed here."

Tom Lacey is a fifth generation apple farmer from the area. He used to run a pick your own apple business, growing mostly McIntosh, Spartan and Golden Delicious. Now it's entirely converted to cider production. He's one of the first farmers to get behind production of hard cider in the region, and I've always thought of him as a friend.

"Tom, what's wrong?" I ask. "Why are you so angry?" He's apoplectic with rage.

"*What's wrong?*" He mocks me and steps up so he is right in my face. "Like you don't know exactly what's happening," he yells. I start to get angry. Who the hell does he think he is?

"What exactly is your problem?" I shout at him. He blinks and steps back from me. He wipes his hand over his face and sits heavily on a stool.

"Do you honestly not have any idea what's going on around

you?" he says after a moment, his voice quiet. I feel a sick sense of dread wash over me.

"What do you mean?" I'm not even sure if I want to know the answer.

The accordion player starts in on a Motown classic, followed by the guitar player. A deep husky voice joins in on the beat. It's the drummer.

"Your husband has been working with the developers." Lacey spat. "Including that guy who bought next to you. He's been in talks to sell them your property. And the hundred acres you back onto. And Kozlowski's across the road." *That's impossible.* The guy next door? After I'd sent the wife and her ugly plans packing I know I'd gotten rid of them. They'd disappeared. But that didn't mean Raymond hadn't spoken to them first. That he hadn't met with them.

"I don't understand. How would my husband even have influence over Anna Kozlowski?" Lacey ignores me and keeps talking.

"They've been trying to muscle me. They're trying to take over my farm. My family's farm. It's been in our family for almost a hundred and fifty years. And they think they can take it away." He points his finger at my chest.

"And your husband is working with those evil bastards."

"That can't be true," I say, even though the moment Lacey says it I know it is. "Why? Why would he do that?"

"Is there a problem here?" A familiar voice says. It's Wright. He's standing close to Lacey, arms crossed. Lacey glances at him, then back to me.

"For the money," Lacey shouts. "What else?" My stomach drops as if I'm on a roller coaster.

Wright watches the two of us. I feel reassured having him there, in case Lacey loses it again. But my head is spinning. Everyone knows about the land developers who are trying to buy up farms in the area. But they'd never approached me. Or so I thought.

"But that hundred acres is greenbelt. It's a conservation area," I say in a whisper, trying to process what Lacey is saying.

"Money talks. These guys have influence. They can buy off government, pull strings with banks." Lacey looks at me with pity before he erupts again.

"Wake up!" he yells, stepping toward me.

"That's enough!" Wright says. Lacey backs off. "Sir, you need to cool off," he says. Lacey stands, panting with rage and frustration. He glares at Wright.

"I know you," Lacey finally says, his eyes on Wright. "You're a cop."

"Yes. I'm Detective Constable Wright, Niagara Regional Police."

"Wright…"Lacey repeats, his eyes narrow. He steps toward Wright, his voice aggressive. "Didn't I hear something…"

"You need to move along now Sir," Wright interrupts. Lacey complies, and as he walks away he keeps his eye on Wright.

Wright turns to me. "Are you okay?" he asks. I'm stunned and shaking.

"He just lost it when he saw me," I say. "Maybe he's been drinking too much of his own cider. How much did you hear?" I ask.

"Enough."

"Great." I shake my head. "Things just keep getting worse." Wright comes into the booth and stands next to me, lowering his voice so we won't be overheard.

"Would your husband have done that?" Wright asks. "Worked with the developers behind your back? Tried to sell your place?" I stare at my hands and see they're clenched into fists.

"Yes." I have to admit the truth. "In a minute." I've already told Wright about the missing cash from our bank account. Why hold back now? "If he needed the cash to finance another *brilliant idea*." Wright nods.

"But the developer next door disappeared months ago," I continue. "They abandoned their project and left." Even as I say the words I realize the truth. There will always be another developer. I feel dizzy and sit down on the stool, my hand gripping the table to steady myself.

"But the farm is mine!" I say. "It was left entirely to me when my sister died. His name isn't even on the deed. He couldn't sell it without my permission."

"Maybe he thought he could convince you somehow," Wright suggests.

"Over my dead body," I say. And I realize that is exactly the point.

Wright goes to bring me a coffee and I sit for a minute trying to calm down and collect my thoughts. The band plays some classic rock mixed with Frank Sinatra and even a few standards like *Stormy Weather* and *Someone to Watch Over Me*. I could listen to the drummer's dark, smoky voice all day, and luckily I'll be able to since I'll be at the booth until the market closes at four.

I realize that even though Lacey's revelation has shocked me, nothing has really changed. Chef is still away—or missing. There's no sign of him, except that postcard from Los Angeles and the texts to Montana's phone. There can't be a sale to the developers without my permission, and I can fight any threat to the conservation land. I take some deep breaths, trying to calm my anxiety. I've managed this far. I hope I'll be able to keep it up as long as I need to.

Wright hands me a coffee and a fresh blueberry muffin, still warm from the oven. I smile my thanks.

"So," I say, trying to lighten the mood. "I guess now I'm on my own for the rest of the day. Since you scared away the other staff."

"Would you rather have him around?" Wright smiles.

"Good point." I shake my head and bite into the muffin.

"So, what's the set up here?" Wright asks. It's clear he's trying to get my mind off what just happened.

"Cider." Wright raises his eyebrow. "We're giving out samples from local cideries. Promoting the industry."

"Okay. Why are you here?" he asks.

"I'm just an enthusiast," I say. "And it's a chance to promote Thorny Rose."

"I like cider. It's more refreshing than beer." He pats his stomach. "Less filling."

"Bet you haven't tasted any as good as these," I say. "Nothing like the multi-national brands you are probably used to." I pour him a sample of an opaque, light brown apple cider, fragrant with fruit and citrus.

Wright drinks it down and nods his approval.

I hand him another sample. "What about this one?" He smells it cautiously then sips, raising his eyebrows.

"That's a perry. It's a hard pear cider. New on the market this year." I pour myself a small amount, leaving lots of headspace in the glass for the aromas to gather. I swirl it, then take a couple of short sniffs with my nose an inch out of the glass. Then I put my nose into the glass and take a long, deep sniff. I notice Wright watching me with interest.

"This is how we taste. Cider, beer, wine," I explain. "You need to swirl the glass, sniff like that. Now I'll cover my glass with my hand to trap more aroma, then sniff again." Last I take a sip and hold the liquid in my mouth for a few seconds before swallowing. I breathe out through my nose, to see if I can pick up any off-flavours retronasally.

"You really look like you know what you're doing," he says. "For someone who's *just an enthusiast.*" He folds his arms and studies me. "Are you being modest, or just keeping secrets?"

"We've all got secrets. I'm a Sommelier. And I'm about to take my Master Cicerone exam," I say, evading his question.

"What's a Cicerone?"

"It's like a Sommelier, but for beer. I may even get my certification as a Sincero as well, for the hell of it. That's a cider expert."

"Why?"

"Why not? I enjoy learning. And you never know, I may have to get an honest job one day, the way things are going." I sigh. "It appears that one thing I have going for me is outstanding tasting abilities."

"Yes, I'd definitely say so," Wright says. "Though I'm not sure I can believe a word you say now."

"Maybe you shouldn't." I have a feeling he hasn't believed much of what I've been saying all along. He's still coming around, still asking questions, still looking for my husband.

"Why don't you work for one of the wineries," he suggests. "That is, if things go sideways…" I don't welcome his suggestion and I guess my expression tells him so. "I mean, given your obvious talent for tasting, maybe you could work with a distiller or something like that. Create some new flavours."

"I'll keep it in mind," I say. "But I sure don't want it to come to that."

I glance across the market and notice a small stall has been set up, with a hand lettered sign on a piece of floppy bristol board: PAWPAW. My heart leaps with excitement.

"Could you do me a favour?" I ask. "Can you watch the booth for a minute? I'll be right back." Wright looks like he might have objections, but I'm already gone.

"But what if somebody asks me a question?" he calls after me.

"You'll be fine," I shout over my shoulder. "I just gave you a tutorial."

I run up to the Pawpaw stall, already pulling my wallet out of my handbag. The booth is staffed by a young First Nations woman, who has two small children with her. She looks a little alarmed seeing me rush up.

"I'd like to buy your Pawpaws," I pant. The family smiles happily at me. Most people have never even tasted a pawpaw. They taste like a mix of banana and mango, with the luscious texture of rich ice cream. They are ripe in only a small window between late summer and the first frost and are really difficult to find unless you know a local farmer or are lucky enough to know where some might grow wild, along the bank of a river.

"How many would you like?" she asks, reaching for a paper bag.

"All of them," I answer. "I'll buy your whole stock."

She stares at me in disbelief. "All of them? I have three crates full."

I nod. "How much?"

"Well…" she hesitates. I've never seen her before at the market. She has probably picked the fruit wild and hopes to make a bit of extra money for the family. I bet she doesn't even know what to charge for them.

Pawpaws are amazing fruit, and are the definition of local produce since they are extremely perishable and far too fragile to ship. They'll begin to turn black and spoil within twenty-four hours of being picked. I'll have these on the menu tonight as a special and they'll be gone by tomorrow, one way or another.

"I'll give you," I say, going through my wallet and pulling whatever cash I have out. "Two hundred dollars now, and another two hundred if you deliver everything to my restaurant. Four hundred for the lot."

She holds out her hand, nodding in shock. "When?"

"Now," I say, handing her a card with the Thorny Rose address. "We're just up on the escarpment." She cradles the card in her hand, studying it. The expression on her face is one of stunned disbelief.

"I'll be happy to buy them from you all season," I say. "I'll take whatever you can give me." I stick out my hand. "I'm Rose, by the way. I'm the owner of Thorny Rose."

She shyly puts out her hand. I'm sure she's never made an agreement to supply a restaurant before, but she isn't going to be bowled over by me.

"Nice to meet you Rose," she says, taking the cash. "Make it five hundred and we've got a deal." Her children look up at her, beaming with pride.

TWENTY THREE

Wright

I DRIVE SLOWLY into the driveway and park where Rose did last week. I don't want to alarm Anna Kozlowski. I expect she doesn't get many visitors and she'd feel vulnerable if a strange man roars up in a car, even if I do tell her I'm a police officer.

I climb the steps and see the lace curtain in the front window move. She's watching me as I knock. I can see her shadowy outline through the frosted glass of the front door as I knock a second time. The door opens and I see a tall elderly woman, with white hair tightly pulled back in a bun. She returns my smile when I identify myself and invites me in without a question. I love it when that happens.

Her house is filled with religious pictures and there are icons on every wall. There's a smell of spice from a votive candle that's burning on a small shelf in the corner, in front of an arrangement of icons. There's no television or bookshelves, which makes sense to me if she's blind.

"I wonder if you could answer a few questions for me," I say as I open my notebook and sit on the chair across from her. She's led me into the kitchen at the back of the house, where she busies herself making a pot of tea. Anna Kozlowski seems to know exactly where everything is, exactly as if she can see. Her eyes look fine to me and she isn't wearing dark glasses, so I wonder about what Rose told me.

"What questions?" she asks in a strong Slavic accent.

"I'm looking into the disappearance of the chef, from the restaurant." She turns her head and looks at me out of the corner of her eye.

"Rose's husband? He disappear?"

I nod. "He hasn't been seen since late July sometime." She keeps studying me sideways, with her face turned away. It's disconcerting.

"I know nothing about her husband. She never told me he is gone."

"When was the last time you saw him?" I ask. She thinks about the question before she replies.

"Easter. He brought me *paska* and smoked fish. After Lent."

"That was five months ago," I press. "You're sure you never saw him since then? Maybe in a car? Driving past your house?" She shakes her head. So much for Lotte's statement that the old woman had seen chef driving her home every night. I wonder what else Lotte lied about. And why.

"I mostly sit here in kitchen, not looking at road."

"Did he visit you often?"

She shakes her head. "Only when he want something," she sneers. "Bringing me food, gifts." She gestures toward the kitchen counter where there are several gift-wrapped boxes of chocolates and biscuits, unopened.

"You don't like sweets?" I ask. She stares at me out of the corner of her eye before answering.

"Beware the man who comes bearing gifts and invoking flattering words," she says. It sounds like a Bible verse, but I'm not familiar with that book. So Anna Kozlowski is nobody's fool. She knew chef wanted something from her, maybe like her signature on the property developer's deal.

"He was not good man," she says. "No good for Rose."

"You know Rose well?"

She looks irritated with my question. "She is family. Like my own daughter." She folds her hands on her lap, her lips tight. "Rose helps me with everything, more than my own son. For years, since before my husband died, she looks after things."

"How did he die?"

Again she looks annoyed and I think for a moment she won't answer. "An accident. The tractor rolled over him." That seems like a common way to die on a farm, I think. "He was not good man either," she says. She shakes her head slowly at the memory, her gaze fixed somewhere I can't see.

I think I'll try another approach. "What can you tell me about Rose's sister?"

"Lily?" She's clearly surprised. "She died." She turns away from me and faces the window, looking out over her apple orchard. She presses her lips together.

"How did she die?"

"An accident." I can barely hear her. "She fell."

"She lived alone in the house? Before Rose came here?" Mrs. Kozolowski turns away from the window and looks at me out of the corner of her eye again.

"Why you asking this?" she demands. "It was years ago. Nobody ask questions then." I don't have an answer for her and I'm not really even sure why I'm asking.

I thank her for her time and rise to leave without drinking my tea. She stands and walks me to the door. On an impulse I ask another question.

"Can you tell me anything about that house there?" I point to the abandoned construction project next to Thorny Rose.

She snorts. "What about it?"

"What happened to the owners? The people who were building it?" She shrugs.

"They have money," she says, rubbing her fingers and thumb together. "Rich people. They found another place. Who cares?" That sounds a lot like Rose and Maggie. Nobody cares what happened to the Monks, as long as they're gone.

"I saw their car one night. I heard a very loud motor. So I look out window. Car is bright orange. Can't miss it." Her gaze drifts away. "It looked like Rose driving," she says, shaking her head at the memory.

"Rose? Are you sure?"

"Of course I'm sure," she snaps. "Do you think I'm blind?"

TWENTY FOUR

Rose

TONIGHT'S WEDDING DINNER is being held in the garden, despite the relentless heat. The couple decided they would have a garden wedding, no matter what, so comfort be damned for them and their guests. Never mind about the serving staff or cooks. Everyone is wilting in the heat. The bride looks limp and her bouquet bedraggled. The men all take off their jackets and ties and hang them on the backs of their chairs and the women look envious they don't have that option. Everyone is drinking heavily to escape the sultry night. Lucky for Thorny Rose it's an open bar, so the servers keep refreshing the drinks the minute they are low, which will get the bill up. Since the tip is based on a percentage of sales, everyone is happy. Except maybe the couple when they get the final bill.

A large tent has been set up over the far parking lot nearest the barn and kitchen garden. The rental company brought in tables and chairs, all covered in white cloths. Two small risers are set up at either end of the tent: One for the wedding party and the other for the band. Once the planters, lights, candles and other decor items are set up you'd never know it was our overflow parking lot. It just looks like a beautiful space surrounded by gardens where the wedding guests can drink, eat and dance, and enjoy themselves.

The ceremony was held in the formal garden, since the open

gravel paths and symmetry make it easy to set up seating for the guests and an altar for the minister and couple to exchange their vows. As the vows were made, when the minister announced them as husband and wife, there was a mass release of butterflies, to signify something romantic, I forget what.

The butterflies had arrived the day before, shipped by FedEx in a large cardboard box that felt like it weighed nothing. I hadn't wanted to do a butterfly release and fought hard against it. It's an additional hassle on a day that's already full of potential disasters, from an event management and catering point of view. Not to mention I think it's cruel. I hope nobody reports Thorny Rose to PETA. But the wedding planner and couple had insisted, and I needed the business. So there you go; morality goes out the window when it comes to survival, as always.

According to the company brochure, the butterflies were *sustainably raised by mentally and physically disabled workers*, which might be a point in their favour. Assuming it's true. Still, we had to order extra because a lot of them arrived dead, or half dead. I let Jacob pick through the box and remove those. It would definitely send the wrong message at the wedding if the guests saw a bunch of dead butterflies in the release cage at the critical moment.

At least they are being released in late summer, when the weather is warm and there will be plenty of nectar available for them in their new environment. Apparently the butterflies that manage to survive shipping, release and predators do migrate south, and do manage to find their way back to their winter hibernation grounds in Mexico, thanks to their DNA coding, which is the real miracle. Thankfully the Thorny Rose garden would support them well, since we've got many thousands of pollen and nectar plants here. And we're just a short flight across Lake Erie for their long journey home. At least they'll have a shot at survival.

The wedding party was only one hundred people, which we

could have accommodated in the restaurant, in air-conditioned comfort. But the couple wanted to hold both the ceremony and the reception in the garden, so we'd rented the large marquee and all the necessary tables and chairs to hold it there. The restaurant was closed to the public however. We couldn't handle any extra people in one evening, even if chef were here to cook.

Regulars at the restaurant, the bride and groom are complete foodies. They love chef, love the attention he gives them whenever they have dinner at Thorny Rose. I doubt they even remember meeting me; most people are invisible when chef is in the room.

Maggie and I had fun planning the menu, though it had been chef who'd sold the couple on the various courses. It had been awkward telling the wedding planner that chef is away. She'd called the couple right away and I could hear their reaction through the phone.

"He's gone? Where?" I listened to the placating murmurs from the wedding planner, telling them I'd be handling it. That it would be fine. That we had it all organized and Maggie was on it.

"But she's just the manager," the bride had whined. "She's not the chef." She didn't have any idea that I was the one who'd planned the entire wedding meal, since chef was already bored with them. He'd lost interest five minutes after they told him they weren't interested in one of his elaborate tasting menus, one featuring twelve small courses including milk fed lamb with *boudin blanc*, and catfish with chickweed and birch syrup.

But Maggie and I had created a fantastic seasonal menu for them that was a celebration of Canadian flavours: mussel *eclade*, BC salmon grilled on cedar planks, and maple glazed root vegetables. All the wines were local Niagara VQA: a juicy Tawse Quarry Road Riesling and an elegant Hidden Bench Pinot Noir.

Dessert is of course wedding cake, a stunning tiered white cake iced with elderflower buttercream and filled with raspberries and lemon curd. And with coffee a selection of truly Canadian desserts: Nanaimo bars, butter tarts and Thorny Rose *timbits,* with raspberry filling covered with decadent chocolate *ganache.*

The band is set up in front of the barn, and they are now playing instrumental versions of classic songs and jazz standards. They'll play through the cocktail hour before dinner as the guests make their way from the formal garden where the ceremony has been held. Then they'll take a break during dinner and speeches, and pick back up for the dancing to close out the night. On an impulse I'd hired the buskers from the farmers market, even though I'd initially had a DJ booked. Once I heard the drummer's husky, mellow voice and how she delivered the romantic standards I knew they'd be perfect for this wedding crowd.

They are dressed up for the evening. The accordion player is wearing the dinner jacket that matches the dress pants he wears every weekend at the market. The hipster guitar player's wearing a tartan kilt, complete with fur sporran, knee socks and Ghillie brogues. But because of the heat he's left out the Prince Charlie jacket. The drummer wears an elegant strappy blue evening gown that shows off her arm sleeves to full effect. I could see her Doc Martins peeping out from under the hem of her dress as she sat behind her drum kit.

The servers move through the crowd, offering trays of sparkling *rose* and *Prosecco.* The budget didn't stretch to champagne, but we've floated fresh raspberries in the flutes and nobody seems to mind a bit.

I feel relaxed and confident that the meal will go well. The staff have done a great job of setting the tables for dinner; the centerpieces look fabulous, thanks to Sophie and the team at Womyn Collective. But I can't shake the uneasy feeling that something is wrong. I keep thinking of my husband and feeling irritated that he isn't here tonight. Here it is, another big event for the restaurant, and he's gone. It's like he's haunting me. Several times in the evening I actually thought I'd seen him—in the crowd, or in his kitchen whites standing at the grill. Of course it isn't him. I know it can't be. Then I'd blink and the illusion would vanish. I must be losing my mind.

Once the guests have been served their second glasses of wine, it's time to put on the mussel *eclade*. I give the sign to the servers to start seating the guests and turn to the appetizers.

Eclade is rustic Canadian cooking, and the aromas and flavours it creates are perfectly redolent of the boreal forest. Originally introduced to Canada by Samuel de Champlain in the 1600's, it's the perfect way to cook the appetizer course for this foodie crowd.

Yesterday Jacob dug a pit alongside the parking lot, next to the area where we'd set up the grills. It was lined with sand and filled with pine needles. Just before service a layer of scrubbed mussels was laid in the pine needles, hinged side up. That was covered with another layer of pine needles, and another layer of mussels. And then another until we had enough mussels to feed a hundred guests. Then we set fire to the pine needles and let them burn until they were ash, which took less than ten minutes.

We'd made pine smoked butter in the kitchen. We put several pounds of butter in a pot on stove. Added a couple of pounds of dried pine needles, set them alight and burn them to ash into the melting butter. That way the flavour of the pine smoke is infused into the butter. We strained it a few times to remove all the burnt particulate and the result was a beautifully aromatic flavoured butter that we add to the dish when complete.

When the mussels are done they are removed from the pit and *sautéed* in a pan with the pine smoked butter, olive oil and shallots. We have six *saute* pans going at once, with three cooks manning the station and it still feels like it takes too long to get the mussels all served in good time. It's probably less than ten minutes to serve the entire wedding party, which is good for any large group, but still. If chef had been here it may have gone faster. I don't know. But I think about it.

Once the mussels are served, we start to cook the salmon. The cedar planks have been soaking all afternoon so they'll smoke the fish and not catch fire. The idea is that they'll season the salmon with the spicy aroma of cedar while protecting the filet from the direct heat of the grill.

Most of what we think we taste is really aroma. Our nose experiences taste first, and how something smells is responsible for how much we enjoy our meal. How something looks on the plate, and how it smells when it's presented are really what create the meal. As I watch the servers take the plates out, I know we've nailed it. Plated with maple glazed root vegetables the salmon is fragrant, looks colorful, and will definitely be delicious.

After an hour the salmon plates have been cleared, are back in the kitchen, with Paul cleaning them and I can finally breathe a sigh of relief. The meal went off without a hitch. Before I know it the wedding cake is being cut to applause and photos are being taken of the bride and groom feeding each other cake. Desserts are being plated in the kitchen—each guest gets three: mini Nanaimo bar, "timbit", butter tart—quintessentially Canadian desserts, with our twist.

Servers are pouring coffee, offering ice cider and Vidal ice wine. The speeches are happening and the band is setting up for dancing. I don't think it will be a late night. It's a second marriage for both the bride and groom so I figure they'll be gone by midnight or one at the latest.

The band begins to play and the bride and groom start their first dance, *Le Vie En Rose* and the singer's smoky voice fills the marquee. The couple moves together across the dance floor, smiling and whispering intimately as if they are the only people in the marquee. The groom laughs and spins the bride around then dips her low and her delighted laugh sparkles. They are so happy it makes my heart ache.

In the early days my husband used to grab me and dance me around the kitchen. Or he'd try to, but I'd balk and retreat shyly. It's no wonder he found someone else to dance with. There was always someone young and willing. Someone who adored him and his passions.

Fun women. Women who laughed at this antics, who found him charming, who thought he was smart and sophisticated, who gave a shit about *terroir*, and would at least pretend to distinguish the faint aroma of morels in his stock. Or to care about whether you really could serve cheese with fish.

The singer switches to French and the song sounds even more beautiful and it hurts me even more, so I go into the kitchen to oversee the clean up. The grills and workstations are being cleaned, dishes washed and put away, the walk-in cleaned and swept. Once that was done most of the kitchen staff would go home, leaving only Paul to run the last of the glasses and coffee cups through the dishwasher.

Once the last of the guests leaves the servers and I will strip the table linens but leave the tables, chairs and tent to be removed by the rental company in the morning. They are scheduled to arrive by seven am, so I can make sure the restaurant and gardens look back to normal for Sunday dinner service.

Finally at midnight the bride and groom leave. They say their good-byes to the guests, toss the bouquet and garter and drive off in a Town Car. Ubers and taxis fill the driveway, chauffeuring drunken guests safely home or to nearby hotels. The band loads their equipment into their van and drives off. Finally it's quiet and all I can hear is the tired chatter of the wait staff and the crickets in the field.

As I'm going back into the kitchen with another tray of dirty wine glasses I notice a box wrapped in gold foil lying on the porch swing. Slipped under the sparkly bow is a small card, with *Thank You* written in calligraphy.

I open the box and see it's filled with dark chocolate truffles. They look a bit soft and melted from sitting out in the heat, but I can never resist chocolate. I bite into one and spit it out instantly. Marzipan. Disgusting. I leave the box where it is and carry on into the kitchen.

The servers make sure all the glassware is back in the kitchen, strip down the tables and stuff the linens into the bags for the rental company. Finally everything is done and I cash them out. The twenty percent gratuity has been added to the bill and that's split between the servers, bartender, and kitchen staff including the dishwasher. Not a bad night for all of us.

I lock the door and go to bed.

TWENTY FIVE

Rose

ONCE AGAIN I sleep through my alarm, something I've never done until this last month since chef disappeared. Now it feels like I do it every morning. Working every day and every night takes its toll and I've been running on empty for a while now. I must have hit snooze a few times before something in my subconscious forces me awake. When I look at the time on the alarm I fly into a panic and leap out of bed, rushing around, grabbing my clothes and running down the stairs. It's seven o'clock and the rental company will be downstairs any minute to pick up the tables and take down the tent.

I fling open the back door and exhale with relief because they aren't here yet. Then I'm irritated because that means they are late. Then I see Jacob lying on the porch swing. He's mumbling something and clutching at his stomach.

"Jacob!" I rush over and kneel next to him. "What's wrong?" I feel his face and it's sweaty but cold. He's staring at me and trying to speak but not making any sense. I grab my phone out of my pocket and punch in 911.

I sit on the porch, looking at the flashing lights of the ambulance as it races down the driveway. The ambulance attendants had arrived within minutes of my call. They'd loaded Jacob onto a stretcher once he was stabilized and he was being taken to the hospital in town. This is the second time within two weeks that an ambulance has been called out to the Thorny Rose. But unlike this morning, the ambulance that took away Montana's body didn't speed away and they didn't use the lights, since there was no need to rush. She couldn't get any more dead.

A police car is still on the driveway, and the uniformed officer approaches me. It's the same young police constable with red hair I saw at the market, and who was here when we found Montana.

She pulls out her notebook in that now too familiar manner and asks if she can sit down. Then she smiles at me and leans forward.

"You don't remember me, do you?" I stare at her.

"I-I'm sorry," I say. "Not really, no." She laughs.

"I'm Lucy Gauthier." That doesn't help. "I used to work here, when you first opened." I go through my mental Rolodex, tying to remember. "I started as a dishwasher, when I was in high school," she says. "Then I worked weekends when I went to University."

"Of course!" Now I can place her. A good kid, hard working, reliable. "And now you're a police officer," I state the obvious.

"Constable Gauthier now," she smiles. "I was lucky enough to get hired onto the force when I graduated four years ago."

"So you remember Jacob," I say. "From when you worked here."

"Absolutely," she says. "He's a great old guy. I hope he makes it." I wipe away the tears that well up in my eyes. She looks at her notebook, giving me a moment to compose myself. Then she smiles gently and begins asking questions.

"What can you tell me about what happened to Jacob?" She corrects herself. "To Mr. Knudson?"

"I don't really know." I exhale, exasperated. "At first I thought maybe he'd had a heart attack."

"At first? You don't think so now?" I shake my head and she raises her eyebrow, waiting for me to explain.

"I came down at around seven this morning. No one else was here. I made coffee, then I opened the kitchen door for some air and saw him lying there," I gesture to the chair where I'd found Jacob lying.

"He was conscious, but he was really pale and his breathing was rapid. He was complaining about stomach pain. He seemed really confused, and he had tremors in his hands. I called 911 right away." Lucy nods for me to continue.

"By the time the ambulance arrived he was unconscious and his breathing was really shallow. I thought at one point he was dead. He's very old…" I stare at the spot on the porch swing where Jacob had been lying. It's empty, with no trace he'd even been there. Like life I suppose. We leave so little behind.

I remember Lucy is waiting and I continue my story. "The paramedics took over. Then I saw the chocolates near him, and I guess I noticed he had some chocolate on his lip…It was weird. I don't know. Could it be the chocolates?"

"Why would you think it's the chocolate?"

"It's just…I thought they smelled funny. There was this weird bitter aroma in the box. I didn't recognize it, but it wasn't right somehow. I have a very good sense of smell." Lucy nods.

"Where did they come from?"

"It was left on porch, at the end of the wedding. With a Thank You card. I just assumed it was from the bride, or the wedding planner. Or the band. Or…anyone."

"Did you eat any?

"Yes. I did. I tasted one—and spat it out. It was marzipan. I hate marzipan."

"When would Mr. Knudson have found them?"

"I don't know. First thing this morning I suppose. About six-thirty or seven. That's when he usually starts. I asked him to come to help with the rental company. They were supposed to be here at seven to take down the tent, and remove the tables and chairs. All the wedding stuff." I paused for a second as I realize they still haven't arrived. Great, they're now over an hour late. Another thing to worry about.

"And you're sure you don't know who left the box of chocolates?" I shake my head.

"This place was a madhouse—the band, the guests, the rental company. You probably remember what those events were like, from when you worked here."

"Definitely," she says. "There was always a lot going on."

"I never even noticed the box until I'd almost finished clearing up. I just left it there, for people to help themselves. I didn't really think about it. I was tired and distracted."

Lucy nods in sympathy. "I get it." She puts away her notebook and gets up to leave, first picking up the chocolates and placing them into a clear plastic bag.

"It's my fault," I say. "If I hadn't left them out like that Jacob wouldn't have found them. He loves sweets."

"We don't know yet exactly what happened," she says. "It might not have anything to do with the chocolates." But I know it does. "We'll know more once they get him admitted. I can call you when I get more information, okay?"

"Thank you. Yes, please," I say and she turns to leave. "Excuse me a second Lucy," I ask. "Do you know Detective Constable Wright? He's on the Niagara Regional force too."

She pauses then turns to me. I feel a prickle of anxiety when I see her expression. After a moment she nods. "Yes, I've heard of him. He was in the guns and gangs unit," she says. "Why?"

"Nothing really," I say. "He's been coming around a fair bit lately, working on my husband's case." Lucy looks surprised. "The chef is missing," I add.

"Missing? For how long?" She seems confused. "And you say Detective Constable Wright is *investigating*?"

"About a month. I didn't report it at first…"

"That's not possible," Lucy interrupts. "Detective Wright is on suspension," she says, sitting back down.

I'm stunned. "There must be a mistake. He's been here, several times…"

"Rose, I shouldn't be telling you this," Lucy interrupts, "since they haven't released his name to the public. But he's been under investigation for the past couple of months." I stare at her, shocked and confused.

"I understand there may be a number of charges against him. Serious allegations of misconduct and criminal activity."

"Charges?" I echo. "What kind of charges?"

"Obstruction. Conspiracy. Breach of trust," she says. "Trafficking." I'm speechless. "I'm going to have to report this. There's no way Wright should be *investigating* anything."

I'm sitting on the back porch going over everything in my mind. I don't know what to do. What is Wright's game? He's on suspension, but he keeps coming around looking for chef? Pretending he's on some legitimate investigation? It's obvious he's after my husband, but why? I think back to when he first showed up the week before. He never showed ID, wasn't in a patrol car. That should have been a clue. And when I denied chef was missing, when I didn't want to make a report at all, he still found reasons to come around, to talk to me, like that day at the farmers market.

His being on suspension explains why he was never on the scene when I'd called 911, like when Montana died, or this morning when I found Jacob. And why he always showed up after the police had gone.

And when we found Luca's body he insisted on driving me home, on my not being there to make a statement to the police. He said it was for my benefit, but now I see it was for his own. He didn't want to be there when the police arrived. How would he explain his being present at the scene of a crime?

Lucy said he was on suspension for trafficking and obstruction. Does that have anything to do with my husband? What don't I understand? What am I missing?

The phone rings. It's Lucy, with an update on Jacob as she'd promised.

"They've intubated him, and he's on a respirator," she says. "It's definitely poisoning." I feel sick with guilt. If I hadn't left the chocolates out this wouldn't have happened.

"Will he be okay?"

"Jacob is going to be fine," Lucy says. "And lucky for you that you don't like marzipan. They tested the chocolates and found they've been injected with nicotine. It's highly toxic."

"I know," I say, my mind racing. "It's a pesticide. It's organic, so we could use it here, but we don't."

"Would Jacob have any around the farm?" Lucy asks.

"I don't think so," I say. "But my grandfather used to make his own. It's not difficult to do."

"It's very dangerous," she says, her voice breaking up a bit over the cell phone.

I remembered my father and grandfather both making nicotine poison to use on the farm. I was allowed to watch, but not help. They took pipe tobacco and soaked it overnight in a bowl with just enough water to cover it. Then in the morning it was strained and the liquid boiled down and reduced to the consistency of syrup. All the old guys knew how to make it.

"Jacob did have tins of loose tobacco in the barn," I say after a moment. "He smokes. I just thought he rolled his own."

"He might have made some if you have a pest problem he wanted to control," Lucy suggests.

"Maybe. But who'd use it to poison the chocolates?" I rake my hands through my hair, trying to process what has just happened. This is not the way it was supposed to go. I'm not sure if I should say anything, but then feel I have no choice.

"Lucy, those chocolates were intended for me," I say. "I think someone is trying to kill me."

Within an hour Lucy is back, with Detective Constable Popovic, clearly an older and more senior detective. I guess they wouldn't trust a young Constable to take this report on her own.

"Tell me what's been happening," Lucy says. It looks like Popovic is letting her take the interview since we're acquainted, so he's the one taking notes. His dark eyes appraise me. I feel him judging everything I say, but his facial expression never changes.

"Last week someone locked me in my walk in freezer," I begin. "It was the middle of the night and I heard someone downstairs, so I came down to investigate. I got shoved inside." They both look predictably alarmed.

"Didn't the emergency release work?" Lucy asks. "How did you get out?"

"The door was jammed somehow. I had to disable the cooler fans so I didn't freeze to death," I say. "Maggie let me out when she got into work."

"Someone broke in?"

I hadn't thought of that. "There was no sign of a break in," I say. "The back door was locked when Maggie came in. Which means someone had a key."

"Someone on the staff?"

"Maybe. But only Maggie and I have a key." I hesitate before I go on. "To be honest, afterwards I thought it might have been my husband. He also has a key."

"Your husband? Why would he want to lock you in the freezer?" I throw my hands up. I don't want to say. Again they exchange a look.

"May I ask why you didn't call the police after it happened," Popovic asks. I feel embarrassed. How could I possibly explain everything that had gone through my mind when it happened? And after Maggie said there was nothing wrong with the door it all seemed so unlikely, so confusing.

"I didn't want to call 911," I say. "We'd just had an accident here a few days before, and I was concerned about the publicity, what with all the emergency vehicles, the media. So I called Detective Wright." Lucy and Popovic exchange a look. "I didn't really know what to think at the time. I was telling myself it was just some weird accident."

"How do you know Detective Wright?" Popovic asks. It looks like he's taking over the interview. Lucy gets out her notebook.

"I don't," I say. "Or I didn't, until last week. He showed up here, investigating the disappearance of my husband. He said there had been a missing person's report filed." I look down at my hands. This is awkward. And embarrassing. I feel stupid for not realizing Wright was up to something. I also resent having to explain, again, where my husband is. "I didn't know then that he was on suspension. I assumed at the time that he was just doing his job."

"And is your husband missing?"

"No!" I blurt. "I told him he's not missing, that he's just gone on a *stage*. But Wright keeps coming around and asking questions, about my husband. He doesn't seem to believe me. I have no idea what he wants." And for the most part that's true.

"Detective Constable Wright should not be conducting any

sort of investigation," Popovic says. "Not on behalf of the Niagara Regional Police in any event. Our records show there was a report made about your husband being missing, but it was handled by an officer over the phone. Nobody visited here."

"He told me there had been several calls," I insist. Popovic and Lucy exchange another look.

"Is your husband acquainted with Detective Constable Wright," Popovic asks. "Are they friends?"

I shake my head. "I've never seen him before he showed up here last week." That isn't exactly an answer, but I can't tell them the truth: I don't have any idea if chef and Wright know one another. I realize now that I don't seem to know very much about my husband. And the truth is, he doesn't have any friends. Just people he uses for a while. But I can't say that either.

"I told him chef's just away for work," I continue. "I even showed him a postcard my husband sent me, from LA," I say. "As far as I know that's where he still is."

"But you just said you thought he'd locked you in the freezer," Lucy says.

"I know. I'm sorry, it makes no sense. It's just what I thought at the time. But the strange thing is," I continue. "I thought I saw him last night…at the wedding we catered. I must be losing my mind."

"And the poisoned chocolates were left here, on your porch last night, during the wedding?" Popovic asks, his dark eyes on mine. I nod. At least that is definitely true.

I give them all the same information I gave Wright last week: my husband's passport numbers, car license plate and full legal name. They get up to leave, promising to get back to me with anything they find out.

"In the meantime," Popovic says, handing me his card. "Do not speak with Detective Constable Wright. Don't let him into the restaurant. Call us if he makes contact with you again." I pretend to agree, but I'm making my own plan. I want to know what Wright is after, who he's really working for and why he's looking for my husband. I can't let this go.

TWENTY SIX

Rose

I LEAVE MY car at the Point Abino Yacht Club and make two trips out to the dock with supplies for my day: fishing gear, food, and wine. Basically everything I'll need for a day out on the water, alone with my thoughts. Away from the Thorny Rose and any more questions without answers and problems without solutions.

There aren't many reservations in the book for this evening, and honestly even if there were I'd still make a run for it. Sometimes you just need to get away and clear your head. Maggie could handle the Festival and oversee service tonight, and I'd called in Amy, my friend who works in a hotel in Niagara on the Lake to help work the line.

I'm dripping with perspiration by the time I finish and can't wait to get out onto the lake. Hopefully there will be an offshore breeze that'll help with this humidity. Day after day, the relentless heat and mugginess is exhausting. Everything feels scorched and limp. We need a big storm to blow through and clear the air.

I've just untied the lines ready to cast off and am heading for the helm when I hear a voice calling from the dock.

"Ahoy matey!" It's Wright. He's standing on the slip next to the boat, wearing aviator sunglasses and a baseball cap that hides his eyes. I can't tell if he's joking, or if he has any clue how ridiculous he sounds. "Permission to come aboard?"

I struggle to not sound hostile. "How did you find me?"

"I'm a Detective, remember?" He grins. I don't reply. "Okay. Maggie told me." He takes my silence for permission and hops up onto the swim platform, then onto the deck.

"What can I do for you, Detective?" I'm careful to not let on that I know he's on suspension, or that he's been misleading me this whole time.

"Wow, this is a nice boat," he says, ignoring my question. "Is it yours?"

"It belongs to a friend." He lets out a low whistle. "She lets me borrow it."

"Nice friends to have." I nod. It is in fact a very nice boat: A Carver 37 Coupe two-deck cruising yacht, with twin inboard engines and a top speed of 37 knots.

"Where are you going?"

"Fishing." He removes his sunglasses and I can see he's surprised. "I like fishing," I say. *Today I plan on catching a lot*, I think, smiling at him.

"I have some news to share with you," he says. "About your husband. And Montana." I'd love to ask him *How would you know, given the fact that you're on suspension?* But I don't. I just smile and keep it to myself, like I do most things.

"Can it wait?" It's probably not the right thing to say, based on his expression, but I don't care.

"Maybe I can come along?" He gives me a sly smile. "I like fishing too." Now that I know he's been lying to me ever since we first met it's tough to not let my mistrust of him show. He's trying to manipulate me, but I can't let him know who's really pulling the strings.

"Either you're getting off now or you're along for the whole ride. I'm not coming back until late." I give him a look to make sure he knows I mean it. "If you get bored you'll have to swim home." He just smiles and settles down on one of the sofas in the salon. Well that's decided then. He's made his move, and I can make mine. I've got everything I need, no matter what I find out.

I put both the engines into reverse, increase the throttle on the starboard engine then have to use the stern thrusters to manoeuvre out of the tight berth in the crowded marina. Wright doesn't say a word, which I appreciate. Most men would be giving helpful unsolicited advice or offering to take over, which I sure don't need. I quickly manage to get us out of the marina and within minutes we're in open water.

The breeze is fresh and it feels as if everything bad is being left behind on the dock. Except for Wright, who's sitting on the sofa, watching the shoreline disappear. What to do with him isn't the question; it's a matter of how and when.

I take her out about ten miles from shore, then head west toward the trenches that divide the east and central basin of Lake Erie. It's a quiet day on the water, with just a few powerboats out. They cut through the water leaving deep Vs in their wake. There isn't much wind, so the sailors haven't even bothered to set out.

I'm not sure we'll catch much fish in this weather. Perch prefer a light chop and the water is too calm. Maybe that's why so few boats are out. There are usually lots of fishing boats out here, but it's Sunday and the commercial fishermen are taking a day off. Perch fishermen are a sociable bunch. They all weigh anchor in a flotilla over a school of perch, their boats about fifty yards or so apart and wait for hours, chatting and passing the time. I prefer to fish away from the pack. And today especially I want some privacy.

It looks like we have the lake to ourselves, apart from a couple of boats that are just dots on the horizon. Which is perfect for what

I've planned. I set anchor and cut the engine. Slight waves gently rock the boat as I join Wright on deck.

"Would you like a drink?" I offer, as I opened a bottle of *Premier Cru* Chablis and pour myself a large glass. He shakes his head and I sit down across from him. I take a big drink.

"We've got Montana's autopsy results back," he says, watching me for a reaction.

"I'm surprised they did an autopsy," I say. I'm even more surprised that he found out about it. He must have access to someone still on the force. "It was obviously a bee sting, wasn't it? She was allergic."

"That's what's interesting," he says. "She died of anaphylactic shock, that's true. But all the trauma and swelling was in her mouth and throat. It looks like that's where she was stung. No idea how that could have happened." I can think of a few ways. But I have no interest in Montana. Now that she's dead she's no longer a problem of mine.

"So what have you learned about my husband?" I ask.

"I heard back from both the US Customs and Border Patrol and the Canadian Border Services Agency," Wright says. "Your husband crossed the border into the US at Fort Erie on July 30. They scanned his passport and plate readers scanned his vehicle as having passed through the boarder checkpoint." I nod. None of this is surprising and it's not shedding any light on why he's really after my husband.

"Someone bought a ticket using his credit card, to Los Angeles."

"Someone?" I interrupt. "Why would you assume it wasn't him?" Wright shrugs.

"It could have been him. But there is no record of his taking the flight. And his car wasn't left at the Buffalo airport."

"So, maybe he drove there?" Which makes no sense I realize. Why would you buy a plane ticket if you're going to drive?

"It's about 2,500 miles to Los Angeles," Wright says. "I hope he likes driving."

"So where is he?" I ask. "Still in the US?"

"I'd love to know," Wright says. "I can tell you there's no record of his returning to Canada."

"And you don't know where his car is either."

"For all we know he's driving around somewhere, on a *stage*. He could have sold his car and bought another. He could be anywhere."

"If he never came back across the border," I begin, dreading the answer. "Then who locked me in the freezer?" Wright says nothing.

"There's another way he could have returned." Wright stares out at the water, sparkling in the sunlight. "Does he know anyone with a boat? It's less than an hour across Lake Erie from Buffalo."

"This is ridiculous!" I'm frustrated and angry. "You're suggesting my husband somehow faked his own disappearance. That he left the country, and then snuck back across the lake. That he may have locked me in the freezer, tried to kill me. It's all too complicated. Why wouldn't he just leave me? Divorce me, the way people do?"

I'm irritated by Wright's game, whatever it is. Clearly he knows more than I do about my husband and though he may not know where he's gone, I bet he knows why. I need to figure out a way to get him to tell me so I can fill in what I'm missing.

Wright smiles. "For the money. If you divorce he'd get half of the business, which from what you told me isn't worth much. But the farm, that's a different story. And if you happened to die I guess he'd inherit it all."

"I don't want to talk about this any more," I say, standing up. "I came out here to get away from all this crap." I get out my fishing tackle and set up two six foot, ultra light rods with spinning reels. I set them on rod holders so I can hold my wine and relax until we get a bite. I set the sinkers at the bottom and ran two red hooks on each of the lines, about twelve inches apart. Wright comes over and watches as I get some live minnows out of the bait bucket.

"Here," I say, as I hand him a minnow. "You can bait your own hooks." Wright recoils.

"I don't know how." He sounds panicked. "I've never been fishing in my life," he admits. I try not to roll my eyes and do it for him. Once both lines are set, I pour myself another glass of wine, then pull up a chair and sit by my rod with my eyes on the horizon.

Within a few minutes Wright sits in a chair next to me, holding a beer. "I found this in the fridge. Think your friend will mind that I helped myself?" I shake my head. I'm sure she will not mind a bit.

We sit for a long time in silence, eyes on the point where the water meets the sky. I sip my wine and think about what I need to do now. Should I confront Wright with what I know? Tell him that the police have been around, that I now know he's on suspension? What would he do then? A wave of anxiety washes over me when I realize it's a conversation I should have had when we were still on land, not out here in the middle of the lake where no one can help me.

I watch Wright out of the corner of my eye, considering my options. He's restless and gets up after a while. He looks around the boat, making impressed noises as he touches everything, like a child. He notices the large package on the deck, wrapped in a white plastic tarp.

"What's this?" he asks, bending to inspect it.

"It's a new anchor." In that moment I know exactly how to handle Wright. I know who he is, but he doesn't know me or what I'm capable of.

"The one you're using doesn't work?" he asks.

"They need a spare," I say. I'm certainly not going to go into my plans for the anchor.

He tries to lift it. "It's heavy," he states the obvious. Wright clearly is not very bright.

"It is an anchor," I say pointedly. "Can't exactly have it floating away." Wright thinks about that then finally sits down. He stares out at the water and stops talking, for a few minutes.

"What made you open a restaurant out here?" Wright asks in far too short a time. I'd appreciated it while it lasted—a man who didn't need to talk. That was so completely unlike my husband, who'd insert himself into every conversation, turning everything into being about him. Life with chef was operatic, with him always singing his one-note arias "*me me me me*".

Wright switches to wine when he tasted the delicious Chablis I'm drinking, and we're on our second bottle. We're snacking on appetizers I've brought—*palmiers* with roasted garlic and rosemary, prosciutto rolls with goat cheese and figs, spiced nuts and Lay's Original plain potato chips. A classic.

"We had the little bistro in the city," I tell him. "With a *prix fixe* tasting menu. It was a tiny place, only seated twenty six."

I watch Wright's expression as he listens to me talk about my husband, and about Thorny Rose. I'm telling him my story, spinning out like fishing line and waiting for him to bite. I offer him the plate of figs and proscuitto. They say the way to a man's heart is through his stomach, but it's not Wright's heart I'm interested in. I still don't know what he's after. I hope this fishing expedition I'm on will fill in the blanks. In any case, I'm going to make sure it's the last conversation I'll be having with Wright.

"We'd been thinking of moving into a bigger space, or even moving out of the city. Maybe buy a farm somewhere, do the whole *Farm to Table* thing right. Then two things happened: First, our restaurant burned down. And then my sister died, so we were able to move back here. We used the fire insurance money to retrofit the farmhouse."

"Thorny Rose was your sister's house?"

"It belonged to both of us, left to us by our grandparents. But she lived in it."

"How did your sister die?"

"An accident. She fell down the stairs at the house." I can tell Wright wants to know more, but he doesn't ask. "She was drunk." I fall silent and look at the horizon. Wright doesn't speak.

"So we moved out here and opened Thorny Rose. We provide a *seasonal prix fixe experience*. Each course has its own wine—all chosen by chef. And we have the tasting menu, for showing off his new ideas and culinary experiments.

"And we do special events as well. Like the Pig's Head Dinner we had in April. Our special guests enjoyed *nose to ear* eating with Chef. They could all partake of roasted pig's head, with wine pairings. Prix fixe, just two hundred dollars a guest." Wright whistles in admiration.

"Don't you mean nose to tail?" he asks.

"No," I say. "I mean a pig's head. Literally. Luca and chef worked it out. Roasted pig's heads—with all the bits: cheeks, ears, brain, and tongue."

Wright shudders and took a big gulp of wine.

I think for a few minutes, drinking wine and staring at the water. "When we first opened he had a lot of extreme ideas on the menu. But after losing money for the first year I told him he had to change. We fought a lot."

"He didn't want to compromise?"

I shake my head. "Honestly, he was becoming bad for business."

TWENTY SEVEN

Rose

AFTER A COUPLE of hours we have pulled up ten fat striped perch, and finished the second bottle of Chablis as the boat drifts at anchor. Its gentle swaying and the rocking of the waves have pulled the tension and fear out of me. I feel more relaxed and happy than I have in weeks. I think I might even feel a slight breeze, though the water is dead calm.

I open another bottle of wine and Wright raises his eyebrows.

"You do realize you are impaired right now," he says. "I believe that you'll find that is against the law to pilot a boat on three bottles of wine."

"Don't worry about it," I reply. "I know a cop." I could tell by the way Wright laughs that he's drunk. I'm not. I've been pacing myself and making sure I eat to keep a clear head. I'll need it.

I top up his wine and put out a plate of Le Cendrillon goat cheese from Quebec, its beautiful rind covered with dark vegetable ash. I hand Wright a baguette so he can tear off his own piece and sit down.

"It was tough to get staff then," I say, cutting a piece of cheese and spreading it on bread. "Still is. We pay minimum wage and we're out in the country, so mostly we get local kids who just want a job."

"Like your dishwasher," Wright mumbles through a mouthful of cheese.

"Yes, like Paul. But chef had a reputation from our last restaurant, so a few apprentices or people doing *stages* would come in. And we'd take some interns on from the local culinary college." I catch Wright looking at me. I know he's thinking about Montana and Lotte.

"At first it was just the two of us, on this great new adventure. I planned the garden. He was obsessed with cuisine, and I thought it was all good."

"Then he cheated. Again." I drink more wine. "And again." I look at Wright, measuring his response to what I'm saying.

"Montana wasn't the first. He's had lots of affairs, all of which he thought he'd hidden from me." I stare out at the water for a moment, watching the sun sparkle across the surface like a million diamonds.

"But you stayed with him." The question he doesn't ask is *Why?*

"After a while I didn't care. I knew the affairs were meaningless." For Raymond, a seduction was like the anticipation of a great meal. The planning, the preparation, imagining how it would be, then savouring every moment, sucking the very marrow from his lover's bones. But then he was done. The meal was over, and he rarely had seconds.

"The first time I found out he'd cheated I packed and went to a hotel for a few days," I say. "But I came back."

"Because he asked you to?"

"No. He never did actually," I admit. "I'm not even sure he noticed I was gone." Wright shakes his head in disbelief.

"And the second time?" Wright asks.

"The second time, the third time, the fourth...I stopped counting," I say. "Then I stopped noticing." I shrug and watch Wright's face, but he reveals nothing. Maybe I'm telling him too much, but after today nothing he knows will matter anyway. I glance over at the new anchor.

"I realized a while ago that I didn't love him anymore. That was a big revelation to me," I say quietly. "Then the real problem becomes what do you do with that information, once you say it to yourself? It was if I'd lived my life in a dark room and someone finally turned on the light. Even if the light is turned out again, I have still seen it. It's done."

"Were you going to leave him?"

"Probably," I say. "But he beat me to it." I jump to my feet and put on a big smile. "Are you hungry?" I ask. "Let's eat."

"We've been eating for hours," Wright groans.

"That's just appetizers," I scoff.

I gut and clean the perch off the side of the boat, while Wright looks the other way. He really has never been fishing before. Then I take them into the galley to filet them.

I bring out my knife roll and find my Wusthof filleting knife. It's nine inches long, perfectly thin and flexible, and I get to work on removing the heads, then the backbones from the perch. Last I run the blade carefully between the fish skin and the flesh, until I have a pile of lovely clean filets, ready for flour, butter and the frying pan.

I start bringing everything out of the cooler and setting it up on the counter. Cheeses, bread, tomatoes, *mache* lettuce, basil, vinaigrette and fresh fruit, everything I'd need to make a great meal to accompany the fresh fish.

"You've got a lot of food packed," he teases. "Were you planning on eating it all yourself?"

I stop what I'm doing but don't look at him. "No. Not really," I say after a moment, with a glance at Wright. "I was hoping for some company." He looks curious. The bait is set. "I was hoping

you'd show up," I admit. "You've been doing a lot of that lately."
He looks embarrassed.

"You sure seemed hostile back on the dock."

"Hostile? I didn't mean to be," I say. "Ambivalent I guess…"
His eyebrows rise in a question.

"I'm attracted to you, Detective. And I'm not sure how I feel
about that."

"That's a bold statement," he says, meeting my gaze.

"My friend here," I raise my wine glass. "And I have been dis-
cussing it all afternoon. We decided to let you know."

"Ambivalent," he echoes. "About what?"

"What I want from you."

"What do you want?" He moves closer to me and I can feel
the heat coming off him.

"I don't know. Yet." But I feel like my fishing expedition so
far has been a waste of time. I haven't found out anything useful
about Wright, like why he's looking so hard for my husband. Any
time I've asked him questions about himself he's deflected, or given
answers so spectacularly boring I can't imagine he's got anything to
hide. He's a dumb guy. Good looking, but stupid.

I dredge the perch fillets in flour and egg wash, then gently
fried them in butter, turning them once, then draining them on
some paper towel. With a simple salad made from ripe tomatoes
and fresh basil and fragrant olive oil, and a loaf of rosemary *foc-
cacia*, dinner was served. I open another bottle of wine and we sit
down to eat.

"This is delicious," Wright says in appreciation, tearing off a
chunk of bread and dipping it into the olive oil and juice from the
tomatoes.

"It's just the ingredients. Fresh food, prepared simply, and don't
get in the way of the natural flavours. Cooking is not hard," I say.

"Not quite what you have on the menu at the Thorny Rose though, is it?"

"Not always, no," I admit. "But if you were to ask my husband, he'd claim he makes *simple food*. Hard to believe sometimes when you look at what we serve. Tiny bits of food on a hot stone or on charred planks of old oak, with an intense reduction for dipping."

"That's a *meal?*" Wright laughs.

"It's absurd, honestly. He got into very show-offy cooking: using foams, froths, gelatins, freeze-dried foods that disintegrate when you eat them, leaving only this intense flavor memory."

"Freeze dried?"

"Oh yeah," I roll my eyes. "Freeze drying sublimates the water from the food, so the flavours go straight to a gas and a powder. You then add those freeze-dried ingredients back in as additional flavours to the food. Basically you flavour the dish with the essence of itself, to intensify the taste experience, rather than adulterate the food with other seasonings or herbs. It's all about purity and intensity." Wright shakes his head.

I sip my wine. "Do you have any idea how much a freeze-drying machine costs? Or a molecular distiller?" Wright shakes his head slowly, his eyes glassy. He's staring at my lips. "But we had to have one. Regardless of the cost." At least the molecular distiller was something I'd been able to put to good use with the Womyn Collective. We use it to distill herbs at low temperatures and separate out the impurities and create a pure extraction for the herbal liqueurs.

"Or what about this?" I say, toasting Wright with my wine glass. I am definitely feeling the wine, but my mind is still clear. I know what I need to do. "Blackberries and raspberries twice frozen using liquid nitrogen so they break apart into tiny individual intense flavor beads. Then sprinkling those over a smoked almond milk *anglaise* with fennel pollen. That was on the menu last month." I drain my glass.

"How is that *simple food,* I ask you? A reduction that takes days and some arcane process to make, as well as a technological feat, all in order to achieve the mythical essence of flavour. Really?!" Wright laughs, a high-pitched giggle you'd never expect from a big guy like him.

"At first I was in love with him, with his passion, and his vision," I say staring at the water as it laps against the side of the boat. "But in the end it became a little creepy. His obsession with minutiae, with food, and with fame. It felt like the emperor has no clothes."

That was only one of the reasons I killed him. Frankly I'm amazed it took me as long as it did. Anyone else would have done it years sooner. I'd seen it all: the trysts in the walk-in cooler, flirtations with the cheese vendor, and affairs with food writers. His taking credit for ideas as if they were his own, acting as if the Thorny Rose's success was all his doing, as if I'd had nothing to do with building it. Of course I killed him. He deserved it.

I researched it thoroughly, learned how to lure wild boars with corn mash and Kool-Aid. Honestly I'd have thought my husband would choke a pig, but Luca's boars made a fine meal of him.

Now I just have to take care of Wright and it will be smooth sailing.

After dinner we sit on the deck, watching the last of the light fade. Across the water the lights of Buffalo and Port Colborne light up the shoreline on either side of the boat. Running lights of the few boats still out sparkled where just an hour ago sunlight danced on the water.

"I love this lake," I tell him. "I love the entire Niagara region: The lakes, the escarpment, the beach. It's in my blood."

"Sometimes when I'm out on the water the fog rolls in quickly, completely obscuring the shore. You can be out in the boat and in just a few minutes you can't even see beyond the prow. It's as if the world has disappeared and you are completely alone."

"Scary," Wright says.

"No, peaceful," I reply, shaking my head.

"But you've got a GPS, right?"

"Of course. Full navigation, depth finder, fish finder…"

"Fish finder? That's efficient," Wright says. "Guess it saves you from sitting around all day without getting a bite."

"Lake Erie is shallow, mostly around thirty to fifty feet, and it heats up quickly in the summer, especially when the weather has been hot like this. Fish prefer cooler water. Like over toward Long Point where it drops down to around two hundred feet in a couple of spots." I'll be heading over to that trench soon, but Wright isn't going to enjoy the trip.

"And a depth finder could get find those deep spots?"

"That's what it's designed to do," I say, looking at him. Wright looks lost in thought, oblivious.

"What are you thinking about Detective? That my husband got thrown off a boat? Lake Erie's not deep enough to get rid of a body." He says nothing and I smile.

"If you were getting rid of a body," I continue, "it would make more sense to drop it into Lake Ontario. It's around eight hundred feet deep and a lot colder."

"Lake Erie is shallow and intense storms blow in really fast. I've seen this lake go from gentle swells to ten-foot waves in just a few minutes. It's terrifying. And exhilarating. If there were a body at the bottom it would be brought up, no question." Unless it was in one of those deep trenches, tied to something heavy, like an anchor.

"You sound like you've given this some thought," Wright says. I nod. I have indeed.

"That's not against the law, is it?" I ask, looking at the new anchor, just a few feet away on the deck. It's time to put it to good use.

He shakes his head. If he only knew what I've been thinking about this whole time he'd have been more careful. He might have stayed on shore. He might have stayed sober. But I'd have found another way to dispose of him.

I get to my feet and make my way to the galley. I'm opening my knife roll when I hear the rumble of a boat motor, getting nearer. I look out the port side window and see the lights of the Coast Guard Auxiliary Rescue boat cruising past. Two men are at the helm, and they carefully look over at my boat and wave.

Wright calls out to them. "Hi! Great night, isn't it?"

"Beautiful, now that the sun's gone down," one of them shouts back. I grit my teeth and wrap the knife roll back up. I can't take a chance that they'll forget having seen Wright onboard, if he suddenly goes missing. I guess I won't be using the anchor tonight.

I drink a glass of water and consider my options. After a minute I make my way back to Wright, handing him a glass of soda water with lime.

"Here you go," I say. "You don't want to get dehydrated, after all that wine." He accepts it and takes a few big drinks. Then he sighs with contentment, setting the glass down.

"This has been a perfect day," he says. The wine, the food, the company." He smiles at me, making the point. "You really love food, don't you?"

"Food is life. It's a sensual experience," I say, stretching my arms wide and arching my back. "The aromas, the textures, the luscious tastes and colours. It nurtures our bodies and our souls. It's everything."

He smiles at me, his expression contented and unaware.

"Here," I say. "Taste this." I hold out a tiny Red Currant

tomato to him. It's like a jewel, sparkling as it catches the last of the evening light. I know it will be an intense burst of flavour, an explosion of summer's essence.

He takes it into his mouth, then leans over and kisses me, as I knew he would.

TWENTY EIGHT

Wright

I WAKE UP with a splitting headache. Lying there, I try to remember why, then I open my eyes and don't recognize the room. Not good. Then it comes back to me, the day on the boat, the night with Rose. Coming back to the house, to her bed. I smile and turn to the other pillow. But her side of the bed is empty.

I find my clothes and pull them on, then make my way downstairs. Rose is in the kitchen, drinking coffee and reading something online. She closes the laptop when I come in.

"Good morning," she says. "Sleep okay?"

"I'm not sure if *sleep* is the right word for it," I say, sitting down across from her. "I think I may have passed out." She grins. "No idea how I got here. I don't remember leaving the boat."

She pours me a coffee and slides the cream and sugar across the table to me, along with a container of ibuprophen. "Take two. You'll feel fine in twenty minutes."

I watch in a stupor as she slices some bread, rubs it with garlic and olive oil and places it on the grill. After a minute she flips the toast, then pulls out a baking sheet from under the broiler. It's filled with cherry tomatoes that have roasted until they are tender and split open, spilling their juice. When the toast is done, she spreads it thickly with *ricotta* cheese and layers the roast tomatoes on top, then drizzles on some more olive oil, salt and fresh ground pepper.

"Perfect hangover cure." She sets a plate in front of me. I eat two thick slices and begin to feel human.

"It's delicious," I mumble with my mouth full. She tops up my coffee but when I try to add cream I find the pitcher is empty.

"There's more in the cooler," she says. "I'll get it." I hold up my hand.

"I'm closer. Let me," I say. She watches as I swing open the heavy cooler door. The metal shelves on the right side are full of metal and plastic trays, all clearly labeled and the floor is covered in buckets and bins. The entire left side is crammed full of vegetables and fruit. I stand there, wishing I'd let Rose get the cream. I have no idea where to find it.

"It's on the shelves at the back. With the other dairy stuff," she calls. Sure enough, there it is: several liters of 10% coffee cream. I pick one up and am about to close the door when I glance again at the produce shelf.

There are three large, clear plastic bags, stuffed with bundles of neatly stacked, familiar serrated green leaves. Weed. I pick one up. It's heavy and weighs maybe five or six pounds. Or about eighteen to twenty four months.

"What's this?" I ask, which is a stupid question I realize, for a police detective to ask. "*Really?*" She stares at me. "It's cannabis."

"It was a rhetorical question," I say. "What I mean is, why do you have three large bags of cannabis in your cooler?"

"It's Maggie's," she replies. "It's just some leaves." As if that's any kind of an explanation. I stand there, waiting for her to give me more.

"She cold-presses the leaves with glycerine and extracts the oil. Takes several drops under her tongue to help manage her pain, as needed. She also juices them, or sometimes makes tea. Smoking weed isn't ideal since the effects don't last that long, but it does work fast if she's in a crisis. The sub-lingual drops or spray she makes work much better."

I must look confused. "The CBD spray helps with her pain management," she clarifies. "But it still allows for her to have a clear head and energy. She's not sleepy or stoned."

"CBD?"

"It's the non-psychoactive part of weed. It's the THC that gets you high. The CBD is medicinal."

"Does it work?" Rose looks out the window.

"Maggie's terminal. According to the doctors she should have already died months ago. Yet here she is, coming to work every day, working busy shifts. So yes, it works." Her voice breaks. "I couldn't manage without her. I don't know what I'll do when she's gone."

"This isn't legal. You know that, right?" Rose shrugs as if challenging me to do something about it.

Now I feel even more awkward and strained being there, if that were possible. "I should go," I mumble. I have to get out of there. The last thing I need is to be around quantities of cannabis, legal or not. Luckily I can tell she's happy for me to leave. "I just need to get my phone," I realize. "And my belt. I left them upstairs. I think."

"I'll help you find everything." She follows me upstairs.

I go through the room, checking under the bed and through the clothes that are flung everywhere. It looks like we'd been in a big hurry to take them off. Shame I can't really remember much of anything. I look under the bed and find one of my shoes. I stand and see Rose holding the other.

Then it hits me. There's nothing of her husband's in the room. No clothes in the closet. Nothing on the chest of drawers or side tables that looks like it belongs to a man.

"Where is all your husband's stuff?" I ask.

Rose looks confused. "What do you mean?"

"Well, there aren't any of his clothes here. Nothing that I

would say look like personal effects." I watch her expression as I speak. "It's almost as if he didn't live here." She looks down at the floor, her cheeks flushed. "Or as if you didn't think he was ever coming back."

"I packed it all up for him. Put it into the barn," she says, raising her eyes to meet mine. "I was going to kick him out, once he got back from Los Angeles, or wherever he went. I'm done."

It seems like a reasonable explanation, but for some reason I don't believe her.

I sit in my car in the restaurant parking lot feeling uneasy. I'd like to believe Rose had packed up her husband's stuff and moved it into the barn. But it was only a few days ago that she'd denied he was even missing. She was clear that he was coming back...just maybe not when. Now, a few days later, she's moved everything out? It feels odd.

I shake my head, still feeling that headache. I'm not surprised I have a hangover. We drank a lot of wine. But still, it wasn't my first time at the rodeo...why don't I remember anything of what happened after we had dinner on the boat?

And if I was so drunk that I'd forgotten last night, how the hell did I manage to drive the car back here? Or did Rose? She'd had as much to drink as I did, maybe even more.

From where I'm parked I can see a small section of the abandoned house, just visible through the screen of trees Rose had planted. Something still nags me about it. I have some slight memory of the story in the papers when the Monks disappeared in Toronto, but since it wasn't a local story I hadn't paid much attention. I've got enough going on here in Niagara to keep me busy.

When I get back home I have a shower, then I open my laptop and scroll through the online news articles about the story. There are dozens, all dated from six months ago, just before Easter. It would have been faster if I had access to the police database, but unfortunately that isn't the case at the moment. This will have to do.

Based on the online stories the couple, Lauren and Stephen Monk, had just disappeared off the face of the earth. Family members had reported the couple missing when they hadn't been heard from in several days. There are dozens of photos of them online. She was your typical rich man's wife: Beautiful, well cared for, with long brown hair and a killer body. Didn't seem to have a job, but did some charity work. Probably spent her afternoons in yoga classes tightening up her yoni. He was an ordinary looking chubby guy who was grinning in every picture, and no wonder. Lots of money, a beautiful wife. The guy had it made. Except for the disappearing part, which for the most part was the same in every article.

Steven Monk, a successful property developer, had missed several business appointments and his assistant had not heard from him. Their Rosedale house was intact, there was no sign of forced entry, and no alarm was activated. Their car, a McLaren 650S Coupe, was found in the driveway.

Since their disappearance there has been no activity on their bank accounts or credit cards and their cell phones have remained turned off.

There is no evidence to suggest foul play. Not signs of struggle, robbery or forced entry. The house was secure and all of their personal items—including clothing and passports, were found in the home.

Investigators were urging anyone with information to come forward. After a few weeks the stories stopped, as no news surfaced and the leads dried up.

What happened to the Monks?

TWENTY NINE

Rose

"**WHY WOULD YOU** risk taking him out on the boat?" Maggie asks, her face flushed with anger. "It's dangerous."

"I wanted to find out what he knows," I reply. I'm trying to say as little as possible. I don't need Maggie to know more than she's already figured out.

"And did you?"

"No." I don't want to lie to her. She sighs and whips off her bandana. I can see her scalp, with her hair just starting to regrow. It's patchy and uneven and she rubs her hands through it in frustration.

"He's a bad cop Rose," she finally says. "He knows people. He could hurt us. Hurt Sophie."

"He's looking into chef's disappearance, that's all." As I say it I know it sounds weak. I don't even really believe it's true. Wright is dim; definitely not much more than a forty-watt bulb. But my gut tells me he knows more than he's letting on, even though I haven't found out what it is.

"What if he digs into things, into the past? He's already curious about the Monks, you saw that yourself. It's not good."

"That's got nothing to do with us," I say. Maggie says nothing. She looks at me, her lips pressed together.

"And what about the freezer? Why did you report that?" she demands. "I thought you wanted to keep it quiet. That's what you said. You wouldn't let me call 911 that morning."

"I didn't want to at the time," I reply, turning the corner onto the side road. "But now that we know about Wright I thought it best that the police—the real police—know. Especially after what happened to Jacob with the chocolates."

Maggie looks worried. She's deep in thought, staring out the window.

"Do you really think chef is trying to kill you?" She sounds skeptical "Why?"

"Money," I reply. "If I die he gets the farm." Maggie nods. "Who else could it be," I ask. Maggie has no idea about what happened to chef, or about anything else I've done. And there's no need for her to ever find out. "Where is he?" I continue the story. "Let's face it, he's been gone a long time now. For a *stage*."

Maggie is silent as she reties her bandana and checks herself in the mirror.

"I just thought it was something else," she says, giving me a look full of sorrow and disappointment.

"What?" I demand. "What did you think?"

Maggie doesn't reply.

We drive up the overgrown driveway and park by the barn. The dogs aren't out, so I'm not nervous about climbing out of the truck. I wave to the guys on the porch and go around to the passenger side to find Maggie is already out of the cab, shouting to them.

"Hi Mitch," she calls to a burly guy with a beard. "I thought you were still in jail!" They all laugh, but it's probably true.

Mitch is another friend from high school, one of the bad boys I'd had a crush on. One of the worst of them, if I recall correctly. Also one of the best looking, and I'm happy to see he's even more attractive now. He'd dated Sophie at one point, though it was hard to imagine the two of them together now. He took the blame for some hash Sophie had on her when they were pulled over one night, in the bad old days.

Mitch was a really good guy at heart, or maybe a really stupid one. Helping Sophie out got him his first criminal charge, since twenty years ago the drug laws were much more strict. But it kept Sophie's record clean, and she was able to go to graduate school and to now carry on with the business today, like a model citizen.

In the end he'd had to leave town because of an outstanding arrest warrant, for an unrelated charge. He disappeared to Alberta and worked the oil rigs for ten years until it was safe to come home, once the police lost interest in his charges. Not that it saved him, because once he came back he got caught smuggling fireworks into Canada and went to prison in Kingston for a while anyway.

"You should know, Maggie," they shout. She lights up with their banter, smiling. It's good to see her happy and alive.

"Let's go," I say. "Jay's waiting."

Maggie follows me into the grow office and Jay meets us inside. "Hi Maggie," he says, embracing her. Maggie hugs him back with all her strength, holding on as if it were the last time she'd see him. My heart clutches at the thought, since it's likely true. Then he leads us through into the back room, and up a small flight of stairs to one of the upstairs offices. There are boxes stacked against the wall, probably full of orders that need to be taken to the Post Office for shipping to clients.

"Here's what I think you might consider," Jay says. Laid out on the desk in front of him is an assortment of products designed to help manage her pain and nausea. Dried buds in a clear plastic jar, a few syringes of oil, and a small baggie of what looked like toffee, next to a vape pen.

"What's that?" asks Maggie.

"Shatter," Jay says. "It's got about ninety percent potency, compared to buds or oil. So it should cut through the pain pretty effectively, until the end." Jay knows Maggie doesn't have any time to waste on niceties. He's honest and direct. "But it's very high in THC. It'll get you high. You're not going to be able to work on this stuff." Maggie nods, taking it in.

She and Jay go through the other options he has available and she makes her selections. Then he packs it all up into a box and carries it out to the truck for her. Maggie writes Jay a cheque for the amount owing and hands it to him.

She gives him another hug goodbye and goes out the door. The minute the door closes Jay tears her cheque up.

I stick my head out the door and shout. "I'll just be a minute Maggie." She waves me off and I watch as she heads toward the porch, where Mitch and his buddy stand to greet her.

I hand Jay a tall stack of bills, tied with an elastic band. He riffles through them without counting then smiles.

"Feels about right," he says.

"I don't think I'll need anymore product for a while after today," I tell him. He nods.

"I'm here when you need me," Jay says. "You just have to call."

"Thanks," I say. Jay will always be there when we need him. "Should I pull up the truck so you guys can load it? Or, will you have someone bring it around?"

Jay thinks for a moment. "I'll get Mitch and the guys to bring it over," he says, his eyes sparkling with mischief. "I bet he'd like to see Sophie anyway. It's been a while."

I nod and head out the door. "About seven years, wasn't it?" I say over my shoulder. "With time off for good behavior." The door closes on Jay's hoot of laughter.

I go back to the truck and wait while Maggie jokes with the guys. We don't need to rush back. Let her have her fun. I've got a lot to think about.

THIRTY

Wright

THE DRIVEWAY INTO the Pelham Woods Long Term Care facility loops around by the entrance, which is blocked by a Care-A-Van unloading some residents. There isn't enough room to pass, so I idle the car by the curb. I watch as a cluster of elderly people wait by the curb, some in wheelchairs, some with walkers, as the personal care workers struggle to get one last man out of the vehicle. He is raging, struggling and cursing and it takes all of them, including the driver, to get him off the van and into a wheelchair, where he is restrained and finally rolled into the building. The rest of the residents follow behind in a caravan, the walkers first, followed by the wheelchairs pushed by the care workers. Finally the van raises the accessibility ramp, closes its doors and moves off, and I'm able to drive into the visitors' parking lot.

I punch in the numbers on the keypad as the sign in the lobby instructs and the doors slide open. Funny kind of security, with locked doors but the entry code clearly posted, but then I remember that Pelham Woods is a secure facility, and most of the residents suffer from various forms of dementia and memory loss. They can't manage to figure out the code and keypad on their own, so they won't be escaping the facility unescorted.

I find the reception desk and ask for Mrs. Efimov, Rose's

mother. Nobody asks me for identification or about my relationship to her; I could be anyone visiting some elderly relative in a nursing home. I find her in the fourth floor lounge, dozing on a loveseat. When I sit beside her she stirs but doesn't wake up, so I look around. I'm in no rush.

There are about two dozen residents in the lounge. Most are asleep, mouths open, in the chairs and loveseats that line the walls. Arranged in front of the television are several people in tilt wheelchairs, though I doubt any of them is actually watching the screen. A care worker pushes a cart through the room, distributing cups of tea or juice, bananas and cups of vanilla pudding.

"Hello," a voice says. "It's good to see you." Mrs. Efimov is awake. She's smiling at me, her head tilted flirtatiously. "I've missed you." She beckons me closer and I carefully lean in a little closer.

"I waited for you last night," she whispers. "After he went to work. But you never came." She lays her hand across mine and looks into my eyes.

To my relief, the care worker interrupts. "Would you like tea, Nadia?" she asks in a loud voice. Mrs. Efimov looks blank. "A cup of tea?" she repeats. Without waiting for a response the worker thrusts a cup of tea into Mrs. Efimov's hands and moves on to the next resident.

Mrs. Efimov sips the tea and looks around the room. Her gaze eventually lands on me again and she stares, eyes wide.

"Ivan!" she cries out. The she continues speaking, in Russian I think. I sit there mute, wondering what exactly I'd thought I'd find out by coming here to speak with her.

After talking with Lotte I thought that maybe Rose's mother would know something about where Raymond Ellis had gone. If he did visit here every week, and if they were close as Lotte said, maybe he'd spoken of his plans. But it's pretty clear that even if he did, she won't remember any of it.

Mrs. Efimov stops speaking in Russian, but continues to stare at me.

"So, what are you cooking today?" she asks. "Whatever it is it will be better than the garbage they serve here." I smile, baffled, but I decide to play along.

"Well Nadia, I thought maybe poached salmon. And ratatouille." I'm not even sure what ratatouille is, but it feels good saying it. She nods in approval.

"Sounds delicious. And for the party? What will you cook for that?" I realize she thinks I'm the chef. Maybe he did visit her and talk with her about food, or about menu ideas. As her mental clarity dulled maybe there were still some topics that she was clear on, where could still engage. She might not know who she was talking to, but maybe some things were still present for her.

"Prime Rib. Scalloped potatoes." She looks confused then shrugs, her lip curled in distaste. Who doesn't love scalloped potatoes? Her gaze drifts off and she stares across the room at nothing in particular.

"And how is Lily?" she asks. "I haven't seen her for a while."

"She's good," I lie. "She's…working a lot." It seems like a reasonable reply, but Mrs. Efimov's head spins around and she glares at me suspiciously.

"Working?" she repeats, staring at me. Then her eyes drift away and her attention is caught by a volunteer leading an overweight black Labrador dog into the room. Her face breaks into a grin and she reaches out both her hands for the dog, then rubs its ears and allows it to lick her face until it's time to move on to the next resident. She then settles back into her chair and gazes ahead, looking at nothing in particular. The dog is gone and I'm sure the memory of it is too, even though the visit was only moments ago.

I realize this visit is a waste of time and I'm thinking of how I can get out of there, when she speaks. "I told her to stop drinking."

Her face goes dark. "Every day I told her." Mrs. Efimov looks at me, her eyes searching mine for answers. "Why did she drink so much?" Who's she talking about now? Lily?

She stares at me for a moment then suddenly shrinks back into her chair, eyeing me with fear.

"You pushed her down the stairs," she hisses. "I know you killed her."

"What are you talking about?" I look around, embarrassed in case anyone heard her. "Why would I do that?"

"You know why."

I shake my head. "No, tell me Nadia," I persist. This feels important, but I'm not sure why. "Why would I push her down the stairs?"

"For the farm. So you could have it. It's all you ever wanted." She's shrunk as far away from me as she can, squeezing herself into the corner of the loveseat. "You took both my daughters," she hisses. "Get away from me."

I wonder how much truth there is in her demented ramblings. Did chef kill her daughter? Did he push Lily down the stairs? Did Rose know about it?

I decide I'll see how far I can push this. And maybe I'll have a bit of fun.

"Have you seen Raymond lately," I ask her. She looks at me, confused. Wasn't I Raymond? I see the shifting reality play across her eyes. Who was I? What had just happened?

"No…" she whispers. "Why?"

"I'm looking for him," I say. "He has something of mine I want." Her expression returns to one of pleasant empty curiosity.

"That's nice," she says.

Then I lean in close to her and whisper in her ear. "And when I find it, I'm going to kill him." I get up and leave as she gasps in shock. It's a shame she'll forget I was ever there.

THIRTY ONE

Rose

I DROP MAGGIE back at the Thorny Rose so she can get ready for tonight's service. The reservation book is filling up and it looks like we'll do two full turns. Then I double back to the Womyn Collective to see Sophie.

I find her in the back kitchen of the barn, straining some olive oil through a fine mesh filter. She flashes me a brief smile then brushes her hair back from her forehead and returns to her task. She seems overwhelmed.

"How's it going?" I ask.

"Good," she says. "Busy. I can't believe how many orders we've got coming in."

"That's a good thing, right?" She nods.

"It's tough to keep up. I could use an extra set of hands." I know what she means and I feel guilty. Usually Maggie helps her during the week. But with chef gone she's been doing extra shifts to cover. Not only am I overworking Maggie, but now Sophie's short staffed.

I look over at a new piece of equipment standing next to the large commercial floor mixer. It is several feet tall, a complex construction of tubes, glass beakers and instrumentation. The vacuum pumps and condensers, chilling units, filters, extractors and evaporators are baffling and intimidating.

"This distiller will make all the difference," I say.

Sophie rolls her eyes. "If I can figure out how to use it," she says. "I think we'll need to keep Jim on full time to operate it." I nod in agreement. That makes sense.

Then Jim walks in, carrying a bag from the local hardware store.

"I needed a new pressure gauge," he says to Sophie then he sees me and smiles.

"How was your day in court, Jim?" I ask.

"Funny thing," he grins. "The complainant didn't show up to testify how I'd threatened his life over some pears. So the judge dropped the charges."

"Funny thing indeed," I agree, my eyes wide in mock surprise. "Wonder what happened there?"

Jim laughs. "He's your husband Rose. If anyone knows what happened to him, my money's on you."

"How's it going with the new molecular distiller?" I ask, changing the subject.

"Good," he says. "I've got it all assembled now. Just want to do a few test runs to see how it does." He walks over to the table and starts to unwrap the new pressure gauge. "I'm going to miss old Bessie though," he says, patting an old piece of equipment next to the table. Bessie is the old supercritical CO_2 extractor Jim made himself, from watching a YouTube video. Jim can make anything.

Bessie has served the Womyn well over the past few years, but it's time to invest in some new equipment to make the process more efficient, and more profitable. The CO_2 extractor had worked well, but the end result retained too many of the terpenes from the original herb, which affected the flavour of the final product it was used in. The new distiller will produce a clear, flavourless extract with high potency that they'll be able to easily incorporate into many topical lotions or other products.

"Yeah," Sophie says. "It's been tough since Bessie broke down. We've had to decarb the herbs in the old fashioned way."

Herbs need to be decarboxylated before they can be infused into cooking. That means they need to be slowly heated to around two hundred degrees Fahrenheit for an hour, which releases their active medicinal ingredients and increases their effectiveness. Then after they're infused into oil or butter they need to be filtered several times to remove the plant matter that might affect the appearance of the finished sauce or oil.

"The smell it makes is pretty strong so we'd have to do it after hours, when no customers are here," Sophie says. "It was tense when that cop showed up last week, looking for Lotte." She shakes her head. "He made some idiotic comment about smelling cannabis."

"Well the distiller will take care of that problem," I say. The herb is distilled to its essence, doesn't need to be filtered, there's no green colour or aroma and all the original terpenes are removed that that might alter the flavour of the final product.

"You'll be able to introduce whatever flavours you want into the products. Maybe honey or lavender?" I suggest, even though she's ignoring me and carrying on with her straining. I pause until I get her attention, then I smile.

"I just wanted to let you know that Jay is coming over later," I tell her. "With a delivery."

"What's that smile for?" she asks, suspiciously.

"He's bringing Mitch." I laugh at Sophie's stunned expression and how she reflexively starts to smooth her hair.

I'm still laughing as I turn to leave, waving goodbye to Jim who's wondering what the joke is.

I'm on my way through town to visit my mother, but there's one thing on my mind that I need to check first. I drive downtown, crossing the canal bridge where I see the work crew rolling grey paint over the LIDSVILLE graffiti, again. No idea why they bother. It'll be right back up as soon as that paint is dry.

I turn left onto Clarence Street then slow down to a crawl. I can see the back parking lot behind the shoe store, with the stairs leading up to Montana's apartment. I've driven by here many times over the past few months, checking to see where chef was, like some pathetic betrayed wife. And I'd found what I was looking for: his car parked at the foot of the metal staircase. Not that it gave me any gratification to have my suspicions proven right. I can still recall the sick feeling in my gut when I realized the truth. There's no satisfaction in proving your husband is cheating on you. Just some justification for what happens next in the story.

I'm about to turn in, knowing Montana won't be there to disturb me. I think I'll take a quick look around to see what I might find in her things.

But then I see Wright's muscle car parked next to the dumpster. What is he doing here? I speed up and drive back out of town.

THIRTY TWO

Wright

SHE ANSWERS ON the first knock. Her eyes are swollen so they look even smaller than usual. I can tell she's been crying. She tries to hold the door closed, but I push it open and she doesn't resist.

"Lotte." I'm not smiling. "I have some more questions." She steps back and I walk past her into the apartment. There are clothes on hangers draped across the futon, and a few boxes packed with books and kitchen utensils.

"Moving out?" I ask. She nods.

"It's Montana's lease. The landlord has another tenant coming in."

"Where are you going?" I ask. "Back to the farm?" She keeps her eyes down and shrugs.

"Should I make a guess?" I say. That gets her attention and her head snaps up. "I think you are meeting chef somewhere." Lotte looks stunned.

"No!" She shakes her head. "I haven't heard from him in weeks." I make myself comfortable on the edge of the futon.

"I don't believe you." Her eyes well up with tears and she slumps in the chair across from me. She looks defeated and wary.

"You know Lotte," I begin with a smile. "Some of what you told me just doesn't add up." She looks at me, eyes narrowed. "You told me that chef was teaching you how to cook with cannabis, after hours at the restaurant." She nods. "Now why would he be doing that?"

"I asked him," she mumbles.

"Because you asked him," I repeat. "And that would make him break the law, even possibly lose his restaurant and his reputation. Because some intern he didn't know, who he'd just randomly met at some event, asked him?"

"It was for my Oma..."

"Right," I interrupt. "I doubt he cared about your sick grand-mother." Lotte stares out the window, her shoulders slumped.

"When my Oma got sick I did try to cook for her, but it all tasted awful. That part is true. I asked chef to teach me how to infuse cannabis oils and concentrates into edibles that taste good. He's got culinary skills that could mask the taste of the THC."

"Then I got thinking that learning to cook with cannabis, to make edibles, would be a great opportunity for me when it's all legalized. I could..."

"Make some money," I finish her thought.

"And chef was interested in this great opportunity?" She nods. "What about Montana?" She nods again.

"I found out that chef and Montana were already experi-menting with different products. They were making truffles and caramels, nut brittles and pralines. And not just sweet things—savoury items like chicken wing sauces and dips. They let me work with them."

"So they were making edibles," I ask. "Before you even worked at Thorny Rose?"

"Yes. Gourmet stuff—not just the usual gummies and cookies you can buy in the dispensaries now." Lotte is excited. "Chef was teaching me how to make edibles that would be legal and govern-ment approved. Prepared in a professional kitchen, with accurate dosage and nutritional information." That sounds like a nice fantasy to me, to make it seem safe. Probably the sort of thing chef would tell her so she'd help out in his *experiment*.

I thought over what she'd just told me, seeing if it adds up with what I know. "How much were they making?"

"Every few weeks or so they made a lot of product," she says. "There were lots of boxes chef put into his car." I know then what I have to do.

"What happened to it all?"

She throws up her hands. "I just figured they made them for a private party somewhere, maybe some corporate event. It wasn't my business. I didn't ask." Lotte isn't bright enough to be curious. I can tell she has no idea where the product had gone.

"And that's all you know?" She nods. "Who else knew about this little experiment of chef's?"

"No one. Just chef, Montana and me." I stand up and go over to her.

"Not Rose?" I ask. She shakes her head, her lips twisted. "You don't like Rose," I say.

"No one does," she says. "But I like Maggie. She's great."

"Did Maggie know what chef was up to?"

Lotte looks terrified. "No," she whispers. I don't believe her.

"No?" I lean in close to her. "Are you sure?"

Lotte's eyes dart back and forth as she tries to think of what to say. "Maggie didn't know about us cooking at Thorny Rose," she says. "Just at Womyn. We were cooking there too."

"Who's we?"

"Me and Maggie. And Sophie, her daughter." Now this is interesting. I might have to go take a closer look, to see if they're going to be trouble for me. Maybe I could get a piece of their action. I'd bet the ladies could use a strong man with my skills. They just don't know it yet.

"Thanks Lotte," I say. "You're sure no one else knows what you and chef were cooking?" She nods and looks up at me with misplaced trust. I smile as I reach for her. "I'm going to have to make sure we keep it that way, okay?"

THIRTY THREE

Rose

SHE FORGOT MY name today. She tried to cover and pretend she knew, but the look in her eye told the truth. She doesn't quite know who I am. My face is familiar to her, but she's not sure of why. What was the context? Could I be her sister? Her mother? Or maybe a neighbour? And when I gently remind her she gets defensive. *Of course I know who you are! I know my daughter Lily anywhere.* She thinks I'm Lily.

So for her I'll be Lily. And that's okay. I can give her that.

"How are you?" I ask as usual, patting her hand and waking her again from her perpetual doze in the lounge. She opens her bright blue eyes, as empty as the sky, and smiles.

"Hello there," she says. "It's so nice to see you." This was what she said to everyone who sat next to her, even if they'd been there for an hour already. It's a cover dementia patients learn, to make it seem like they really remember the person they are talking to. I used to believe it, hoping she really did know me. That it really was nice to see me. But now I just pretend along with her. I pull up my chair a bit closer and sit next to her, putting my back to the sad old woman who pulls at my sleeve, trying to engage me in conversation every time I visit. It's easier to ignore her this way.

"I'm good," I say. "Everyone is fine." I am always vague, since

I'm not sure who she'll ask about, if anyone. *Everyone* seems like the safest bet, when I'm never sure what decade or country she'll think she's in. Whether she knows her parents are dead, or her brothers. Or my sister. So I lie. Of course I lie and I play along until she gives me some clues.

"How is the restaurant?" she asks. Sometimes she surprises me. Sometimes she'll be right there for a moment, fully present.

"Great," I say, my eyes tearing in gratitude. "We're really busy, with the Wine Festival." As I tell her about what I've been doing I can see the light start to fade in her eyes. She's left the conversation, but I keep talking since I never know what else to do when she loses the thread. Maybe she'll pick it up again.

"He was here, asking about you, Lily," she interrupts me.

"Who was?"

"Oh you know," she snaps. She is impatient. "That husband of yours." My head spins. My husband was here? That's impossible.

"What was he asking about?" She stares over my shoulder at nothing.

"He asked me who killed you."

"Okay…" I play along. I am careful. "And what did you tell him?"

"That he did it," she laughs. "As if he didn't remember."

I struggle with how I should respond to her. She was imagining the visit, obviously. I have no idea why.

"Lily fell," I stroke her hand. "She was drinking."

"I know she fell," she snaps. "After he pushed her." She pushes my hand away. Her face is flushed and she becomes agitated. "Boring me with his silly talk about food," she mutters. "Flashing his ring."

His ring? Chef never even wore a wedding band. Anxiety floods my chest. Wright wears a ring. I feel the panic rise. Has he been here too?

My mother grumbles to herself for a minute then closes her eyes. She's tired. Within a minute I can see from the steady rise and fall of her chest that she's asleep. It must be exhausting trying to find your way through the fog of your own mind.

Week after week I visit her here. Some days she's better. Mostly she's worse. I'm not even sure why I come anymore. It's not like she remembers me, or even when I was last here. Sometimes she'll rage at me because she hasn't seen me in weeks, when I'd just visited the day before. Other times I'm busy and I miss a few visits and she never notices. So what am I even coming here for? In the end sometimes it feels like I'm putting on a show so the nurses can see I'm a Loyal Daughter. I'm looking for their approval now that I can't get my mother's. If I ever could.

This could on for years as she goes through the predictable stages of decay: memory loss, incontinence, inability to feed herself, then to swallow what's she's fed by the caregivers. Then the last few days when food and fluids are withheld until she dies. There's no alternative. Unless I hold a pillow over her face and suffer the consequences. I could probably get away with it. I'm sure I could figure out a way to hide what I'd done.

But could I do that? It's not a question of whether I could be so cruel—it's not cruelty to put an animal out of its misery. We treat our pets better than we do our demented parents. It's not even whether I'd have the courage. I know I could manage it. It's just a decision. One that I'm not ready to make yet.

Or do I just let her live out her time as her mind dissolves and her body disintegrates? Her memories are already scattered like bits of ash after a fire. I sometimes get a glimpse of the smouldering embers of her personality, but those too are going out. We all fade away, and usually there isn't even anyone left to remember us. Only the land remains. It's all that matters in the end.

I stand and creep away without waking her. There's no need. I've been saying goodbye to her for a long time.

I walk to my truck in the parking lot and sit for a minute, staring out the window. It is stifling inside so I start to drive, opening all the windows hoping for a cross breeze. God I wish it would rain. Anything to give us a break from this heat and humidity.

I turn on the radio to the news channel listening for the weather report, even though I can see there isn't a cloud in the sky. I almost weep with relief when I hear the thunderstorm advisory, issued by Environment Canada.

"Given the high heat and humidity, a few of these thunderstorms could be intense resulting in localized torrential downpours, and the potential for flooding," the announcer says. *"Some regions could quickly receive 25 to 50 millimeters of rain, and wind gusts of up to 65 miles per hour could also occur. The Niagara Region remains under a heat warning, with high temperatures expected to continue into the weekend."*

The announcer's voice comes on after the severe weather alert:

Niagara Regional Police are investigating the suspicious death of Lotte De Vries of Port Colborne, whose body was discovered earlier today in an apartment in the downtown area. No other details have been released at this early stage of the investigation.

Homicide investigators are appealing to anyone with information to contact police.

I slam my foot on the gas pedal and drive home.

THIRTY FOUR

Rose

When I pull up in the driveway I see Maggie sitting on the porch. She has her vape pen beside her and she's nodding off.

"Hi Maggie," I say. "How's it going?" She smiles and closes her eyes. It's obvious she's high as a kite. This is not good. We have service in a couple of hours. I peer through the door to see if the rest of the staff are at work. To my relief they seem to be carrying on, without her supervision, doing their *mis en place* as instructed. Maybe we'll be okay.

"This shatter of Jay's is something," Maggie says. "Wow."

"You okay?" I ask, sitting beside her. She's slumped on the swing, clearly not feeling any pain.

"I've been thinking," she slurs, leaning into my shoulder. "About chef."

"What about chef?" I ask, wishing she hadn't spoken. I wondered who else has seen her this way, who else she's been talking to.

"What do you think really happened to him?" she asks. "All these deaths, these accidents. First Luca, then Montana. Even poor old Jacob." She drifts off for a moment, staring into the middle distance. Then she starts laughing.

"If he's trying to kill you, he's not doing a very good job, is he?" She keeps laughing until the tears stream down her face. "The freezer, poison chocolates."

She takes another hit off the vape pen then closes her eyes again. It's quiet on the porch. I can hear her breathing heavily next to me.

"There was nothing wrong with that freezer, Rose," she mumbles. "Marzipan? Everybody knows you hate it, even chef." She is drifting off as she talks, her voice just a whisper. "It's almost like he's not really trying, do you see? Chef would have done the job right the first time."

I sit beside her, thinking hard. Maggie is slipping, she's needing more and more medication to get her through the day, and to help her manage her pain. And the more she takes, the less capable she is, and the less discreet. And the more she might say, without thinking of the consequences. I can't have her acting like this in front of the rest of the staff. They look up to her; she's the leader on the line. And now she's a hot mess.

"I think you took care of it all," she mumbled. "Like the Monks. Like you manage everything so well."

I take a deep breath and slip the vape pen out of her hand. I quietly go into the kitchen and look up my friend Amy's number. Hopefully she isn't already working because I need her to take over Maggie's shift tonight.

Then I get Will to help me walk Maggie to my truck. "It's time to go Maggie," I say. "I'm taking you home." She doesn't protest, and just quietly allows herself to be driven home.

When I pull into the Womyn's Collective I can see them finishing up in the fields. It's almost dusk and the light is fading. Soon the sun will be behind the trees and they'll have a hard time seeing what to pick. I wave as I drive past the barn to the back of the property where Maggie has her trailer.

I leave Maggie dozing in the passenger seat and go to open the door and get everything ready. Then I get her out of the truck and, with my arm firmly around her waist, I help her up the steps into the trailer. I sit her down on the couch in front of the television and prop her up with some pillows, then do what I have to do. Then I pour her usual glass of Scotch, remove her shoes and raise her feet onto an ottoman.

"Hey Maggie," I say, jostling her shoulder a little to wake her. "How are you feeling?" Maggie's eyes open. She looks at me and smiles, and my heart breaks.

"Here," I say, handing her the glass of Scotch. "Let's have a drink together and watch some television." I sit next to her with my own glass, just like we always did, and click on the remote and begin scrolling through the channels looking for a nature program, Maggie's favourite.

This was what I've missed for weeks now, what I should have been doing instead of working every night at Thorny Rose. If chef hadn't done what he did, then I wouldn't have this regret. I would have had this time supporting Maggie and being with her and with Sophie. I'll never get that time back but I can be with her now.

We sip our drinks in easy silence, watching the images flicker across the screen. By the time the program is over, she has finished her scotch and is drifting off. I remove her Scotch glass and pour a fresh glass of water. Then I set it beside her and try to make her as comfortable as I can, given her condition. She's quiet and I don't disturb her.

I give her a kiss on the cheek. "Goodnight Maggie," I say, wiping the tears from my eyes.

I keep the television on so she's not alone. Leaving a light on against the growing darkness I quietly slip out, shutting the door behind me.

THIRTY FIVE

Rose

FINALLY THIS MORNING, after weeks of relentless sun, the sky is overcast. The air already feels cooler and I think I may even feel a breeze, a slight stirring of the thick, moist air. I turn on the radio in the truck and just catch the end of the severe weather advisory.

"... northern Pennsylvania, Ohio and Ontario. A state of emergency has been declared in Pennsylvania, with storm surge warnings for the Lake Erie shoreline.

Expect heavy rainfalls, in excess of 40 millimeters. Strong winds and wind gusts up to 65 miles per hour. There is potential for power outages due to broken tree limbs and high risk of localized flooding as creeks and streams overflow their banks."

The massive tropical storm hitting the US coast is almost one thousand miles wide, and promises to be one of the most destructive and dangerous storms in decades. It has shifted course and is now predicted to track north/north west once it moves inland. We'll get rain and high winds as the outermost bands of the storm reach us. I'm just relieved the heat and humidity might finally break.

I drive past the Womyn sign and see that it has been tagged

with graffiti again. Some meaningless scribbles with spray paint, as well as the predictable cartoonish penises, as you'd expect a misogynist idiot to scrawl on a feminist collective sign. It wasn't the first time and sadly probably won't be the last. I'm sure they'll have it cleaned off before breakfast.

Before I go in to check on Maggie, I stop into the barn to see Sophie. As usual, she's already at work, packing bottles of liqueurs for shipping to one of their major retailers.

"Hi Sophie," I say. "You're at it bright and early." She smiles and comes out from behind the counter to give me a hug. "Sorry to tell you your sign's been tagged again." She sighs and takes out her cell phone, then sends a text to someone, probably the clean up crew.

"Thanks for the head's up," she says. "What are you doing here at this hour?" She glances at her watch. "It's barely eight o'clock!"

"I was just passing by and wanted to check on your mom." Sophie's face falls.

"What's happening?" she asks.

"Don't get upset," I say, placing my hand on her arm. "But I had to bring her home early last night from the restaurant." Sophie looks devastated. "I'm sure she'll be okay. I think she took too much pain medication. She was pretty out of it." Sophie nods. This is not new. We've both seen it before.

"I'll come with you, okay?" She gets into my truck and we drive up the lane to Maggie's trailer.

She gets out and knocks on the door.

"Mom? Are you awake?" She knocks again, louder, while I wait behind her. "Mom?" Then she turns to me, tears in her eyes. Maggie is always up before the birds, no matter how ill she is. We both know what's waiting behind the door.

Sophie turns the knob and steps into the trailer. I'm right behind her. Maggie is exactly as I'd left her last night, sitting on the couch, with the light on and her feet up on an ottoman. The television is still on, tuned to the same channel. She has a peaceful smile on her face. She is dead.

I burst into tears. Even though I knew it was inevitable and that Maggie would be dead when I saw her, I find it hard to accept. Sophie is crying and we clutch at one another, sobbing in grief. She steps outside to call 911 and I look around the trailer, one more time.

I sit on the sofa in the trailer watching the police officer look around. Maggie's body has already been removed and Sophie has gone with it to the funeral home to make arrangements. I've turned off the noise of the television.

"It looks like she took an overdose of her pain medication," the paramedic says, after they'd arrived and confirmed Maggie was dead. "We see this a lot with terminal cancer patients."

"She wouldn't kill herself," I argue. "Maggie was a fighter. She wanted to live."

"I apologize," he says. "I didn't mean to imply suicide. I meant an accidental overdose. It happens. Tolerances change. People might forget they'd taken a dose and then take another if they're confused."

I watch as the police officers go through the trailer, checking in the drawers and under the bed. I'm not sure what they're looking for, since Maggie's pain medications are all laid out on the kitchen table: her fentanyl patches, morphine and hydromorphone tablets. They will not find any of Jay's cannabis there, because I'd removed it and anything else incriminating when Sophie stepped out of the trailer to call 911. It's all in my bag, now stowed safely in the truck. The last thing I need is anyone asking awkward questions about where Maggie had acquired the cannabis. She had a prescription and it was all more or less legal. I'm not entirely sure the shatter or wax would fall under the legal definition of her medical cannabis prescription—and I don't care. There's nothing the law can to do Maggie now, but I don't want to get Jay into trouble.

"What's this?" one of the officers says, pulling a plastic water bottle out from under Maggie's bed. It's filled with yellow liquid.

"Urine," I say. "I think." The police officer looks horrified and almost drops the bottle. Then he recovers himself and slips the bottle into a clear plastic evidence bag, followed by two more bottles he finds.

"Why would she have bottles of urine under her bed?" he asks no one in particular.

"She saves it for the collective," I say. He looks at me in disbelief.

"What to they do with it?" He looks like he really didn't want to know.

"It's a repellant," I say. "They spread it around the flower fields, to keep rabbits and deer away from the crops." He stares at me, apparently unable to process what I'd just told him.

"What are you going to do with it?" I ask him.

"Test it," he says. I nod. Presumably for traces of toxins or drugs that might have contributed to Maggie's death.

They won't find anything unusual, that I know. There will be cannabis of course, morphine, and her nightly glass of Scotch. And possibly, if they were looking for it, they'd find the amygdalin from her Laetrile treatments. Nothing out of the ordinary.

After he leaves I sit in the empty trailer. I've never felt so alone. Maggie is gone. She was my rock. My only family since Lily died and my mother faded away. Losing her like this is the hardest thing I'd ever had to do. But I didn't have a choice.

THIRTY SIX
Rose

I LEAVE THE trailer, locking it behind me as I head back to my truck. I can see the lake in the distance, its indigo blue now almost black. To the south I can see the heavy black clouds moving in across the water. The horizon is gone and the lake is blended into the heavy sky, a menacing darkness rolling toward me.

The storm is coming fast now. I turn the radio on and hear the severe thunderstorm watch has been updated to a warning:

> *...severe thunderstorms are imminent or occurring, likely to cause large hail, damaging winds and torrential rainfall. Heavy downpours may cause flash floods and water pooling on roads. Expect wind damage to roofs, siding and trees."*

The sky is already dark as I pull into the Thorny Rose parking lot and it looks like dusk, though it's barely noon. The automatic security lights come on, triggered by the low light. Now the parking lot and restaurant entrance are illuminated in an eerie half-light.

I feel the wind picking up and I rush to stack all the chairs on the porch and bring in all the candles and cushions. Then I run around to all the sheds and outbuildings, locking doors and putting away or tying down any loose tools or equipment. I park my truck in the barn and I'm just securing the barn door when I see Wright pull into the parking lot. Icy fear washes over me and I hide.

I watch as he goes into the restaurant, first looking to see if anyone is around. He must have assumed I was out since he didn't see my truck and there are no other cars in the lot. He knows no staff would be here today, since it's Monday. Now I don't wonder what he's looking for or what he wants. I know.

I wait a few minutes in the darkness of the barn while he's in the restaurant. Then I creep up to his car and peer inside. I pull on the handle. It's locked of course. I'm not even sure what I'm looking for. My mind races in desperation. Then I pull my secateurs out of my pocket and crouch down behind the passenger side.

A few minutes later I hear him calling my name.

"Rose!" he shouts from inside. "Are you here?"

I walk up the porch steps just as the first fat raindrops fall.

"I was just securing some things," I tell him casually, as if I hadn't noticed him sneaking in and spending ten minutes snooping around inside. "Looks like the rain is finally coming." He smiles as I pass him in the doorway. "I'm just about to make some coffee," I say. "Would you like some?"

"Sure. Sounds great." He sits on a kitchen stool while I put the kettle on to boil, put several heaping spoons of coffee grounds into the *cafetiere* and set out the sugar. I move deliberately, trying to buy some time. I think about how I should manage him, what I can say or do to get him out of here, for good this time.

I go into the display case and carefully plate a selection of pastries, then place them on the counter in front of Wright. He looks pleased and begins to study them as he makes his choice.

Then I go into the walk in for some cream. I see Maggie's supplies, still on the shelf, and an idea comes to me. I watch out of the corner of my eye as Wright selects the *mille-feuille* and begins to eat, ignoring me, which I'd counted on. I make my decision and then I allow the cooler door to swing shut. In less than a minute I'm back out, bringing the cream with me.

As the water boils I watch the rain pouring down outside the door. Several millimeters have fallen in just a few minutes and water sheets across the porch and pools in the parking lot. Far off I can see forks of lightning strike the ground and I hear thunder, rolling closer. I pour boiling water into the French press and wait, watching as the storm rages.

Finally the coffee is ready and I press down on the *cafetiere's* plunger then pour two mugs. Wright pays no attention as I carefully prepare then set his mug in front of him and slide the cream and sugar over.

He drinks the coffee and makes a face.

"Is it okay?" I ask. "We've got a new supplier I'm testing out. It's fair trade and shade grown, from Ethiopia."

"It's good," he says. "A bit bitter, maybe." Then he adds more sugar and takes another sip.

"I've been thinking about a few things," he says, sipping his coffee. "Like Montana's autopsy results." I try to stay calm and take my time selecting a pastry. I need to make sure he stays under control for about thirty minutes. I bite into a *macaron*.

"About how she was stung in the throat." He watches me. His eyes are cold. "How do you suppose that would have happened?" I shrug. "Then I remembered about Maggie's bee venom therapy," Wright continues. "And I thought about how easy it would be to pour some venom into Montana's water bottle. The mucosal tissue in her mouth and throat would swell and shut off her airways, even more quickly than if she'd been stung."

"And who would want to do that?" I ask.

He looks at me for a moment before he replies. "You, for one," he says. "Or Maggie, to help you out."

"That's ridiculous," I scoff. "To help me out how, exactly?"

"To get rid of your husband's girlfriend?" he says. "You told me yourself you couldn't fire her."

"That's not a reason to kill anyone," I say. "And Maggie would never do something like that."

"But you would." His laugh is like a bark and his eyes are fixed on me. "I bet you'd do whatever you had to do." I watch him carefully, trying to figure out where this is coming from.

"You're accusing me of murdering Montana?" I say. "Why? Because she was sleeping with my husband? She wasn't the first and she won't be the last."

"I'd say she definitely was his last," he says. "Since I'm pretty sure he's dead." I don't like where this is going.

"How would you even know about Montana's autopsy results," I sneer, changing the subject. "Since you're on suspension?"

Wright gives me that killer smile, surprised that I know. "I'm on *administrative leave* at the moment," he shrugs, trying to seem indifferent. "That's what it's called, by the way. I've still got friends on the force," he says. "They provide me with information if I need it." He is so arrogant, so smug, I feel like hitting him with a *saute* pan. I wish I'd done it on the boat.

I stare him down. "What do you want, Wright?"

"Like I said, I'm looking for your husband."

"Why?" It isn't on behalf of the Niagara Regional Police, that much I now know.

"He and I have a business arrangement. I'm surprised you don't seem to know about it."

"What kind of arrangement?"

"He provided me with some product which I have distributed in the US, through my partners' network."

"Product?"

"Cannabis edibles," he says. "High end sauces and desserts,

thanks to your pastry chef. We've been thinking of expanding our market, to include gourmet edibles. And luckily for me, your chef has the skills, and the appetite…for cash."

I understand now where all the extra baking supplies have been going. All those nuts, butter and chocolate. I guess he did have some kind of side job after all.

"I don't know anything about your *business arrangement*," I say. "And I didn't kill Montana." Wright rolls his eyes. "And I have no idea where your product is."

"It's not the product I'm looking for. That was safely delivered by your husband, since I wasn't able to."

"*Not able to*," I sneer. "Because you're under surveillance for trafficking and corruption charges?"

He holds up his hand to silence me, a pitying expression on his face. "Please Rose, we're friends. That's not nice way to talk to me. And anyway, it's not corruption, it's obstruction."

"Whatever. It means you tipped off your drug dealer friends when there was going to be a police raid. And for that I'm sure you got paid nicely."

"Money's good to have," he says. "Your husband was happy to be in business with me. He did all right by me." I wonder how long Wright and my husband been working together, in their little arrangement. And how much money he'd made that I didn't know anything about.

"My husband did all right by me too," I say. "Cleaned out our savings, stole money from the restaurant."

Wright sips his coffee. "That's where we have so much in common. Your husband disappeared with all my money too." I stare at him, speechless. "He met my partners out on the lake— probably using your friend's boat I'm guessing."

"You made him do your dirty work."

Wright bursts out laughing. "You've got to be kidding. He

begged me to do it. He set the whole thing up, the meet with the other boat." I knew that was probably true. I didn't take much to imagine my husband doing that. "He was into the thrill of it. Thinking he's a real bad boy." That sounded exactly like the man I was married to.

"He gave them the product and got the payment. Then he disappeared. Leaving no trace of my money. My three hundred thousand dollars."

"I imagine he took it with him, don't you think?" I say, thinking hard. "Along with our savings and whatever else he could grab." I move slowly behind the counter, getting it between us. The magnetic knife strip is to my left, with cleavers and knives now within reach. Wright catches me looking at it.

"You're not seriously thinking of using one of those, are you?" He smiles then lifts the bottom of his t-shirt, revealing his gun.

"Don't you have to turn that in when you get thrown off the force?" I sound braver than I feel.

"I have spares." He's so cool and offhand about it. Brutal, like I'd thought the first time I laid eyes on him.

"You know, for the longest time I thought he'd just taken the money and run," Wright says. "Didn't seem like you two were getting along. He was playing around. It looked like he just drove across the border and disappeared. Making a fresh start somewhere, with all the money. I guessed he figured I wouldn't be in a position to look for him, given my situation."

"You mean when you end up in jail?"

"I won't go to jail," he laughs. "Maybe I'll lose my job. But in the meantime I'm suspended with full pay. I've got lots of time to look for him."

"So I got curious," he continues. "I asked some questions around town about him. Spoke to some people. I followed you to the grow op on the Concession, by the way," he says. I glare at him. "After that it looked to me like maybe you knew more than you let on. Maybe you knew where your husband is after all. And maybe even where my money is."

"I've already told you. I have no idea where my husband is," I say. "I was getting that cannabis for Maggie."

"So you say. Who knows?" I watch him drink the rest of his coffee and wish he would choke on it. "Poor Maggie. Shame she had to die."

"Shut your mouth about Maggie," I snarl. "She was my best friend." There is a blinding flash of lightning, followed a few seconds later by a deafening crash of thunder. It has struck very close. The rain pours down, heavy drops bouncing off the porch and pounding the roof in a deafening roar.

"I'm guessing you killed her too," Wright continues, ignoring me. "Maybe she knew too much." He pops a *macaron* into his mouth. "Did you use more of that bee venom, like with Montana? Or maybe just an overdose of morphine?" He wipes his mouth with a napkin. "She was dying anyway. It would be easy to make it look like an accident or natural causes.

"It's too bad really," he says after a moment. "Because I wanted to talk to Maggie."

"About what?" I look at the clock.

"I understand she's been cooking cannabis, over at the Womyn farm." My blood runs cold. "I think maybe I should pay them a visit. See what they're up to. See the beautiful Sophie again." My mind is racing but I try to look calm. I need to make sure he never goes near the farm, or Sophie.

"That's ridiculous," I sneer. "Who told you that?"

"Lotte, your former intern." I felt sick with fear.

"Lotte's dead," I hear myself say. "I heard it on the news."

Wright looks disinterested. "Shame really," he says. "But I

couldn't have her talking about chef's project. She was helping him." I can't believe what I'm hearing.

"You killed Lotte." I now understand what Wright is capable of.

He laughs. "So what? You killed Maggie."

"I loved Maggie," I say, my eyes narrow with hatred. "I would never hurt her."

"Love," he sneers. "Things don't seem to end well for people who love you. Your husband, Maggie, Luca…"

"Luca?" My voice is shrill with fear. "That was an accident. You were there yourself!"

"Why'd you kill him, Rose?" Wright talks right over my objections. "He was crazy about you. He'd do anything for you. He told me." I look at the kitchen clock. Fifteen minutes have passed since he'd arrived.

"Funny thing," he says, his voice sounding a bit slurred. "Montana told me that Maggie would do anything for you too. All these people, so loyal to you, ending up dead." I look away, wondering what I can do.

"The way I see it," Wright continues. "Someone else could have driven your husband's car across the border, using his passport. Someone who looks enough like your husband to fool a border guard. Someone like Luca Ricci."

"All he had to do then was leave your husband's car in Buffalo, say in some high crime area, unlocked with the keys in the ignition. The car would be gone in a few hours, untraceable. And then Luca could just come back into Canada using his own passport. Or, maybe someone met him at the Buffalo marina… someone with access to a boat." He looks at me.

The lights flicker off then back on as lightning strikes close by. I jump out of my skin, but Wright barely seems to notice.

"And that's why you had to kill Luca," he continues. "He knew too much. You got him drunk on Amarone, killed him and left him to get eaten by the boars. You staged the whole thing with the ladder to make it look like an accident. Hid any trace that you had been there with him that night. Washed the second wine glass. You needed to bring me along as an objective witness when you found the body. Who better than a cop?"

"You're hardly a reliable witness," I say. "And you're not even a cop."

"You didn't know that then," he says, which is true.

It wouldn't matter what Wright said or what he thought he'd figured out, if I could just survive long enough to get away from him. I look out the window and see that it is now dark as night, even though it's still afternoon. The rain is coming down sideways and the high winds blew the trees back and forth like rag dolls shaken by an angry child. I hear a loud crack as a limb breaks and falls to the ground.

"Maybe it was you who locked me in the freezer and tried to kill me," I say, grasping at straws. "Did I interrupt you snooping around that night? Were you looking for your money?"

He laughs. "You faked those attempts on your life—being locked in the freezer, the poisoned chocolates," he says. "To make it look like your husband might still be around here. Maybe pin the murders on him." He starts counting on his fingers as he speaks. "He sure looks good for it. He killed Montana to cover up her help with this arrangement. He killed Luca out of jealousy because you two were having an affair. And, it makes sense that he would also be trying to kill you. But he wasn't. Because he's already dead, isn't he?" I shake my head, denying what he was suggesting.

"Poor little you," he continues. "I totally bought your act. Little *wifey*, cheated on, didn't know where your husband went. You knew all along. You're the one who emptied the bank account.

You knew exactly where he is. Or where his body is anyway." He leans across the counter, his face close to mine.

"And you knew it from the first time I showed up looking for him. Because you killed him."

"Why would I do that?" My voice catches in my throat.

"Lots of reasons people kill their husbands. Maybe you're tired of him sleeping around. Maybe you figured out he was leaving you, and taking all your money. Maybe you found my money and wanted it for yourself."

"He's not dead," I say. "There's no body."

"True. There's no trace of him left, is there?" he says, tapping the side of his head. "I thought, funny how you stopped eating pork suddenly. You know what those pigs eat. Fitting end for a chef, you must have thought." He laughs again at his own joke. I look at the clock.

Wright stops laughing and stares at me. His pupils are dilated. It's been almost twenty minutes since he drank the coffee. The effects of the cannabis distillate I slipped into his mug are setting in. But I need to buy more time.

"I may not be the smartest guy, Rose," he says. "But I think I've got this all figured out." I stare at him, saying nothing.

"I think your husband murdered your sister." I'm afraid to speak. "So you could inherit the farm and then you'd both move out here to create your dream restaurant. You probably even torched the old one for the insurance money to help you open this place. What's a bit of arson when you've already committed murder?"

"My only question is when did you find out about it—was it before or after he pushed her down the stairs? If it was before, then you were in on it together. It makes sense that you killed him to cover up the crime, in case he ever talked. If it was after, then I guess you killed him for revenge when you found out. Personally,

I'd rather it was the latter," he says. "I wouldn't like to think of you murdering your own sister." I try to stay cool.

"My sister wasn't murdered by anyone. She died of natural causes. There was an investigation."

"Investigations can be compromised. They often are. Mistakes are made. I wonder if I looked into it, maybe talked to some of the investigating officers, what I'd find." He meets my eye, holds my gaze.

"Not sure how you'd look into it, given your situation."

"*Touché.*" He smirks. "Not that I could prove anything. It was a few years ago."

Wright stands up and goes over to the gas stove. I consider running out the door into the storm, but I'd have to slip past him to do so. I don't think I'd make it and I'm afraid of making him angry.

He begins flicking the burners on, one by one. Blue and orange flames flicker across the grills, the glow of the fire eerie in the gloomy kitchen. He smiles at me and my blood runs cold.

"How long have you known I'm on suspension, Rose?" He leans across the counter and stares at me. "Did you know when you took me out on the lake?" His eyes study my face, then move down and linger on my breasts. "Before we had sex?"

I look away and he laughs. "Don't go all shy on me now," he says. "You were all over me on the boat." He leers at me.

"I've had better," I say. He steps back in surprise and his smug smile slips. "Anyway we didn't have sex."

His pitiful look of astonishment is worth the risk of making him angry. "You don't remember anything, do you," I taunt him. "That's no surprise. I gave you a roofie."

He looks confused. "A roofie? Why?"

"I wanted to get some information. About what you're after. About who you work for."

He looks nervous. "And what did you find out?"

"You drank too much. Couldn't get it up," I smirk. "But I had fun anyway. I couldn't make much sense of what you said. Sadly." He stares at me, slack jawed. "But I did hear some interesting names, and I learned all about the obstruction charges. About who you were tipping off, who you were protecting. Fascinating stuff." That really rattles him and he looks confused as he tries to process what I'm saying. I glance at the clock. Another five minutes have passed.

"You don't know how close you came to going overboard that night," I continue, pushing my advantage. He stares at me in disbelief. "That was the plan, anyway. Tied to that lovely new anchor you saw." His face goes pale. "Into the two hundred foot deep trench off Long Point. But we were seen by another boat. So I had no choice but to bring you back here."

That had been frustrating. Wright was a pig and so drunk I couldn't wait to crack open his skull with the pan I'd used to *saute* the perch filets. But when the Coast Guard Auxiliary Rescue boat cruised by I couldn't take the chance.

Wright looks stunned. "You're even more of a killer than I thought," he says after a moment." Then he laughs, the same high-pitched shrill giggle I'd had to endure when he was drunk on the boat. "I was wondering about the Monks—your next door neighbours, but I think I have my answer now. Funny how they just disappeared, isn't it? It's almost like anyone who gets between you and your precious farm has to go. Your sister, the Monks, your husband…and the rest were just cleaning up the mess."

"I didn't have anything to do with their disappearance."

"Anna Kozlowski said she'd seen you driving their orange car…" He waggles his finger at me and I feel like biting it off.

"She's blind."

"No, she's got macular degeneration. She can see great—only

just out of the corner of her eye. The Monks' McLaren is unmistakable—even to a blind woman, and it was found at their home in Toronto."

I just watch him as he talks and try to stay calm as I look for my opportunity to escape.

"…driven there by you," he continues. "I bet their bodies are buried somewhere where they'll never be found. Maybe under your stone garden, with a thick cover of lime? Where that dog was sniffing around? Or wherever project you were working on when they disappeared." I just glare at him. I'm not going to give him the satisfaction of an argument.

Suddenly he reaches out and grabs my arm, pulling me up to my feet. He drags me over to the stove, and then wrenching my forearm, he holds my hand out over the flame. I can feel the heat, but it isn't close enough to burn me. Yet.

"Where's my money, Rose?" I shake with terror.

"I don't know." I plead with him. "Please, stop this." Wright just stares at me, a smile on his face. He pushes my hand down into the fire and I scream in pain. Then he lets me go.

He's swaying slightly. Does he even notice he's under the influence? Or are adrenaline and rage keeping him going?

"Let's be reasonable, Rose," he says. "I'm not interested in what happened to the Monks. Or to your husband." He slams his hand down onto the counter in front of me. "I just want my money."

Then his hand is on my throat, choking me. He leans in, his face inches from mine. "Where's my money?" I pull at his hand and free myself and he steps back, grinning, his hands up. I back slowly away from him, trying to keep as much distance between us as I can. I glance at the clock. Over twenty five minutes now. I'd given him enough to get an elephant high. Even though it was diluted with coffee enough of the cannabis distillate should have been absorbed by now. At 90% effectiveness it's only a matter of time. Something I don't have much of.

Wright pulls out his gun. "I'm tired of asking nicely," he says. "You're going to tell me where the money is or I'm going kill you." I know he means it. One of the effects of an overdose of THC distillate can be anxiety and paranoia. Maybe my solution was going to see me dead before he passes out.

"I-I think I know where it might be," I say. He tilts his head and smiles. "I found a bag in my husband's stuff."

"See? I thought you might remember. Where is this bag?" I glance toward the walk in cooler. "In there?" he asks, following my look.

I say nothing. I just stand with my back against the wall, watching the clock.

"Why do you keep looking at the clock?" he erupts. Then he fires the gun and the clock blows to pieces. "No one is coming to save you. The restaurant is closed today, remember?" He's definitely impaired, but not in the happy, passive way I'd planned on. He's aggressive and unpredictable.

"Why don't you go in there and get the bag for me?" He gestures with the gun. "Now."

I keep my back to the wall and slip across to the walk in cooler then pull the door open. Wright is behind me, watching as I move some boxes of lettuce and a few bins of produce out of the way and uncover the bag, just where I'd left it. I can feel him swaying slightly.

"Pick it up." I do as I'm told and bring the bag out of the cooler and place it on the counter. "Open it," he says. I unzip the bag partway and reveal bundles of bills lined up. It looks as if the bag is full of them. Wright smiles and I zip it up again. When I raise my head, Wright is looking at me, his head tilted to one side.

"Now what do I do with you?" Then he smiles and I feel my stomach turn over.

"I know you faked that attempt on your life the last time. Your miraculous escape," he says. "Let's see how you manage it for real." I stare at him in horror. "Open the freezer door." I shake my head. He wrenches the door open himself then grabs my arm and shoves me inside. I slip and fall on my hands and knees as I hear the door slam shut behind me. I hear him wedge something into the door handle then all I can hear are the freezer fans.

I push on the emergency exit knob and I'm unable to move it. Something is blocking the mechanism from releasing the latch. My face and ears are already feeling the cold and I plunge my burned hand into a bag of ice to soothe it while I look around for some way to escape.

The freezer walls and door are made of four-inch thick polystyrene, with a thin galvanized steel skin. I could hack my way out with an axe, if only I had one. Maggie suggested we keep a fire axe in the freezer after what happened last week, but we hadn't gotten around to it yet.

I turn and see a pile of veal bones have been left out of their crate, probably by Will. He'd been making a *demi glace* yesterday before we'd fallen behind in service. We were in the weeds and he'd probably been too busy or too distracted to make sure he'd cleaned up afterwards. And Maggie hadn't been here to make sure he did. The bones lay in a heap; shanks, knuckles and marrow bones strewn carelessly on the cutting board, along with the meat axe and the cleaver.

I pick them both up and start to hack at the door. My hand throbs with pain but I ignore it and grip the handle as hard as I can. The pain won't matter a damn if I freeze to death. The cleaver skids across the smooth steel surface and I press harder in one spot until I've created a dent. Then I keep hitting the same spot until the steel skin splits and I can pry the crack open to widen the gap. Within ten minutes I manage to cut through the first layer of steel skin, prying and levering it open with the heavy meat axe so I can gouge out the foam insulation. Then another ten minutes and I've made a hole large enough in the door skin on the exterior side and I'm able to get my arm through. I scrape myself and tear open the flesh of my inner elbow on the sharp steel edge but still I thrust my arm through as far as I could reach.

I feel blood trickling down my forearm, making my fingers slip across the outside surface of the freezer door as I feel around blindly for the handle. My face is pressed against the steel door and my arm is through up to my shoulder. My fingertips make contact with something, but I can't quite get my hand around it. My arm isn't long enough to reach. Again I shove my shoulder deep into the door until I feel something tear, and I'm just able to push away the chunk of wood Wright has wedged into the handle. It falls to the floor on the other side and I carefully pull my arm back through the bloody jagged hole in the freezer door. Then I'm able to use the emergency door release to escape.

THIRTY SEVEN
Rose

THE STORM IS still raging outside. Torrential rain is sheeting down the windows and when I look out I can see Wright's car is gone. He was thoughtful enough to turn off the lights and close the door on his way out, as he left me to die in the freezer. I wonder whether he'd thought to wipe away his fingerprints that would be all over the freezer and stovetop. If I'd died in the freezer and they'd have found me trapped in there by a wedged door, the investigation would have pretty quickly caught up with him. The idiot. He isn't very bright, that's obvious, and I'm sure the overdose of cannabis distillate I gave him with wasn't helping his limited cognitive faculties.

First I tend to the cuts on my arm and wash away the blood on my hands. I apply some burn ointment to my hand and wrap it lightly in gauze. Then, after changing my clothes, I put away the coffee cups and clean up any trace that Wright has ever been here, including the cream and sugar, the pastries, and the now empty vial of Maggie's THC distillate, all of which had all gone into Wright's coffee. I'm a lot smarter than he is.

I noticed he was starting to slur his words when he was threatening me, and again as he'd locked me into the freezer. That meant that by now, over forty-five minutes after he'd been dosed, he was very impaired. Too high to drive legally or safely, even in a car with working brakes. And in his car, all bets were off.

Before I'd come inside to meet Wright I'd crawled under his car and used my secateurs to crimp the metal brake lines to both front brakes. He wouldn't have even noticed the brakes feeling soft when he pressed on the pedal, especially in his condition. But when he tried to stop suddenly or slow down to get around the sharp turn on the steep escarpment hill, he'd go into a rear wheel skid. I just hoped he'd be too impaired to correct it before he crashed.

I pour myself a big glass of Sancerre and hold the cold glass in my burned hand. It feels good. Then I pick up my phone and call 911. When the operator answers I do my best to sound upset.

"I'm calling to report a driver who almost ran me off the road. I'm sure he's drunk, or crazy." I give her the information she needs to know. "No, I didn't get his license plate, but he's driving an old car, a classic grey Mustang. On Concession 6 north of Ridge Road." I smile as I put down the receiver.

The wine is delicious. I sip it slowly, enjoying the grassy bouquet and the trace aroma of lemongrass and grapefruit. It's a great vintage and I make a mental note to get more of it in for the new wine list.

I wonder idly what the charges will be when they finally catch up with Wright. Impaired driving. Possession. Something for the gun he has on him—which is probably illegal and unregistered. And he'll have a lot of explaining to do about that big bag of weed, covered with a single layer of bundled bills that they'll find in his car. I'd stuffed at least ten thousand dollars there, I think. Wright is a crooked cop, already under investigation for trafficking. It will look very bad for him indeed.

The rest of the money is safely hidden upstairs under the floorboards. My money. I've worked hard enough for it. I put it there weeks ago, after I'd first found the bag of cash in my husband's things. Right after I'd killed him.

You can only take so much and I learned my limit the day I found him packing his bags to leave. He told me that he'd be taking his share of the business in the divorce. I'll never forget his smug face when he informed me the only way I'd be able to buy him out was to sell the farm to pay him his share. And that was never going to happen.

He should have known that I'd do anything to keep the farm. He thought he could scare me. Pity he forgot what I'm capable of.

I arranged for chef to go on a *stage,* but I'm sure it wasn't one he'd have chosen. I was working out the story of how he'd left me; how he had decided to not return from Los Angeles once we had our trial time apart. I could have managed it perfectly; it was a great story, and one familiar enough that nobody would question it. Couples break up every day. With his reputation nobody would have a hard time imagining him leaving me for another woman.

I had no idea where the bag of cash had come from. Not at first. I still hadn't put all the pieces together, or figured out about his little scheme with Montana. I should thank Wright for filling in the blanks for me. I didn't know who chef was working for, but thought it was likely somebody might come looking for the money at some point. But I figured they'd assume he'd taken the money and run. It would have been fine if Montana hadn't called in a missing person's report, which brought Wright here, nosing around before I'd properly set up the story.

I'd arranged for Montana to die, of course. She deserved it. I didn't kill her, exactly. Wright isn't smart but he had the general idea. But it wasn't bee venom I put into her bottle. It was bees. All summer I'd watched her greedily gulp the honey water from her stainless steel flask while she was in the garden. She'd just unscrew the lid and drink carelessly. In this heat I knew she'd be drinking a lot; it would just be a matter of time and I was waiting patiently for it to happen that day. It was hard to keep the smile off my face when Jacob brought me out to the garden after he'd found her body.

While she was looking for the trimmers I'd hidden from her that morning, I just put about a dozen bees I'd captured from the hives into her flask and shut them inside. That upset them and when they were upended into her mouth they'd all have stung her at once. It would only be a few seconds before her airways started to close and her heart stopped. She was probably so confused by how it happened she wouldn't have had time to use her EpiPen, if she'd had it on her. But I'd hidden that too.

When Jacob brought me out to find her body, I sent him away to call 911. Then I quickly pulled her cell phone out of her pocket and used her fingerprint to unlock it. Before I joined Jacob on the porch I went into her Settings and removed her passwords and privacy settings, to make sure the police would be able to discover the texts I'd sent from chef's phone. And that worked perfectly. It proved chef was still alive, had been texting her for weeks after he'd supposedly gone away.

It had been easy to send them to her, once he was dead. I had his phone after all and knew all his passwords. He'd never been clever enough to hide them from me. Or maybe he was just being cruel, since he knew what I'd find if I ever looked.

I watched the storm roll across the gardens, bending everything before its lashing rain and wind. I saw the tall sunflowers snap and their massive heads fall to the ground, watched as the corn stalks broke and the tomato cages blew over. The destruction was terrible, and at the same time thrilling. I sipped my wine and reveled in the majesty of the storm.

Wright wasn't the brightest guy, but he was right about Luca. I'd convinced him to drive across the border and ditch my husband's car there, and I had picked him up afterwards at the marina in Buffalo. We'd had many great nights together on the boat, where I'd persuaded Luca to do it, convincing him it was just an insurance scam. I told him that I really needed the money and could claim the car was stolen while chef was in the US on his stage. Of course he believed me. Luca was such a sweet innocent guy.

But of course I couldn't risk him becoming suspicious at some point, maybe once he realized my husband was never coming home. So I brought over two bottles of his favourite Amarone and a twenty year old Cuvee Riserva Grappa and we celebrated the success of his first farmers market. Once he passed out I made sure he was dead, then I carted his body into the boar pen and staged the accident with the ladder. I made sure to remove the extra glasses, the Grappa and second wine bottle, and any trace I'd been there that night. That was why I needed someone with me the next day to pick up my *filetto*. I needed to go back to check I hadn't missed anything and make sure that the story played out the way I needed it to. The story is so important. So is making sure people understand what you need them to.

It's all about the story. Like with my husband. Once he'd gone on his *stage*, I used his cell phone to text Montana for weeks, building the story that he'd left me and would send for her. I sent her intimate messages about how he missed her, calling her at times when I knew she'd not be able to pick up but would see missed calls from him. I don't know what finally tipped her off that he wasn't alive, or what made her call the police to report him missing. If she hadn't done that she wouldn't have had to die. It's really all her own fault, to be honest. I'd just have terminated her employment at some point, once I'd told everyone the story of his having left me and moved to the Los Angeles.

I do feel bad about Maggie. I really did love her. But she was asking too many questions, putting the pieces together. And she'd become careless when she was high. Her talk might give people ideas, make them ask questions and look more closely. My only comfort is that she was dying anyway. At least she felt no pain. That's something I could give her.

Now the most important thing in my world is protected, my farm. So is my flourishing business with Sophie at the Womyn Collective. It's actually a great success story, not that we can tell it, about a group of local entrepreneurial women creating hand made products from local ingredients.

It's been easy for people to overlook us as just a bunch of women running a little craft business, making jams and selling flowers. But the real money is in the herb-infused liqueurs, distilled on the premises, as advertised in our pamphlets. We extract THC from the cannabis we buy in bulk from Jay and create truly intoxicating cordials. There's a huge market for them and we are only just starting to distribute widely across North America.

We've already made a great deal of money from the enterprise. I've bought a very nice boat and Sophie has a beachfront cottage in Barbados. All the Womyn are paid well, and a great deal of money goes into supporting social justice issues in town. We make anonymous donations to pay for the class action suit against the refinery, to help pay Jim's legal bills, and especially to help women and children at risk. With my managerial skills the Womyn Collective's success promises to continue for years, bringing all kinds of economic benefits to the entire region.

Weed has already made us, and lots of other people, rich. There has always been money to be made and opportunity there for those who know how to take advantage of it. It just takes courage and a disregard for the small thing called the law.

EPILOGUE
Rose

I STAND OUTSIDE the hospital room, holding a small bouquet of red dahlias. They signify betrayal and dishonesty, which seems appropriate. There's an empty chair in the hall, but no one else is in the corridor. I guess it was getting late for visiting hours. I peek into the room and see it's empty, apart from the figure in the bed, so I step inside.

Wright is lying in the bed, hooked up to a respirator and several monitors. His eyes are closed and I lay the dahlias next to him on the bedside table. I look at him in silence for a minute then jump in surprise as the door opens and a police officer enters.

"Excuse me, ma'am," she begins then he stops short. "*Rose*? What are you doing here?" It's Constable Lucy Gauthier. "You're not supposed to be in here," she says. "No visitors allowed."

"Sorry, I didn't realize," I say and make my way toward the door.

"Rose, are you a friend of his?" Lucy asks, placing her hand on my elbow to stop me.

I shake my head. "No. Not friends," I say. "I don't even know his first name."

"Why are you here then?"

"I'm not sure, exactly," I say. What could I possibly tell her? To see if Wright is dead?

"It was a really bad accident," Lucy says. "He went right over the cliff on the escarpment, off Concession 6. At that bend near your place." I nod. "And in a classic car like his he didn't stand much of a chance. No seatbelts. No airbags."

"The weather didn't help I'm sure," I say, my expression sorrowful. "Wet roads, poor visibility."

"It's not a good idea for you to be here," Lucy says. "You know there's an investigation ongoing. That's expanded now, since the accident. He's implicated in some very serious crimes." I nod. "Is there anything you'd like to tell me?" she asks, looking pointedly at me. Lucy is a perceptive young woman; she knows there has to be more to the story.

I think again about how much to tell her. How difficult it is to know how honest to be. I shake my head.

"I'm not sure it matters anyway," Lucy continues as she turns to leave. "He's in a coma. Chances aren't good that he'll survive."

I hear the door close behind her, look out the window at the view over the lake and smile. The sun is setting, just dipping below the horizon in a ball of golden light, spilling pink and blue clouds across the sky above. I hear a noise and turn to the bed.

Wright opens his eyes.

ACKNOWLEDGEMENTS

Thanks to the multitude of motley, misguided, creative and crazy chefs, servers and bartenders I knew in my restaurant life, as well as those who gave me insight into the cannabis industry—legal, shady and illegal. I'm also forever grateful to the passionate gardeners, vintners and farmers—the people who grow things both delicious and beautiful. You'll all find yourselves somewhere in this book.

As always, thank you to my dear friend Martha Mason, who welcomed me into her beautiful family cottage on Lake Erie, which provided the early inspiration for the Niagara Noir series. The characters and situations in this novel are my own invention and any mistakes in the book are my own.

Thanks also to Dr. Sammy Barakat for his pharmaceutical and medical advice, and for his support over the years—and to the Damonza team for fabulous cover design and formatting.

Most of all, I'm grateful to my mother for inspiring me with a love of reading and of books, and to my children for their love and support.

ABOUT THE AUTHOR

Liza Drozdov is the author of the Niagara Noir series, including Blood Relative, Dark Water and The One That Got Away. She worked as a bookseller and book publicist, as a garden designer and a college professor, and as a producer of lifestyle television, before settling down to writing full-time. She lives in Oakville, Ontario.

www.lizadrozdov.com

twitter.com/lizadrozdov

instagram.com/lizadrozdov